Tristan
and
Isolde

T0284480

Tristan
and
Isolde

Introduction by
Dr. Mairi Stirling Hill

General Editor: Jake Jackson

**FLAME TREE
PUBLISHING**

This is a FLAME TREE Book

FLAME TREE PUBLISHING
6 Melbray Mews
Fulham, London SW6 3NS
United Kingdom
www.flametreepublishing.com

First published 2024
Copyright © 2024 Flame Tree Publishing Ltd

24 26 28 27 25
1 3 5 7 9 8 6 4 2

ISBN: 978-1-80417-817-1
Ebook ISBN: 978-1-80417-961-1

Cover image created by Flame Tree Studio and featuring the illumination *Tristan
and Isolde Drinking the Love Potion* by Évrard d'Espinques, from the manuscript
Roman de Lancelot by Walter Map (Gaultier de Moap), 1470, and elements courtesy of
Shutterstock.com/antonpix.

The images on page 7 are Caroline Watts' illustrations to *Tristan and Iseult*, translated by
Jessie L. Weston and published by David Nutt, 1902. All other inside images courtesy of
Shutterstock.com and the following: GRSOYMRV, Flat_Enot, VectorV.

This book is compiled and edited, with a new introduction, featuring texts as follows:
The Romance of Tristan & Iseult, by J. Bédier, translated by H. Belloc, London: George
Allen & Company, Ltd., 1913; and extracts from Vols XIII and XIV (*King Arthur*) of
Historical Tales: The Romance of Reality by Charles Morris, Philadelphia and London:
J.B. Lippincott Company, 1891–1908.

Printed in China

Contents

Series Foreword

STRETCHING BACK to the oral traditions of thousands of years ago, tales of heroes and disaster, creation and conquest have been told by many different civilizations in many different ways. Their impact sits deep within our culture even though the detail in the tales themselves are a loose mix of historical record, transformed narrative and the distortions of hundreds of storytellers.

Today the language of mythology lives with us: our mood is jovial, our countenance is saturnine, we are narcissistic and our modern life is hermetically sealed from others. The nuances of myths and legends form part of our daily routines and help us navigate the world around us, with its half truths and biased reported facts.

The nature of a myth is that its story is already known by most of those who hear it, or read it. Every generation brings a new emphasis, but the fundamentals remain the same: a desire to understand and describe the events and relationships of the world. Many of the great stories are archetypes that help us find our own place, equipping us with tools for self-understanding, both individually and as part of a broader culture.

For Western societies it is Greek mythology that speaks to us most clearly. It greatly influenced the mythological heritage of the ancient Roman civilization and is the lens through which we still see the Celts, the Norse and many of the other great peoples and religions. The Greeks themselves learned much from their neighbours, the Egyptians, an older culture that became weak with age and incestuous leadership.

It is important to understand that what we perceive now as mythology had its own origins in perceptions of the divine and the rituals of the sacred. The earliest civilizations, in the crucible of the Middle East, in the Sumer of the third millennium BC, are the source to which many of the mythic archetypes can be traced. As humankind collected together in cities for the first time, developed writing and industrial-scale agriculture, started to irrigate the rivers and attempted to control rather than be at the mercy of its environment, humanity began to write down its tentative explanations of natural events, of floods and plagues, of disease.

Early stories tell of Gods (or god-like animals in the case of tribal societies such as African, Native American or Aboriginal cultures) who are crafty and use their wits to survive, and it is reasonable to suggest that these were the first rulers of the gathering peoples of the earth, later elevated to god-like status with the distance of time. Such tales became more political as cities vied with each other for supremacy, creating new Gods, new hierarchies for their pantheons. The older Gods took on primordial roles and became the preserve of creation and destruction, leaving the new gods to deal with more current, everyday affairs. Empires rose and fell, with Babylon assuming the mantle from Sumeria in the 1800s BCE, then in turn to be swept away by the Assyrians of the 1200s BCE; then the Assyrians and the Egyptians were subjugated by the Greeks, the Greeks by the Romans, and so on, leading to the spread and assimilation of common themes, ideas and stories throughout the world.

The survival of history is dependent on the telling of good tales, but each one must have the 'feeling' of truth, otherwise it will be ignored. Around the firesides, or embedded in a book or a computer, the myths and legends of the past are still the living materials of retold myth, not restricted to an exploration of origins. Now we have devices and global communications that give us unparalleled access to a diversity of traditions. We can find out about Indigenous American, Indian, Chinese and tribal African mythology in a way that was denied to our ancestors; we can find connections, match the archaeology, religion and the mythologies of the world to build a comprehensive image of the human adventure.

The great leaders of history and heroes of literature have also adopted the mantle of mythic experience, because the stories of historical figures – Cyrus the Great, Alexander, Genghis Khan – and mytho-poetic warriors such as Beowulf achieve a cultural significance that transcends their moment in the chronicles of humankind. Myth, history and literature have become powerful, intwined instruments of perception, with echoes of reported fact and symbolic truths that convey the sweep of human experience. In this series of books we are glad to share with you the wonderful traditions of the past.

Jake Jackson
General Editor

Introduction

THE TRAGIC LOVE STORY of Tristan and Isolde is one of the most enduring tales in Western culture. Born out of Celtic folklore, the story of these two ill-fated lovers was popular throughout medieval Europe, appearing in a number of languages across Britain, France, Germany, Spain, Italy and Scandinavia. The legend continues to enjoy popularity with contemporary audiences through a number of different mediums including poetry, film and, most famously, the opera *Tristan und Isolde*, composed by Richard Wagner in the nineteenth century. The present volume includes two different versions of the narrative published in the late nineteenth century and early twentieth century respectively. Each has taken medieval versions of the narrative as its main sources.

Celtic Origins

The tale is thought to have its origins in Celtic folklore, with Hellenic, Persian, Roman and Arabic motifs also incorporated into the narrative. A number of Irish tales are considered to be analogues of the Tristan and Isolde legend, among them the tales of *Deirdre of the Sorrows*, included in the Ulster Cycle of Irish heroic legends, as well as *Diarmuid and Gráinne*. Both narratives tell of ill-fated love triangles and marriages between an older king and a younger woman who falls in love with another man. The figure of Tristan has also been identified with Drystan and Essylt of the Welsh Triads.

In these Celtic analogues the female protagonist is often a powerful and magical figure. She chooses her lover and, if he does not return her love, casts a spell over him. The more familiar versions of Tristan and Isolde that come out of continental Europe reduce the heroine's magical agency with the inclusion of the love potion, given to Isolde by her mother.

The location in Cornwall has been associated with the sixth-century 'Long Stone', also called the 'Drustanus Stone' or 'The Tristan Stone'. This stone is inscribed with the name Drustanus, an equivalent to 'Tristan' and similar to the Welsh 'Drystan'. However, there is some debate among historians as to whether the stone relates to the legendary Tristan. Some archaeologists have suggested that the first letter inscribed is in fact a 'C' and an 'I', rather than a backwards 'D'.

Medieval Renditions

The earliest written versions of the legend of Tristan and Isolde date from the second half of the twelfth century and the start of the thirteenth. These early texts are often split into two 'branches' or 'traditions', known respectively as the courtly branch (*version courtoise*) and the common branch (*version commune*). Scholars consider the courtly branch to reflect the culture and priorities of aristocratic society at the time, while the common branch is perhaps more reflective of the earlier Celtic legends. These traditions can be seen in the two earliest surviving versions of the tale written by Thomas of Britain (courtly branch) and Béroul (common branch). Both texts are narrative poems written in Anglo-Norman that have survived in fragments. Béroul's *Tristan* was composed sometime between 1150 and 1190, while Thomas of Britain's version dates from around 1170–75. Also linked to the common branch is a contemporaneous text composed at the end of the twelfth century – the Middle High German text *Tristant*, composed by Eilhart von Oberage. Eilhart's version provides the oldest complete version of the narrative, including episodes familiar and unfamiliar to the French works.

Though Thomas of Britain's version survives only in fragments, we can piece together the narrative from later surviving works that associate themselves with Thomas's *Tristan*. One of these is the Middle High German *Tristan und Isold*, composed by Gottfried von Strassburg in the early thirteenth century. Due to the supposed death of the author the text is incomplete, but despite this *Tristan und Isold* remains one of the most famous versions of the legend. Gottfried states that his source is Thomas's text, and coincidentally the surviving text ends just where the Thomas fragments begin. There is little overlap between the two versions, however, which makes it difficult to observe Gottfried's individual style and originality. Another adaptation/ translation of Thomas's *Tristan* is the Old Norse *Tristrams saga ok Ísöndar* ('Saga of Tristram and Isold') written by Friar Róbert. This version, though abridged, is the earliest complete version of the narrative; it was composed for King Hákon Hákonarson of Norway in 1226.

Another very brief version of the Tristan and Isolde tale was composed by the Anglo-Norman poet Marie de France. Featured in her collection of Breton Lays, *Chevrefoil* ('Honeysuckle') narrates a brief scene between the lovers. It also includes a description of the love of Tristan and Isolde as the intertwining of the hazel and the honeysuckle plants – an image that appears following the deaths of the lovers in other versions of the story.

From the middle of the thirteenth century we begin to see the tale of Tristan and Isolde being associated with another legendary figure: King Arthur. We can see this from the French Prose *Tristan*, a highly influential text composed in the thirteenth century. The Prose *Tristan* follows the tradition of the Vulgate Cycle or the Lancelot-Grail Cycle, a series of lengthy and interconnected Arthurian romances. The Prose *Tristan* was clearly immensely popular and paved the way for later writers to weave Tristan and Isolde's story into Arthurian mythology.

In his epic fifteenth-century tome, *Le Morte Darthur*, Sir Thomas Malory dedicates a large portion of his narrative to the exploits of Tristan. He positions him as a knight of such skill and prowess that he is second only to Lancelot du Lac. Located in the middle of *Le Morte Darthur*, Malory's *Book of Sir Tristram* diverges from the earlier Anglo-Norman narratives, as the primary focus shifts from the lovers and their suffering to the martial exploits of Tristram and the other knights of Arthur's Round Table. A large proportion of Malory's version is spent at Arthur's court rather than in the familiar settings of Cornwall, Ireland, the forest or Brittany. The hero is far more concerned with gaining worship and renown, and in maintaining his friendship with Sir Lancelot, revealing a shift away from concerns with adultery and towards loyalty and chivalric fidelity to one's lord. Moreover, Malory makes King Mark a far less sympathetic figure, removing much of the ambiguity towards the lovers' immoral behaviour.

Later Redactions

Following the medieval revival in the Victorian period, the legend of Tristan and Isolde, along with tales of Arthur and his Knights of the Round Table, enjoyed a notable resurgence in popularity. The love story inspired a number of poets and artists who all put their own, distinctly Victorian spin on the familiar story. Alfred, Lord Tennyson included a poem on the Tristan tale in his *Idylls of the King*. He is himself far less sympathetic towards the lovers and their adultery in 'The Last Tournament' (1871), reflecting his own Victorian ideals. Algernon Charles Swinburne, by contrast, treated his lovers far more kindly in his *Tristram of Lyoness* (1882).

Richard Wagner's opera of *Tristan und Isolde* was hugely influential in reviving the legend, both in Germany and beyond. Today it remains one of the most famous versions of the legend, emphasizing in particular a relationship between love and death for the lovers. The final piece of the opera titled 'Liebestod' ('Love-Death') sees the lovers appear to welcome death as a means of reuniting them in eternity and finally giving them peace.

There have been numerous further adaptations of the myth in the twentieth and twenty-first centuries, sustaining characters and their presence in the popular imagination. These include a one-act play by Thomas Hardy, completed in 1923, the presence of Tristan and Isolde in James Joyce's *Finnegans Wake* (1939), a 1988 novel by Diana L. Paxson titled *The White Raven* that tells the story from the perspective of Isolde's handmaiden, and even a high-budget Hollywood movie, *Tristan & Isolde* (2006), produced by Ridley Scott and starring James Franco and Sophia Myles.

Key Characters: The Love Triangle and Love Quartet

Tristan, otherwise called Tristram, Tristain and Drystan, is a Cornish knight and nephew to the king of Cornwall. He is an impressive fighter and talented musician, winning the hearts of both his uncle and Isolde through martial prowess and his skill with a harp. In some versions of the legend the focus remains on Tristan and Isolde's love and their inner turmoil. However, as the legend developed in medieval Europe and began to be associated with the court of King Arthur (with the publication of the Prose *Tristan*), the focus shifted from Tristan's suffering in love to his chivalric adventures, becoming more concerned with his knightly behaviour than his ill-fated love affair.

Isolde, Iseult, Yseut or Isolda is an Irish princess who marries King Mark of Cornwall after falling in love with his nephew, Tristan. She is first seen as the niece of Sir Morholt, an Irish knight killed by Tristan. Once married to Mark she continues her affair with Tristan and usually remains at the forefront of the narrative, where the internal suffering of both her and Tristan is voiced by early narrators such as Thomas of Britain. In versions more concerned with Tristan's knightly prowess, Isolde is sometimes relegated to the wings. In Malory's *Tale of Sir Tristam*, for instance, she is present for much of Tristram's time at Arthur's court, but their love affair is paid very little attention. Instead Isolde lives very much in domestic silence as Tristram continues to build his chivalric reputation.

King Mark of Cornwall is Tristan's uncle who marries Isolde. Sometimes this is done to appease his jealous barons who plot against his nephew; at other times his decision to marry Isolde is done out of his own jealousy towards Tristan, in order to spite his nephew, who he knows cares for her. This pinpoints the key difference between the various versions of King Mark. At times he is a somewhat sympathetic character, torn by his love of both his nephew and his wife and his desire to believe them both innocent. At other times, however, he is depicted as an unambiguous villain, whose desire to bring about Tristan's destruction drives most of the character's cruel behaviours.

Isolde of the White Hands (*Iseult Blanchmains*) completes the love quartet when she is introduced later in the story. She is a princess of Brittany, to which Tristan is banished by King Mark following the discovery of his affair with Isolde. Tristan becomes friends with her brother Kahedin while serving their father, King Hoel of Brittany. He marries Isolde of the White Hands, but is unable to consummate the marriage. In some versions she plays a key role in the deaths of the lovers, in revenge for Tristan's neglect of their marriage. In other versions of the tale, however – especially those more closely linked to the Arthurian myth, such as the Prose *Tristan* and Malory's *Le Morte Darthur* – Isolde of the White Hands disappears from the narrative once Tristan returns from Brittany, playing no part in the lovers' tragic deaths.

The Narrative

Many different variations of the Tristan and Isolde legend have been told throughout the centuries, some featuring significant differences. Below I outline the basic plot and some of the most important variations:

The son of the King of Lyonesse and the sister of King Mark of Cornwall, Tristan's birth is followed by the death of his mother. The child is thus named using the French word *triste* (sad) to indicate the sorrow that surrounded his birth. In some versions of the story his father also dies in battle just before or just after Tristan is born, as happens in Bédier's version (the first tale included in this volume). In other versions, including Morris's adaptation (the second tale included in this volume), Tristan's father remarries and his stepmother attempts to poison him out of jealousy.

Educated in both martial and courtly activities, Tristan becomes particularly adept as a musician, especially playing the harp. He travels to Cornwall in disguise and wins the favour of his uncle, King Mark; he then puts himself forward as champion against the Irish knight Morholt, brother to the Irish queen and uncle to Isolde. During their fight Tristan inflicts a fatal blow upon Morholt, leaving a fragment of his sword in the knight's head, which the Irish Queen and Isolde later recognize and identify Tristan as the killer. In return, Tristan is injured by Morholt's poisonous spear and must ultimately travel to Ireland in disguise, there to be healed by the queen of Ireland and Isolde. In some versions of the story it is here that the love between Tristan and Isolde starts to grow, well before they consume the love potion.

Back in Cornwall, Mark is convinced to search for a wife. The reasons for this vary: in some cases his barons insist on him finding a wife and producing an heir, because they are jealous of Tristan and do not want to see the kingdom pass to him as Mark intends. In other versions, Mark hears of Isolde's beauty through Tristan and subsequently decides to marry her, sending Tristan back to Ireland to ask for her hand.

In Ireland, Tristan slays a troublesome dragon to win the hand of the Irish princess, but is once again injured and needs to be nursed back to health by Isolde. In Malory's version, and in Morris's too, Tristan instead wins Isolde by offering himself as champion for the Irish king in a trial by battle at Arthur's court. On board the ship on the way to Cornwall, Tristan and Isolde accidentally consume a love potion meant for Isolde and Mark. Their passion is all encompassing, and they consummate their love on the boat.

In several versions of the tale there then occurs a bed trick, whereby Isolde's companion Brangane, also spelled as Brangwane, Brangien or Brangaine, is persuaded to substitute Isolde in her marital bed so that Mark does not discover she is not a virgin. Later, fearing disloyalty and betrayal of their secret by Brangane, Isolde attempts to have her friend murdered. The attempt is unsuccessful, however, Isolde repents of her mistrust and the two women are reconciled.

For a time Tristan, Isolde and Mark live in Cornwall in relative peace, with the lovers carrying on their affair secretly. Persuaded by his barons of his wife and nephew's clandestine love, the king sets traps to try to catch them, but is initially unsuccessful. Hiding in a tree, he tries to expose the lovers; however, they are alerted to his presence through his reflection in the river and are able to deceive him into believing in their innocence. Later, another trap is set for Tristan, involving flour laid on the floor by Isolde's bed. Again he sees the trap and leaps to her bed across the floor, to avoid leaving a trail of incrimating footprints. Unbeknownst to Tristan, however, his action opens up a wound that causes him to leave a trail of blood in and around the bed. The blood is discovered and he and Isolde are arrested.

Mark sentences them both to death, but on the way to the pyre Tristan, persuading his prison guards to let him enter a chapel for a final prayer, escapes out of the back window, leaping off a cliff and miraculously surviving. Mark is persuaded to send Isolde to a leper colony instead of burning her. Tristan is able to rescue his lover and they escape to the forest, where the couple live peacefully for some time.

Eventually the king finds them. Initially intending to kill them, he is dissuaded when he finds them sleeping with a sword between them. Mark leaves, taking the sword, and when the pair wake they realize he has shown them mercy and eventually return to court. Here Isolde escapes her trial by ordeal through an unequivocal oath, and is pardoned by Mark and the court.

Tristan departs from Cornwall and goes on his own adventures. Sometimes these lead him to King Arthur's court, where he wins renown as a knight equal to Lancelot du Lac in chivalry and valour. In most versions of the tale he ends up in Brittany, where he encounters Isolde of the White Hands, whom he decides to marry. Tristan is unable to consummate the marriage, however, due to his ongoing affection for his first love, Isolde, Queen of Cornwall.

There are two main narrative endings to the tragic love story. In one, King Mark kills Tristan and Isolde dies of heartbreak. In the more common version, Tristan is fatally wounded by another poisoned weapon and calls for Isolde once again to heal him. He instructs his messenger to raise a white flag if Isolde is with him and a black flag if she is not, reminiscent of the Theseus myth and foreshadowing a similar tragic fate. Isolde of Cornwall does indeed rush to her lover's aid. However, Isolde of the White Hands, inspired by jealousy, falsely informs her husband that the white sail is black and he immediately dies. Arriving too late, Isolde also dies over her lover's body. The two are buried alongside one another. Two trees grow from each grave and intertwine with one another.

The Love Potion

One of the major differences between texts comes from the way in which the lovers come together. As discussed above, the Celtic origins often place the heroine in the driving seat; she initiates the relationship and uses magic to develop it if necessary. Moreover, as we have seen, in some versions of the tale Tristan and Isolde have already begun to love one another before they drink the love potion. Some scholars argue that the potion itself is merely symbolic, a narrative device to show that their love is indisputable, not a force of magic at all. This is often presented as the difference between the common and the courtly branches, with the former assuming a literal love potion and the latter using the potion to explain the lovers' psychological state.

The potion also sometimes differs in its nature. In some adaptations of the narrative, including Béroul's, the love potion is given a time limit of three years; it is while the couple are living in exile in the forest that their love wanes. The two lovers are suddenly aware of the social consequences of their actions, a realization that motivates their return to courtly life.

The variations in the love magic and love potion change the culpability of the lovers in a number of ways. The love potion itself reduces their agency in their passionate love affair, rendering them almost blameless of the inevitable adultery that occurs after Isolde has married Mark. This is emphasized in versions that conclude with Mark's discovery of the love potion after the lovers' death. Realizing that they had no choice in their actions, Mark repents and forgives the pair for their otherwise immoral actions.

There are also variations in the delivery of the potion, resulting in the blame being passed around different characters. In some versions Brangane deliberately gives the couple the potion; in other versions they consume it entirely by mistake. At times it is Isolde who drinks the potion and gives it to Tristan. These changes, though slight on the surface, change how characters and readers interpret subsequent events and dictate who can, and who should, be blamed for the lovers' actions.

The Unequivocal Oath

In several versions of the tale, Tristan and Isolde revel in the word play that allows them to manipulate situations to their advantage. For example, following her return to Mark's court from the forest, Isolde is made to swear an oath of innocence in front of Mark's and Arthur's courts. The trial by ordeal is a familiar feature of medieval romance, as is the unequivocal oath. The ordeal relies on a verbal assertion of innocence, an exculpatory oath, followed by a physical trial: walking across hot coals or plunging one's hand into boiling water. Innocence or guilt is proved when the accused either emerges unscathed or with a festering wound.

In order that her oath be a literal truth, Isolde devises a plan whereby Tristan, disguised as a leper, carries her over a body of water on the way to the trial. Thus, when she goes to swear her innocence, she can assuredly declare that 'no man has held me in his arms saving King Mark, my lord, and that poor pilgrim' (from Belloc's translation of Bédier).

Of course, this carefully manipulated oath cannot deceive divine powers. This raises questions around God's own treatment of the lovers; whether God accepts her exploitative use of language or sees the two lovers as truly innocent. It is not the only time that divine intervention saves the lovers, as Tristan's survival after his leap from the chapel before his execution is also declared an act of God. This could harken back to the love potion, and the lack of culpability the lovers have over their own actions. Alternatively, it could also suggest that their love is true and they are faithful to one another, and therefore God forgives their other trespasses.

Disguise and Mistaken Identity

Disguise and mistaken identity also play a central role in the narrative – sometimes with comic and sometimes with tragic effect. In his attempt to hide his identity from Isolde and her mother when he returns to Ireland following the death of Morholt, Tristan inverts his name and changes it to Tantris (or Tramtrist/Trantris, depending on the spelling). His clever wordplay works, enabling him to remain unrecognized until the missing piece of his sword reveals him to be

Morholt's killer. At other times Tristan dresses up as a leper, a pilgrim and a fool in order to trick Mark and visit Isolde. Many times even Isolde does not recognize him at first; she is only convinced of his identity when his dog recognizes him.

The role of Isolde of the White Hands serves as a kind of mistaken identity that leads to tragedy. Besotted by her name and the way it reminds him of the other Isolde, Tristan chooses her to be his wife – only to regret this decision as soon as he sees Isolde of Cornwall's ring and is reminded of his love for her. This inversion of the two Isoldes ends, as we have seen, in heartbreak: a jealous and neglected Isolde of the White Hands lies about the colour of the sail, and Tristan dies believing that his love has abandoned him.

The Role of Women

The legend of Tristan and Isolde contains several central female characters, who exhibit strength and agency in their decision-making. Isolde herself, derived from the magical women of Celtic folklore, shows herself to be a character of resolve and determination. In Ireland she helps to heal Tristan on multiple occasions and is often described as one of the greatest healers in the world. She also even attempts to kill him when she discovers his role in the death of her uncle (in other versions it is her mother who seeks vengeance). Once Isolde realizes that she must either marry the treacherous steward who has claimed the reward for killing the dragon or go with Tristan, she resolves to head to Cornwall. Isolde often takes the lead in their plotting to evade Mark. She proves especially adept at manipulating language to suit her situation, convincing the king of her innocence on multiple occasions, including under oath.

Isolde is not the only woman who plays a central role in the narrative. Her handmaiden (sometimes cousin) Brangane is instrumental in the plot. In some versions Brangane intentionally gives Tristan and Isolde the love potion in order to stop them from drinking poison; she also agrees to partake in the bed trick as noted above, switching places with

Isolde to save her mistress from discovery. Brangane undertakes many missions for Isolde, often putting herself in danger in order to find Tristan or to deliver a message.

Dr Mairi Stirling Hill (Introduction) is a medievalist who works on English and French literature from the latter half of the Middle Ages. She has a particular interest in women and gender in medieval literature and culture, as well as medieval romance and the myth of King Arthur. She has written on women's work and women's roles in medieval law and literature, as well as the role of women in Arthurian legends.

The Romance of Tristan and Iseult

FRENCH MEDIEVALIST Joseph Bédier's version of the Tristan and Isolde legend, originally published in 1900 as *Le roman de Tristan et Iseult* ('The Romance of Tristan and Iseult'), was immensely popular; it was translated into English by Hilaire Belloc in 1903, and it is this version which we present here. Bédier's version, intended for the general reader, drew on a number of medieval sources, and scholars credit the publication of Bédier's *Tristan* with enhancing the popularity of the tale.

Bédier's version draws on both the common and the courtly traditions of the Tristan and Isolde legend. He merges episodes from the early writers, including Béroul and Thomas of Britain, to create a cohesive and, importantly, a complete narrative. During his extensive research on the history of the Tristan narrative, Bédier came to the conclusion that there must have once existed a French version of the text that pre-dated both Thomas and Béroul. He suggested that this lost archetype, *Ur-Tristan*, served as a source text for both of the early French versions of the Tristan and Isolde legend.

His tale begins with the deaths of both of Tristan's parents, then tells how Tristan proved himself to King Mark and his court. In Bédier's narrative King Mark is a far more sympathetic figure; he cares deeply for his nephew, though he is at times turned against Tristan by his cruelly intentioned and jealous barons. Bédier's love potion is one of permanence, unlike Béroul's, and thus the lovers' passion does not wane after their exile in the forest. Their reasoning for their return is linked instead to their desire to reclaim their courtly lives, rather than waste their youth in the poverty of the forest.

Bédier includes the episode of *Folie Tristan* ('Tristan's madness') which is found in two twelfth-century narrative poems, differentiated by the location of their manuscripts in Oxford and Bern. In this episode Tristan arrives at Mark's court disguised as a fool. Here he begins to recount the story of his love for the queen in order to get Isolde's attention. The death of the lovers follows the traditional story, featuring Isolde of the White Hands and the misidentified black sail. Bédier concludes his tale with a nod to the early recorders of the Tristan legend, naming Béroul, Thomas, Gilbert (Eilhart von Oberge) and Gottfried, and reminding his reader of the long history of the romance of Tristan and Isolde.

Part the First

The Childhood of Tristan

M Y LORDS, if you would hear a high tale of love and of death, here is that of Tristan and Queen Iseult; how to their full joy, but to their sorrow also, they loved each other, and how at last they died of that love together upon one day; she by him and he by her.

Long ago, when Mark was King over Cornwall, Rivalen, King of Lyonesse, heard that Mark's enemies waged war on him; so he crossed the sea to bring him aid; and so faithfully did he serve him with counsel and sword that Mark gave him his sister Blanchefleur, whom King Rivalen loved most marvellously.

He wedded her in Tintagel Minster, but hardly was she wed when the news came to him that his old enemy Duke Morgan had fallen on Lyonesse and was wasting town and field. Then Rivalen manned his ships in haste, and took Blanchefleur with him to his far land; but she was with child. He landed below his castle of Kanoël and gave the Queen in ward to his Marshal Rohalt, and after that set off to wage his war.

Blanchefleur waited for him continually, but he did not come home, till she learnt upon a day that Duke Morgan had killed him in foul ambush. She did not weep: she made no cry or lamentation, but her limbs failed her and grew weak, and her soul was filled with a strong desire to be rid of the flesh, and though Rohalt tried to soothe her she would not hear. Three days she awaited reunion with her lord, and on the fourth she brought forth a son; and taking him in her arms she said:

"Little son, I have longed a while to see you, and now I see you the fairest thing ever a woman bore. In sadness came I hither, in sadness did I bring forth, and in sadness has your first feast day gone. And as by sadness you came into the world, your name shall be called Tristan; that is the child of sadness."

After she had said these words she kissed him, and immediately when she had kissed him she died.

Rohalt, the keeper of faith, took the child, but already Duke Morgan's men besieged the Castle of Kanoël all round about. There is a wise saying: "Foolhardy was never hardy," and he was compelled to yield to Duke Morgan at his mercy: but for fear that Morgan might slay Rivalen's heir the Marshal hid him among his own sons.

When seven years were passed and the time had come to take the child from the women, Rohalt put Tristan under a good master, the Squire Gorvenal, and Gorvenal taught him in a few years the arts that go with barony. He taught him the use of lance and sword and 'scutcheon and bow, and how to cast stone quoits and to leap wide dykes also: and he taught him to hate every lie and felony and to keep his given word; and he taught him the various kinds of song and harp-playing, and the hunter's craft; and when the child rode among the young squires you would have said that he and his horse and his armour were all one thing. To see him so noble and so proud, broad in the shoulders, loyal, strong and right, all men glorified Rohalt in such a son. But Rohalt remembering Rivalen and Blanchefleur (of whose youth and grace all this was a resurrection) loved him indeed as a son, but in his heart revered him as his lord.

Now all his joy was snatched from him on a day when certain merchants of Norway, having lured Tristan to their ship, bore him off as a rich prize, though Tristan fought hard, as a young wolf struggles, caught in a gin. But it is a truth well proved, and every sailor knows it, that the sea will hardly bear a felon ship, and gives no aid to rapine. The sea rose and cast a dark storm round the ship and drove it eight days and eight nights at random, till the mariners caught through the mist a coast of awful cliffs and seaward rocks whereon the sea would have ground their hull to pieces: then they did penance, knowing that the anger of the sea came of the lad, whom they had stolen in an evil hour, and they vowed his deliverance and got ready a boat to put him, if it might be, ashore: then the wind, and sea fell and the sky shone, and as the Norway ship grew small in the offing, a quiet tide cast Tristan and the boat upon a beach of sand.

Painfully he climbed the cliff and saw, beyond, a lonely rolling heath and a forest stretching out and endless. And he wept, remembering Gorvenal, his father, and the land of Lyonesse. Then the distant cry of a hunt, with horse and hound, came suddenly and lifted his heart, and a tall stag broke cover at the forest edge. The pack and the hunt streamed after it with a tumult of cries and winding horns, but just as the hounds were racing clustered at the haunch, the quarry turned to bay at a stones throw from Tristan; a huntsman gave him the thrust, while all around the hunt had gathered and was winding the kill. But Tristan, seeing by the gesture of the huntsman that he made to cut the neck of the stag, cried out:

"My lord, what would you do? Is it fitting to cut up so noble a beast like any farmyard hog? Is that the custom of this country?"

And the huntsman answered:

"Fair friend, what startles you? Why yes, first I take off the head of a stag, and then I cut it into four quarters and we carry it on our saddle bows to King Mark, our lord: So do we, and so since the days of the first huntsmen have done the Cornish men. If, however, you know of some nobler custom, teach it us: take this knife and we will learn it willingly."

Then Tristan kneeled and skinned the stag before he cut it up, and quartered it all in order leaving the crow-bone all whole, as is meet, and putting aside at the end the head, the haunch, the tongue and the great heart's vein; and the huntsmen and the kennel hinds stood over him with delight, and the Master Huntsman said:

"Friend, these are good ways. In what land learnt you them? Tell us your country and your name."

"Good lord, my name is Tristan, and I learnt these ways in my country of Lyonesse."

"Tristan," said the Master Huntsman, "God reward the father that brought you up so nobly; doubtless he is a baron, rich and strong."

Now Tristan knew both speech and silence, and he answered:

"No, lord; my father is a burgess. I left his home unbeknownst upon a ship that trafficked to a far place, for I wished to learn how men lived in foreign lands. But if you will accept me of the hunt I will follow you gladly and teach you other crafts of venery."

"Fair Tristan, I marvel there should be a land where a burgess's son can know what a knight's son knows not elsewhere, but come with us since you will it; and welcome: we will bring you to King Mark, our lord."

Tristan completed his task; to the dogs he gave the heart, the head, offal and ears; and he taught the hunt how the skinning and the ordering should be done. Then he thrust the pieces upon pikes and gave them to this huntsman and to that to carry, to one the snout, to another the haunch, to another the flank, to another the chine; and he taught them how to ride by twos in rank, according to the dignity of the pieces each might bear.

So they took the road and spoke together, till they came on a great castle and round it fields and orchards, and living waters and fish ponds and plough lands, and many ships were in its haven, for that castle stood above the sea. It was well fenced against all assault or engines of war, and its keep, which the giants had built long ago, was compact of great stones, like a chessboard of vert and azure.

And when Tristan asked its name:

"Good liege," they said, "we call it Tintagel."

And Tristan cried:

"Tintagel! Blessed be thou of God, and blessed be they that dwell within thee."

(Therein, my lords, therein had Rivalen taken Blanchefleur to wife, though their son knew it not.)

When they came before the keep the horns brought the barons to the gates and King Mark himself. And when the Master Huntsman had told him all the story, and King Mark had marvelled at the good order of the cavalcade, and the cutting of the stag, and the high art of venery in all, yet most he wondered at the stranger boy, and still gazed at him, troubled and wondering whence came his tenderness, and his heart would answer him nothing; but, my lords, it was blood that spoke, and the love he had long since borne his sister Blanchefleur.

That evening, when the boards were cleared, a singer out of Wales, a master, came forward among the barons in Hall and sang a harper's song, and as this harper touched the strings of his harp, Tristan, who sat at the King's feet, spoke thus to him:

"Oh master, that is the first of songs! The Bretons of old wove it once to chant the loves of Graëlent. And the melody is rare and rare are the words: master, your voice is subtle: harp us that well."

But when the Welshman had sung, he answered:

"Boy, what do you know of the craft of music? If the burgesses of Lyonesse teach their sons harp – play also, and rotes and viols too, rise, and take this harp and show your skill."

Then Tristan took the harp and sang so well that the barons softened as they heard, and King Mark marvelled at the harper from Lyonesse whither so long ago Rivalen had taken Blanchefleur away.

When the song ended, the King was silent a long space, but he said at last:

"Son, blessed be the master that taught thee, and blessed be thou of God: for God loves good singers. Their voices and the voice of the harp enter the souls of men and wake dear memories and cause them to forget many a mourning and many a sin. For our joy did you come to this roof, stay near us a long time, friend."

And Tristan answered:

"Very willingly will I serve you, sire, as your harper, your huntsman and your liege."

So did he, and for three years a mutual love grew up in their hearts. By day Tristan followed King Mark at pleas and in saddle; by night he slept in the royal room with the councillors and the peers, and if the King was sad he would harp to him to soothe his care. The barons also cherished him, and (as you shall learn) Dinas of Lidan, the seneschal, beyond all others. And more tenderly than the barons and than Dinas the King loved him. But Tristan could not forget, or Rohalt his father, or his master Gorvenal, or the land of Lyonesse.

My lords, a teller that would please, should not stretch his tale too long, and truly this tale is so various and so high that it needs no straining. Then let me shortly tell how Rohalt himself, after long wandering by sea and land, came into Cornwall, and found Tristan, and showing the King the carbuncle that once was Blanchefleur's, said:

"King Mark, here is your nephew Tristan, son of your sister Blanchefleur and of King Rivalen. Duke Morgan holds his land most wrongfully; it is time such land came back to its lord."

And Tristan (in a word) when his uncle had armed him knight, crossed the sea, and was hailed of his father's vassals, and killed Rivalen's slayer and was reseized of his land.

Then remembering how King Mark could no longer live in joy without him, he summoned his council and his barons and said this:

"Lords of the Lyonesse, I have retaken this place and I have avenged King Rivalen by the help of God and of you. But two men Rohalt and King Mark of Cornwall nourished me, an orphan, and a wandering boy. So should I call them also fathers. Now a free man has two things thoroughly his own, his body and his land. To Rohalt then, here, I will release my land. Do you hold it, father, and your son shall hold it after you. But my body I give up to King Mark. I will leave this country, dear though it be, and in Cornwall I will serve King Mark as my lord. Such is my judgment, but you, my lords of Lyonesse, are my lieges, and owe me counsel; if then, some one of you will counsel me another thing let him rise and speak."

But all the barons praised him, though they wept; and taking with him Gorvenal only, Tristan set sail for King Mark's land.

The Morholt out of Ireland

WHEN TRISTAN came back to that land, King Mark and all his Barony were mourning; for the King of Ireland had manned a fleet to ravage Cornwall, should King Mark refuse, as he had refused these fifteen years, to pay a tribute his fathers had paid. Now that year this King had sent to Tintagel, to carry his summons, a giant knight; the Morholt, whose sister he had wed, and whom no man had yet been able to overcome: so King Mark had summoned all the barons of his land to Council, by letters sealed.

On the day assigned, when the barons were gathered in hall, and when the King had taken his throne, the Morholt said these things:

"King Mark, hear for the last time the summons of the King of Ireland, my lord. He arraigns you to pay at last that which you have owed so long, and because you have refused it too long already he bids you give over to me this day three hundred youths and three hundred maidens drawn by lot from among the Cornish folk. But if so be that any would prove by trial of combat that the King of Ireland receives this tribute without right, I will take up his wager. Which among you, my Cornish lords, will fight to redeem this land?"

The barons glanced at each other but all were silent.

Then Tristan knelt at the feet of King Mark and said:

"Lord King, by your leave I will do battle."

And in vain would King Mark have turned him from his purpose, thinking, how could even valour save so young a knight? But he threw down his gage to the Morholt, and the Morholt took up the gage.

On the appointed day he had himself clad for a great feat of arms in a hauberk and in a steel helm, and he entered a boat and drew to the islet of St. Samson's, where the knights were to fight each to each alone. Now the Morholt had hoisted to his mast a sail of rich purple, and coming fast to land, he moored his boat on the shore. But Tristan pushed off his own boat adrift with his feet, and said:

"One of us only will go hence alive. One boat will serve."

And each rousing the other to the fray they passed into the isle.

No man saw the sharp combat; but thrice the salt sea breeze had wafted or seemed to waft a cry of fury to the land, when at last towards the hour of noon the purple sail showed far off; the Irish boat appeared from the island shore, and there rose a clamour of "the Morholt!" When suddenly, as the boat grew larger on the sight and topped a wave, they saw that Tristan stood on the prow holding a sword in his hand. He leapt ashore, and as the mothers kissed the steel upon his feet he cried to the Morholt's men:

"My lords of Ireland, the Morholt fought well. See here, my sword is broken and a splinter of it stands fast in his head. Take you that steel, my lords; it is the tribute of Cornwall."

Then he went up to Tintagel and as he went the people he had freed waved green boughs, and rich cloths were hung at the windows. But when Tristan reached the castle with joy, songs and joy-bells sounding about him, he drooped in the arms of King Mark, for the blood ran from his wounds.

The Morholt's men, they landed in Ireland quite cast down. For when ever he came back into Whitehaven the Morholt had been wont to take joy in the sight of his clan upon the shore, of the Queen his sister, and of his niece Iseult the Fair. Tenderly had they cherished him of old, and had he taken some wound, they healed him, for they were skilled in balms and potions. But now their magic was vain, for he lay dead and the splinter of the foreign brand yet stood in his skull till Iseult plucked it out and shut it in a chest.

From that day Iseult the Fair knew and hated the name of Tristan of Lyonesse.

But over in Tintagel Tristan languished, for there trickled a poisonous blood from his wound. The doctors found that the Morholt had thrust into him a poisoned barb, and as their potions and their theriac could never heal him they left him in God's hands. So hateful a stench came from his wound that all his dearest friends fled him, all save King Mark, Gorvenal and Dinas of Lidan. They always could stay near his couch because their love overcame their abhorrence. At last Tristan had himself carried into a boat apart on the shore; and lying facing the sea he awaited death, for he thought: "I must die; but it is good to see the sun and my heart is still high. I would like to try the sea that brings all chances. ... I would have the sea bear me far off alone, to what land no matter, so that it heal me of my wound."

He begged so long that King Mark accepted his desire. He bore him into a boat with neither sail nor oar, and Tristan wished that his harp only should be placed beside him: for sails he could not lift, nor oar ply, nor sword wield; and as a seaman on some long voyage casts to the sea a beloved companion dead, so Gorvenal pushed out to sea that boat where his dear son lay; and the sea drew him away.

For seven days and seven nights the sea so drew him; at times to charm his grief, he harped; and when at last the sea brought him near a shore where fishermen had left their port that night to fish far out, they heard as they rowed a sweet and strong and living tune that ran above the sea, and feathering their oars they listened immovable.

In the first whiteness of the dawn they saw the boat at large: she went at random and nothing seemed to live in her except the voice of the harp. But as they neared, the air grew weaker and died; and when they hailed her Tristan's hands had fallen lifeless on the strings though they still trembled. The fishermen took him in and bore him back to port, to their lady who was merciful and perhaps would heal him.

It was that same port of Whitehaven where the Morholt lay, and their lady was Iseult the Fair.

She alone, being skilled in philtres, could save Tristan, but she alone wished him dead. When Tristan knew himself again (for her art restored him) he knew himself to be in the land of peril. But he was yet strong to hold his own and found good crafty words. He told a tale of how he was a seer that had taken passage on a merchant ship and sailed to Spain to learn the art of reading all the stars of how pirates had boarded the ship and of how, though wounded, he had fled into that boat. He was believed, nor did any of the Morholt's men know his face again, so hardly had the poison used it. But when, after forty days, Iseult of the Golden Hair had all but healed him, when already his limbs had recovered and the grace of youth returned, he knew that he must escape, and he fled and after many dangers he came again before Mark the King.

The Quest of the Lady with the Hair of Gold

MY LORDS, there were in the court of King Mark four barons the basest of men, who hated Tristan with a hard hate, for his greatness and for the tender love the King bore him. And well I know their names: Andret, Guenelon, Gondoïne

and Denoalen. They knew that the King had intent to grow old childless and to leave his land to Tristan; and their envy swelled and by lies they angered the chief men of Cornwall against Tristan. They said:

"There have been too many marvels in this man's life. It was marvel enough that he beat the Morholt, but by what sorcery did he try the sea alone at the point of death, or which of us, my lords, could voyage without mast or sail? They say that warlocks can. It was sure a warlock feat, and that is a warlock harp of his pours poison daily into the King's heart. See how he has bent that heart by power and chain of sorcery! He will be king yet, my lords, and you will hold your lands of a wizard."

They brought over the greater part of the barons and these pressed King Mark to take to wife some king's daughter who should give him an heir, or else they threatened to return each man into his keep and wage him war. But the King turned against them and swore in his heart that so long as his dear nephew lived no king's daughter should come to his bed. Then in his turn did Tristan (in his shame to be thought to serve for hire) threaten that if the King did not yield to his barons, he would himself go over sea serve some great king. At this, King Mark made a term with his barons and gave them forty days to hear his decision.

On the appointed day he waited alone in his chamber and sadly mused: "Where shall I find a king's daughter so fair and yet so distant that I may feign to wish her my wife?"

Just then by his window that looked upon the sea two building swallows came in quarrelling together. Then, startled, they flew out, but had let fall from their beaks a woman's hair, long and fine, and shining like a beam of light.

King Mark took it, and called his barons and Tristan and said:

"To please you, lords, I will take a wife; but you must seek her whom I have chosen."

"Fair lord, we wish it all," they said, "and who may she be?"

"Why," said he, "she whose hair this is; nor will I take another."

"And whence, lord King, comes this Hair of Gold; who brought it and from what land?"

"It comes, my lords, from the Lady with the Hair of Gold, the swallows brought it me. They know from what country it came."

Then the barons saw themselves mocked and cheated, and they turned with sneers to Tristan, for they thought him to have counselled the trick. But Tristan, when he had looked on the Hair of Gold, remembered Iseult the Fair and smiled and said this:

"King Mark, can you not see that the doubts of these lords shame me? You have designed in vain. I will go seek the Lady with the Hair of Gold. The search is perilous: never the less, my uncle, I would once more put my body and my life into peril for you; and that your barons may know I love you loyally, I take this oath, to die on the adventure or to bring back to this castle of Tintagel the Queen with that fair hair."

He fitted out a great ship and loaded it with corn and wine, with honey and all manner of good things; he manned it with Gorvenal and a hundred young knights of high birth, chosen among the bravest, and he clothed them in coats of home-spun and in hair cloth so that they seemed merchants only: but under the deck he hid rich cloth of gold and scarlet as for a great king's messengers.

When the ship had taken the sea the helmsman asked him:

"Lord, to what land shall I steer?"

"Sir," said he, "steer for Ireland, straight for Whitehaven harbour."

At first Tristan made believe to the men of Whitehaven that his friends were merchants of England come peacefully to barter; but as these strange merchants passed the day in the useless games of draughts and chess, and seemed to know dice better than the bargain price of corn, Tristan feared discovery and knew not how to pursue his quest.

Now it chanced once upon the break of day that he heard a cry so terrible that one would have called it a demon's cry; nor had he ever heard a brute bellow in such wise, so awful and strange it seemed. He called a woman who passed by the harbour, and said:

"Tell me, lady, whence comes that voice I have heard, and hide me nothing."

"My lord," said she, "I will tell you truly. It is the roar of a dragon the most terrible and dauntless upon earth. Daily it leaves its den and stands at one of the gates of the city: Nor can any come out or go in till a maiden has been given up to it; and when it has her in its claws it devours her."

"Lady," said Tristan, "make no mock of me, but tell me straight: Can a man born of woman kill this thing?"

"Fair sir, and gentle," she said, "I cannot say; but this is sure: Twenty knights and tried have run the venture, because the King of Ireland has published it that he will give his daughter, Iseult the Fair, to whomsoever shall kill the beast; but it has devoured them all."

Tristan left the woman and returning to his ship armed himself in secret, and it was a fine sight to see so noble a charger and so good a knight come out from such a merchant-hull: but the haven was empty of folk, for the dawn had barely broken and none saw him as he rode to the gate. And hardly had he passed it, when he met suddenly five men at full gallop flying towards the town. Tristan seized one by his hair, as he passed, and dragged him over his mount's crupper and held him fast:

"God save you, my lord," said he, "and whence does the dragon come?" And when the other had shown him by what road, he let him go.

As the monster neared, he showed the head of a bear and red eyes like coals of fire and hairy tufted ears; lion's claws, a serpent's tail, and a griffin's body.

Tristan charged his horse at him so strongly that, though the beast's mane stood with fright yet he drove at the dragon: his lance struck its scales and shivered. Then Tristan drew his sword and struck at the dragon's head, but he did not so much as cut the hide. The beast felt the blow: with its claws he dragged at the shield and broke it from the arm; then, his breast unshielded, Tristan used the sword again and struck so strongly that the air rang all round about: but in vain, for he could not wound and meanwhile the dragon vomited from his nostrils two streams of loathsome flames, and Tristan's helm blackened like a cinder and his horse stumbled and fell down and died; but Tristan standing on his feet thrust his sword right into the beast's jaws, and split its heart in two.

Then he cut out the tongue and put it into his hose, but as the poison came against his flesh the hero fainted and fell in the high grass that bordered the marsh around.

Now the man he had stopped in flight was the seneschal of Ireland and he desired Iseult the Fair: and though he was a coward, he had dared so far as to return with his companions secretly, and he found the dragon dead; so he cut off its head and bore it to the King, and claimed the great reward.

The King could credit his prowess but hardly, yet wished justice done and summoned his vassals to court, so that there, before the Barony assembled, the seneschal should furnish proof of his victory won.

When Iseult the Fair heard that she was to be given to this coward first she laughed long, and then she wailed. But on the morrow, doubting some trick, she took with her Perinis her squire and Brangien her maid, and all three rode unbeknownst towards the dragon's lair: and Iseult saw such a trail on the road as made her wonder – for the hoofs that made it had never been shod in her land. Then she came on the dragon, headless, and a dead horse beside him: nor was the horse harnessed in the fashion of Ireland. Some foreign man had slain the beast, but they knew not whether he still lived or no.

They sought him long, Iseult and Perinis and Brangien together, till at last Brangien saw the helm glittering in the marshy grass: and Tristan still breathed. Perinis put him on his horse and bore him secretly to the women's rooms. There Iseult told her mother the tale and left the hero with her, and as the Queen unharnessed him, the dragon's tongue fell from his boot of steel. Then, the Queen of Ireland revived him by the virtue of an herb and said:

"Stranger, I know you for the true slayer of the dragon: but our seneschal, a felon, cut off its head and claims my daughter Iseult for his wage; will you be ready two days hence to give him the lie in battle?"

"Queen," said he, "the time is short, but you, I think, can cure me in two days. Upon the dragon I conquered Iseult, and on the seneschal perhaps I shall reconquer her."

Then the Queen brewed him strong brews, and on the morrow Iseult the Fair got him ready a bath and anointed him with a balm her mother had conjured, and as he looked at her he thought, "So I have found the Queen of the Hair of Gold," and he smiled as he thought it. But Iseult, noting it, thought, "Why does he smile, or what have I neglected of the things due to a guest? He smiles to think I have for– gotten to burnish his armour."

She went and drew the sword from its rich sheath, but when she saw the splinter gone and the gap in the edge she thought of the Morholt's head. She balanced a moment in doubt, then she went to where she kept the steel she had found in the skull and she put it to the sword, and it fitted so that the join was hardly seen.

She ran to where Tristan lay wounded, and with the sword above him she cried:

"You are that Tristan of the Lyonesse, who killed the Morholt, my mother's brother, and now you shall die in your turn."

Tristan strained to ward the blow, but he was too weak; his wit, however, stood firm in spite of evil and he said:

"So be it, let me die: but to save yourself long memories, listen awhile. King's daughter, my life is not only in your power but is yours of right. My life is yours because you have twice returned it me. Once, long ago: for I was the wounded harper whom you healed of the poison of the Morholt's shaft. Nor repent the healing: were not these wounds had in fair fight? Did I kill the Morholt by treason? Had he not defied me and was I not held to the defence of my body? And now this second time also you have saved me. It was for you I fought the beast.

"But let us leave these things. I would but show you how my life is your own. Then if you kill me of right for the glory of it, you may ponder for long years, praising yourself that you killed a wounded guest who had wagered his life in your gaining."

Iseult replied: "I hear strange words. Why should he that killed the Morholt seek me also, his niece? Doubtless because the Morholt came for a tribute of maidens from Cornwall, so you came to boast returning that you had brought back the maiden who was nearest to him, to Cornwall, a slave."

"King's daughter," said Tristan, "No. … One day two swallows flew, and flew to Tintagel and bore one hair out of all your hairs of gold, and I thought they brought me good will and peace, so I came to find you overseas. See here, amid the threads of gold upon my coat your hair is sown: the threads are tarnished, but your bright hair still shines."

Iseult put down the sword and taking up the Coat of Arms she saw upon it the Hair of Gold and was silent a long space, till she kissed him on the lips to prove peace, and she put rich garments over him.

On the day of the barons' assembly, Tristan sent Perinis privily to his ship to summon his companions that they should come to court adorned as befitted the envoys of a great king.

One by one the hundred knights passed into the hall where all the barons of Ireland stood, they entered in silence and sat all in rank together: on their scarlet and purple the gems gleamed.

When the King had taken his throne, the seneschal arose to prove by witness and by arms that he had slain the dragon and that so Iseult was won. Then Iseult bowed to her father and said:

"King, I have here a man who challenges your seneschal for lies and felony. Promise that you will pardon this man all his past deeds, who stands to prove that he and none other slew the dragon, and grant him forgiveness and your peace."

The King said, "I grant it." But Iseult said, "Father, first give me the kiss of peace and forgiveness, as a sign that you will give him the same."

Then she found Tristan and led him before the Barony. And as he came the hundred knights rose all together, and crossed their arms upon their breasts and bowed, so the Irish knew that he was their lord.

But among the Irish many knew him again and cried, "Tristan of Lyonesse that slew the Morholt!" They drew their swords and clamoured for death. But Iseult cried: "King, kiss this man upon the lips as your oath was," and the King kissed him, and the clamour fell.

Then Tristan showed the dragon's tongue and offered the seneschal battle, but the seneschal looked at his face and dared not.

Then Tristan said:

"My lords, you have said it, and it is truth: I killed the Morholt. But I crossed the sea to offer you a good blood-fine, to ransom that deed and get me quit of it.

"I put my body in peril of death and rid you of the beast and have so conquered Iseult the Fair, and having conquered her I will bear her away on my ship.

"But that these lands of Cornwall and Ireland may know no more hatred, but love only, learn that King Mark, my lord, will marry her. Here stand a hundred knights of high name, who all will swear with an oath upon the relics of the holy saints, that King Mark sends you by their embassy offer of peace and of brotherhood and goodwill; and that he would by your courtesy hold Iseult as his honoured wife, and that he would have all the men of Cornwall serve her as their Queen."

When the lords of Ireland heard this they acclaimed it, and the King also was content.

Then, since that treaty and alliance was to be made, the King her father took Iseult by the hand and asked of Tristan that he should take an oath; to wit that he would lead her loyally to his lord, and Tristan took that oath and swore it before the knights and the Barony of Ireland assembled. Then the King put Iseult's right hand into Tristan's right hand, and Tristan held it for a space in token of seizin for the King of Cornwall.

So, for the love of King Mark, did Tristan conquer the Queen of the Hair of Gold.

The Philtre

WHEN THE DAY of Iseult's livery to the Lords of Cornwall drew near, her mother gathered herbs and flowers and roots and steeped them in wine, and brewed a potion of might, and having done so, said apart to Brangien:

"Child, it is yours to go with Iseult to King Mark's country, for you love her with a faithful love. Take then this pitcher and remember well my words. Hide it so that no eye shall see nor no lip go near it: but when the wedding night has come and that moment in which the wedded are left alone, pour this essenced wine into a cup and offer it to King Mark and to Iseult his queen. Oh! Take all care, my child, that they alone shall taste this brew. For this is its power: they who drink of it together love each other with their every single sense and with their every thought, for ever, in life and in death."

And Brangien promised the Queen that she would do her bidding.

On the bark that bore her to Tintagel Iseult the Fair was weeping as she remembered her own land, and mourning swelled her heart, and she said, "Who am I that I should leave you to follow unknown men, my mother and my land? Accursed be the sea that bears me, for rather would I lie dead on the earth where I was born than live out there, beyond ..."

One day when the wind had fallen and the sails hung slack Tristan dropped anchor by an Island and the hundred knights of Cornwall and the sailors, weary of the sea, landed all. Iseult alone remained aboard and a little serving maid, when Tristan came near the Queen to calm her sorrow. The sun was hot above them and they were athirst and, as they called, the little maid looked about for drink for them and found that pitcher which the mother of Iseult had given into Brangien's keeping. And when she came on it, the child cried, "I have found you wine!" Now she had found not wine – but Passion and Joy most sharp, and Anguish without end, and Death.

The Queen drank deep of that draught and gave it to Tristan and he drank also long and emptied it all.

Brangien came in upon them; she saw them gazing at each other in silence as though ravished and apart; she saw before them the pitcher standing there; she snatched it up and cast it into the shuddering sea and cried aloud: "Cursed be the day I was born and cursed the day that first I trod this deck. Iseult, my friend, and Tristan, you, you have drunk death together."

And once more the bark ran free for Tintagel. But it seemed to Tristan as though an ardent briar, sharp-thorned but with flower most sweet smelling, drave roots into his blood and laced the lovely body of Iseult all round about it and bound it to his own and to his every thought and desire. And he thought, "Felons, that charged me with coveting King Mark's land, I have come lower by far, for it is not his land I covet. Fair uncle, who loved me orphaned ere ever you knew in me the blood of your sister Blanchefleur, you that wept as you bore me to that boat alone, why did you not drive out the boy that was to betray you? Ah! What thought was that! Iseult is yours and I am but your vassal; Iseult is yours and I am your son; Iseult is yours and may not love me."

But Iseult loved him, though she would have hated. She could not hate, for a tenderness more sharp than hatred tore her.

And Brangien watched them in anguish, suffering more cruelly because she alone knew the depth of evil done.

Two days she watched them, seeing them refuse all food or comfort and seeking each other as blind men seek, wretched apart and together more wretched still, for then they trembled each for the first avowal.

On the third day, as Tristan neared the tent on deck where Iseult sat, she saw him coming and she said to him, very humbly, "Come in, my lord."

"Queen," said Tristan, "why do you call me lord? Am I not your liege and vassal, to revere and serve and cherish you as my lady and Queen?"

But Iseult answered, "No, you know that you are my lord and my master, and I your slave. Ah, why did I not sharpen those wounds of the wounded singer, or let die that dragon-slayer in the grasses of the marsh? But then I did not know what now I know!"

"And what is it that you know, Iseult?"

She laid her arm upon Tristan's shoulder, the light of her eyes was drowned and her lips trembled.

"The love of you," she said. Whereat he put his lips to hers.

But as they thus tasted their first joy, Brangien, that watched them, stretched her arms and cried at their feet in tears:

"Stay and return if still you can ... But oh! that path has no returning. For already Love and his strength drag you on and now henceforth for ever never shall you know joy without pain again. The wine possesses you, the draught your mother gave me, the draught the King alone should have drunk with you: but that old Enemy has tricked us, all us three; friend Tristan, Iseult my friend, for that bad ward I kept take here my body and my life, for through me and in that cup you have drunk not love alone, but love and death together."

The lovers held each other; life and desire trembled through their youth, and Tristan said, "Well then, come Death."

And as evening fell, upon the bark that heeled and ran to King Mark's land, they gave themselves up utterly to love.

The Tall Pine Tree

AS KING MARK came down to greet Iseult upon the shore, Tristan took her hand and led her to the King and the King took seizin of her, taking her hand. He led her in great pomp to his castle of Tintagel, and as she came in hall amid the vassals her beauty shone so that the walls were lit as they are lit at dawn. Then King Mark blessed those swallows which, by happy courtesy, had brought the Hair of Gold, and Tristan also he blessed, and the hundred knights who, on that adventurous bark, had gone to find him joy of heart and of eyes; yet to him also that ship was to bring sting, torment and mourning.

And on the eighteenth day, having called his Barony together he took Iseult to wife. But on the wedding night, to save her friend, Brangien took her place in the darkness, for her remorse demanded even this from her; nor was the trick discovered.

Then Iseult lived as a queen, but lived in sadness. She had King Mark's tenderness and the barons' honour; the people also loved her; she passed her days amid the frescoes on the walls and floors all strewn with flowers; good jewels had she and purple cloth and tapestry of Hungary and Thessaly too, and songs of harpers, and curtains upon which were worked leopards and eagles and popinjays and all the beasts of sea and field. And her love too she had, love high and splendid, for as is the custom among great lords, Tristan could ever be near her. At his leisure and his dalliance, night and day: for he slept in the King's chamber as great lords do, among the lieges and the councillors. Yet still she feared; for though her love were secret and Tristan unsuspected (for who suspects a son?) Brangien knew. And Brangien seemed in the Queen's mind like a witness spying; for Brangien alone knew what manner of life she led, and held her at mercy so. And the Queen thought Ah, if some day she should weary of serving as a slave the bed where once she passed for Queen … If Tristan should die from her betrayal! So fear maddened the Queen, but not in truth the fear of Brangien who was loyal; her own heart bred the fear.

Not Brangien who was faithful, not Brangien, but themselves had these lovers to fear, for hearts so stricken will lose their vigilance. Love pressed them hard, as thirst presses the dying stag to the stream; love dropped upon them from high heaven, as a hawk slipped after long hunger falls right upon the bird. And love will not be hidden. Brangien indeed by her prudence saved them well, nor ever were the Queen and her lover unguarded. But in every hour and place every man could see Love terrible, that rode them, and could see in these lovers their every sense overflowing like new wine working in the vat.

The four felons at court who had hated Tristan of old for his prowess, watched the Queen; they had guessed that great love, and they burnt with envy and hatred and now a kind of evil joy. They planned to give news of their watching to the King, to see his tenderness turned to fury, Tristan thrust out or slain, and the Queen in torment; for though they feared Tristan their hatred mastered their fear; and, on a day, the four barons called King Mark to parley, and Andret said:

"Fair King, your heart will be troubled and we four also mourn; yet are we bound to tell you what we know. You have placed your trust in Tristan and Tristan would shame you. In vain we warned you. For the love of one man you have mocked ties of blood and all your Barony. Learn then that Tristan loves the Queen; it is truth proved and many a word is passing on it now."

The royal King shrank and answered:

"Coward! What thought was that? Indeed I have placed my trust in Tristan. And rightly, for on the day when the Morholt offered combat to you all, you hung your heads and were dumb, and you trembled before him; but Tristan dared him for the honour of this land, and took mortal wounds. Therefore do you hate him, and therefore do I cherish him beyond thee, Andret, and beyond any other; but what then have you seen or heard or known?"

"Naught, lord, save what your eyes could see or your ears hear. Look you and listen, Sire, if there is yet time."

And they left him to taste the poison.

Then King Mark watched the Queen and Tristan; but Brangien noting it warned them both and the King watched in vain, so that, soon wearying of an ignoble task, but knowing (alas!) that he could not kill his uneasy thought, he sent for Tristan and said:

"Tristan, leave this castle; and having left it, remain apart and do not think to return to it, and do not repass its moat or boundaries. Felons have charged you with an awful treason, but ask me nothing; I could not speak their words without shame to us both, and for your part seek you no word to appease. I have not believed them … had I done so … But their evil words have troubled all my soul and only by your absence can my disquiet be soothed. Go, doubtless I will soon recall you. Go, my son, you are still dear to me."

When the felons heard the news they said among themselves, "He is gone, the wizard; he is driven out. Surely he will cross the sea on far adventures to carry his traitor service to some distant King."

But Tristan had not strength to depart altogether; and when he had crossed the moats and boundaries of the castle he knew he could go no further. He stayed in Tintagel town and lodged with Gorvenal in a burgess' house, and languished oh! more wounded than when in that past day the shaft of the Morholt had tainted his body.

In the close towers Iseult the Fair drooped also, but more wretched still. For it was hers all day long to feign laughter and all night long to conquer fever and despair. And all night as she lay by King Mark's side, fever still kept her waking, and she stared at darkness. She longed to fly to Tristan and she dreamt dreams of running to the gates and of finding there sharp scythes, traps of the felons, that cut her tender knees; and she dreamt of weakness and falling, and that her wounds had left her blood upon the ground. Now these lovers would have died, but Brangien succoured them. At peril of her life she found the house where Tristan lay. There Gorvenal opened to her very gladly, knowing what salvation she could bring.

So she found Tristan, and to save the lovers she taught him a device, nor was ever known a more subtle ruse of love.

Behind the castle of Tintagel was an orchard fenced around and wide and all closed in with stout and pointed stakes and numberless trees were there and fruit on them, birds and clusters of sweet grapes. And furthest from the castle, by the stakes of the pallisade, was a tall pine tree, straight and with heavy branches spreading from its trunk. At its root a living spring welled calm into a marble round, then ran between two borders winding, throughout the orchard and so, on, till it flowed at last within the castle and through the women's rooms.

And every evening, by Brangien's counsel, Tristan cut him twigs and bark, leapt the sharp stakes and, having come beneath the pine, threw them into the clear spring; they floated light as foam down the stream to the women's rooms; and Iseult watched for their coming, and on those evenings she would wander out into the orchard and find her friend. Lithe and in fear would she come, watching at every step for what might lurk in the trees observing, foes or the felons whom she knew, till she spied Tristan; and the night and the branches of the pine protected them.

And so she said one night: "Oh, Tristan, I have heard that the castle is faëry and that twice a year it vanishes away. So is it vanished now and this is that enchanted orchard of which the harpers sing." And as she said it, the sentinels bugled dawn.

Iseult had refound her joy. Mark's thought of ill-ease grew faint; but the felons felt or knew which way lay truth, and they guessed that Tristan had met the Queen. Till at last Duke Andret (whom God shame) said to his peers:

"My lords, let us take counsel of Frocin the Dwarf; for he knows the seven arts, and magic and every kind of charm. He will teach us if he will the wiles of Iseult the Fair."

The little evil man drew signs for them and characters of sorcery; he cast the fortunes of the hour and then at last he said:

"Sirs, high good lords, this night shall you seize them both."

Then they led the little wizard to the King, and he said:

"Sire, bid your huntsmen leash the hounds and saddle the horses, proclaim a seven days' hunt in the forest and seven nights abroad therein, and hang me high if you do not hear this night what converse Tristan holds."

So did the King unwillingly; and at fall of night he left the hunt taking the dwarf in pillion, and entered the orchard, and the dwarf took him to the tall pine tree, saying:

"Fair King, climb into these branches and take with you your arrows and your bow, for you may need them; and bide you still."

That night the moon shone clear. Hid in the branches the King saw his nephew leap the pallisades and throw his bark and twigs into the stream. But Tristan had bent over the round well to throw them and so doing had seen the image of the King. He could not stop the branches as they floated away, and there, yonder, in the women's rooms, Iseult was watching and would come.

She came, and Tristan watched her motionless. Above him in the tree he heard the click of the arrow when it fits the string.

She came, but with more prudence than her wont, thinking, "What has passed, that Tristan does not come to meet me? He has seen some foe."

Suddenly, by the clear moonshine, she also saw the King's shadow in the fount. She showed the wit of women well, she did not lift her eyes.

"Lord God," she said, low down, grant I may be the first to speak."

"Tristan," she said, "what have you dared to do, calling me hither at such an hour? Often have you called me – to beseech, you said. And Queen though I am, I know you won me that title – and I have come. What would you?"

"Queen, I would have you pray the King for me."

She was in tears and trembling, but Tristan praised God the Lord who had shown his friend her peril.

"Queen," he went on, "often and in vain have I summoned you; never would you come. Take pity; the King hates me and I know not why. Perhaps you know the cause and can charm his anger. For whom can he trust if not you, chaste Queen and courteous, Iseult?"

"Truly, Lord Tristan, you do not know he doubts us both. And I, to add to my shame, must acquaint you of it. Ah! but God knows if I lie, never went out my love to any man but he that first received me. And would you have me, at such a time, implore your pardon of the King? Why, did he know of my passage here tonight he would cast my ashes to the wind. My body trembles and I am afraid. I go, for I have waited too long."

In the branches the King smiled and had pity.

And as Iseult fled: "Queen," said Tristan, "in the Lord's name help me, for charity."

"Friend," she replied, "God aid you! The King wrongs you but the Lord God will be by you in whatever land you go."

So she went back to the women's rooms and told it to Brangien, who cried: "Iseult, God has worked a miracle for you, for He is compassionate and will not hurt the innocent in heart."

And when he had left the orchard, the King said smiling:

"Fair nephew, that ride you planned is over now."

But in an open glade apart, Frocin, the Dwarf, read in the clear stars that the King now meant his death; he blackened with shame and fear and fled into Wales.

The Discovery

KING MARK MADE PEACE with Tristan. Tristan returned to the castle as of old. Tristan slept in the King's chamber with his peers. He could come or go, the King thought no more of it.

Mark had pardoned the felons, and as the seneschal, Dinas of Lidan, found the dwarf wandering in a forest abandoned, he brought him home, and the King had pity and pardoned even him.

But his goodness did but feed the ire of the barons, who swore this oath: If the King kept Tristan in the land they would withdraw to their strongholds as for war, and they called the King to parley.

"Lord," said they, "Drive you Tristan forth. He loves the Queen as all who choose can see, but as for us we will bear it no longer."

And the King sighed, looking down in silence.

"King," they went on, "we will not bear it, for we know now that this is known to you and that yet you will not move. Parley you, and take counsel. As for us if you will not exile this man, your nephew, and drive him forth out of your land for ever, we will withdraw within our bailiwicks and take our neighbours also from your court: for we cannot endure his presence longer in this place. Such is your balance: choose."

"My lords," said he, "once I hearkened to the evil words you spoke of Tristan, yet was I wrong in the end. But you are my lieges and I would not lose the service of my men. Counsel me therefore, I charge you, you that owe me counsel. You know me for a man neither proud nor overstepping."

"Lord," said they, "call then Frocin hither. You mistrust him for that orchard night. Still, was it not he that read in the stars of the Queen's coming there and to the very pine tree too? He is very wise, take counsel of him."

And he came, did that hunchback of Hell: the felons greeted him and he planned this evil.

"Sire," said he, "let your nephew ride hard tomorrow at dawn with a brief drawn up on parchment and well sealed with a seal: bid him ride to King Arthur at Carduel. Sire, he sleeps with the peers in your chamber; go you out when the first sleep falls on men, and if he love Iseult so madly, why, then I swear by God and by the laws of Rome, he will try to speak with her before he rides. But if he do so unknown to you or to me, then slay me. As for the trap, let me lay it, but do you say nothing of his ride to him until the time for sleep."

And when King Mark had agreed, this dwarf did a vile thing. He bought of a baker four farthings' worth of flour, and hid it in the turn of his coat. That night, when the King had supped and the men-at-arms lay down to sleep in hall, Tristan came to the King as custom was, and the King said:

"Fair nephew, do my will: ride tomorrow night to King Arthur at Carduel, and give him this brief, with my greeting, that he may open it: and stay you with him but one day."

And when Tristan said: "I will take it on the morrow;"

The King added: "Aye, and before day dawn."

But, as the peers slept all round the King their lord, that night, a mad thought took Tristan that, before he rode, he knew not for how long, before dawn he would say a last word to the Queen. And there was a spear length in the darkness between them. Now the dwarf slept with the rest in the King's chamber, and when he thought that all slept he rose and scattered the flour silently in the spear length that lay between Tristan and the Queen; but Tristan watched and saw him, and said to himself:

"It is to mark my footsteps, but there shall be no marks to show."

At midnight, when all was dark in the room, no candle nor any lamp glimmering, the King went out silently by the door and with him the dwarf. Then Tristan rose in the darkness and judged the spear length and leapt the space between, for his farewell. But that day in the hunt a boar had wounded him in the leg, and in this effort the wound bled. He did not feel it or see it in the darkness, but the blood dripped upon the couches and the flour strewn between; and outside in the moonlight the dwarf read the heavens and knew what had been done and he cried:

"Enter, my King, and if you do not hold them, hang me high."

Then the King and the dwarf and the four felons ran in with lights and noise, and though Tristan had regained his place there was the blood for witness, and though Iseult feigned sleep, and Perinis too, who lay at Tristan's feet, yet there was the blood for witness. And the King looked in silence at the blood where it lay upon the bed and the boards and trampled into the flour.

And the four barons held Tristan down upon his bed and mocked the Queen also, promising her full justice; and they bared and showed the wound whence the blood flowed.

Then the King said:

"Tristan, now nothing longer holds. Tomorrow you shall die."

And Tristan answered:

"Have mercy, Lord, in the name of God that suffered the Cross!"

But the felons called on the King to take vengeance, saying:

"Do justice, King: take vengeance."

And Tristan went on, "Have mercy, not on me – for why should I stand at dying? Truly, but for you, I would have sold my honour high to cowards who, under your peace, have put hands on my body – but in homage to you I have yielded and you may do with me what you will. But, lord, remember the Queen!"

And as he knelt at the King's feet he still complained:

"Remember the Queen; for if any man of your household make so bold as to maintain the lie that I loved her unlawfully I will stand up armed to him in a ring. Sire, in the name of God the Lord, have mercy on her."

Then the barons bound him with ropes, and the Queen also. But had Tristan known that trial by combat was to be denied him, certainly he would not have suffered it.

For he trusted in God and knew no man dared draw sword against him in the lists. And truly he did well to trust in God, for though the felons mocked him when he said he had loved loyally, yet I call you to witness, my lords who read this, and who know of the philtre drunk upon the high seas, and who, understand whether his love were disloyalty indeed. For men see this and that outward thing, but God alone the heart, and in the heart alone is crime and the sole final judge is God. Therefore did He lay down the law that a man accused might uphold his cause by battle, and God himself fights for the innocent in such a combat.

Therefore did Tristan claim justice and the right of battle and therefore was he careful to fail in nothing of the homage he owed King Mark, his lord.

But had he known what was coming, he would have killed the felons.

The Chantry Leap

DARK WAS THE NIGHT, and the news ran that Tristan and the Queen were held and that the King would kill them; and wealthy burgess, or common man, they wept and ran to the palace.

And the murmurs and the cries ran through the city, but such was the King's anger in his castle above that not the strongest nor the proudest baron dared move him.

Night ended and the day drew near. Mark, before dawn, rode out to the place where he held pleas and judgment. He ordered a ditch to be dug in the earth and knotty vine-shoots and thorns to be laid therein.

At the hour of Prime he had a ban cried through his land to gather the men of Cornwall; they came with a great noise and the King spoke them thus:

"My lords, I have made here a faggot of thorns for Tristan and the Queen; for they have fallen."

But they cried all, with tears:

"A sentence, lord, a sentence; an indictment and pleas; for killing without trial is shame and crime."

But Mark answered in his anger:

"Neither respite, nor delay, nor pleas, nor sentence. By God that made the world, if any dare petition me, he shall burn first!"

He ordered the fire to be lit, and Tristan to be called.

The flames rose, and all were silent before the flames, and the King waited.

The servants ran to the room where watch was kept on the two lovers; and they dragged Tristan out by his hands though he wept for his honour; but as they dragged him off in such a shame, the Queen still called to him:

"Friend, if I die that you may live, that will be great joy."

Now, hear how full of pity is God and how He heard the lament and the prayers of the common folk, that day.

For as Tristan and his guards went down from the town to where the faggot burned, near the road upon a rock was a chantry, it stood at a cliff's edge steep and sheer, and it turned to the sea breeze; in the apse of it were windows glazed. Then Tristan said to those with him:

"My lords, let me enter this chantry, to pray for a moment the mercy of God whom I have offended; my death is near. There is but one door to the place, my lords, and each of you has his sword drawn. So, you may well see that, when my prayer to God is done, I must come past you again: when I have prayed God, my lords, for the last time.

And one of the guards said: "Why, let him go in."

So they let him enter to pray. But he, once in, dashed through and leapt the altar rail and the altar too and forced a window of the apse, and leapt again over the cliff's edge. So might he die, but not of that shameful death before the people.

Now learn, my lords, how generous was God to him that day. The wind took Tristan's cloak and he fell upon a smooth rock at the cliff's foot, which to this day the men of Cornwall call "Tristan's leap".

His guards still waited for him at the chantry door, but vainly, for God was now his guard. And he ran, and the fine sand crunched under his feet, and far off he saw the faggot burning, and the smoke and the crackling flames; and fled.

Sword girt and bridle loose, Gorvenal had fled the city, lest the King burn him in his master's place: and he found Tristan on the shore.

"Master," said Tristan, "God has saved me, but oh! master, to what end? For without Iseult I may not and I will not live, and I rather had died of my fall. They will burn her for me, then I too will die for her."

"Lord," said Gorvenal, "take no counsel of anger. See here this thicket with a ditch dug round about it. Let us hide therein where the track passes near, and comers by it will tell us news; and, boy, if they burn Iseult, I swear by God, the Son of Mary, never to sleep under a roof again until she be avenged."

There was a poor man of the common folk that had seen Tristan's fall, and had seen him stumble and rise after, and he crept to Tintagel and to Iseult where she was bound, and said:

"Queen, weep no more. Your friend has fled safely."

"Then I thank God," said she, "and whether they bind or loose me, and whether they kill or spare me, I care but little now."

And though blood came at the cord-knots, so tightly had the traitors bound her, yet still she said, smiling:

"Did I weep for that when God has loosed my friend I should be little worth."

When the news came to the King that Tristan had leapt that leap and was lost he paled with anger, and bade his men bring forth Iseult.

They dragged her from the room, and she came before the crowd, held by her delicate hands, from which blood dropped, and the crowd called:

"Have pity on her – the loyal Queen and honoured! Surely they that gave her up brought mourning on us all – our curses on them!"

But the King's men dragged her to the thorn faggot as it blazed. She stood up before the flame, and the crowd cried its anger, and cursed the traitors and the King. None could see her without pity, unless he had a felon's heart: she was so tightly bound. The tears ran down her face and fell upon her grey gown where ran a little thread of gold, and a thread of gold was twined into her hair.

Just then there had come up a hundred lepers of the King's, deformed and broken, white horribly, and limping on their crutches. And they drew near the flame, and being evil, loved the sight. And their chief Ivan, the ugliest of them all, cried to the King in a quavering voice:

"O King, you would burn this woman in that flame, and it is sound justice, but too swift, for very soon the fire will fall, and her ashes will very soon be scattered by the high wind and her agony be done. Throw her rather to your lepers where she may drag out a life for ever asking death."

And the King answered:

"Yes; let her live that life, for it is better justice and more terrible. I can love those that gave me such a thought."

And the lepers answered:

"Throw her among us, and make her one of us. Never shall lady have known a worse end. And look," they said, "at our rags and our abominations. She has had pleasure in rich stuffs and furs, jewels and walls of marble, honour, good wines and joy, but when she sees your lepers always, King, and only them for ever, their couches and their huts, then indeed she will know the wrong she has done, and bitterly desire even that great flame of thorns."

And as the King heard them, he stood a long time without moving; then he ran to the Queen and seized her by the hand, and she cried:

"Burn me! rather burn me!"

But the King gave her up, and Ivan took her, and the hundred lepers pressed around, and to hear her cries all the crowd rose in pity. But Ivan had an evil gladness, and as he went he dragged her out of the borough bounds, with his hideous company.

Now they took that road where Tristan lay in hiding, and Gorvenal said to him:

"Son, here is your friend. Will you do naught?"

Then Tristan mounted the horse and spurred it out of the bush, and cried:

"Ivan, you have been at the Queen's side a moment, and too long. Now leave her if you would live."

But Ivan threw his cloak away and shouted:

"Your clubs, comrades, and your staves! Crutches in the air – for a fight is on!"

Then it was fine to see the lepers throwing their capes aside, and stirring their sick legs, and brandishing their crutches, some threatening: groaning all; but to strike them Tristan was too noble. There are singers who sing that Tristan killed Ivan, but it is a lie. Too much a knight was he to kill such things. Gorvenal indeed, snatching up an oak sapling, crashed it on Ivan's head till his blood ran down to his misshapen feet. Then Tristan took the Queen.

Henceforth near him she felt no further evil. He cut the cords that bound her arms so straightly, and he left the plain so that they plunged into the wood of Morois; and there in the thick wood Tristan was as sure as in a castle keep.

And as the sun fell they halted all three at the foot of a little hill: fear had wearied the Queen, and she leant her head upon his body and slept.

But in the morning, Gorvenal stole from a wood man his bow and two good arrows plumed and barbed, and gave them to Tristan, the great archer, and he shot him a fawn and killed it. Then Gorvenal gathered dry twigs, struck flint, and lit a great fire to cook the venison. And Tristan cut him branches and made a hut and garnished it with leaves. And Iseult slept upon the thick leaves there.

So, in the depths of the wild wood began for the lovers that savage life which yet they loved very soon.

Part the Second

The Wood of Morois

THEY WANDERED in the depths of the wild wood, restless and in haste like beasts that are hunted, nor did they often dare to return by night to the shelter of yesterday. They ate but the flesh of wild animals. Their faces sank and grew white, their clothes ragged; for the briars tore them. They loved each other and they did not know that they suffered.

One day, as they were wandering in these high woods that had never yet been felled or ordered, they came upon the hermitage of Ogrin.

The old man limped in the sunlight under a light growth of maples near his chapel: he leant upon his crutch, and cried:

"Lord Tristan, hear the great oath which the Cornish men have sworn. The King has published a ban in every parish: Whosoever may seize you shall receive a hundred marks of gold for his guerdon, and all the barons have sworn to give you up alive or dead. Do penance, Tristan! God pardons the sinner who turns to repentance."

"And of what should I repent, Ogrin, my lord? Or of what crime? You that sit in judgment upon us here, do you know what cup it was we drank upon the high sea? That good, great draught inebriates us both. I would rather beg my life long and live of roots and herbs with Iseult than, lacking her, be king of a wide kingdom."

"God aid you, Lord Tristan; for you have lost both this world and the next. A man that is traitor to his lord is worthy to be torn by horses and burnt upon the faggot, and wherever his ashes fall no grass shall grow and all tillage is waste, and the trees and the green things die. Lord Tristan, give back the Queen to the man who espoused her lawfully according to the laws of Rome."

"He gave her to his lepers. From these lepers I myself conquered her with my own hand; and henceforth she is altogether mine. She cannot pass from me nor I from her."

Ogrin sat down; but at his feet Iseult, her head upon the knees of that man of God, wept silently. The hermit told her and retold her the words of his holy book, but still while she wept she shook her head, and refused the faith he offered.

"Ah me," said Ogrin then, "what comfort can one give the dead? Do penance, Tristan, for a man who lives in sin without repenting is a man quite dead."

"Oh no," said Tristan, "I live and I do no penance. We will go back into the high wood which comforts and wards us all round about. Come with me, Iseult, my friend."

Iseult rose up; they held each other's hands. They passed into the high grass and the underwood: the trees hid them with their branches. They disappeared beyond the leaves.

The summer passed and the winter came: the two lovers lived, all hidden in the hollow of a rock, and on the frozen earth the cold crisped their couch with dead leaves. In the strength of their love neither one nor the other felt these mortal things. But when the open skies had come back with the springtime, they built a hut of green branches under the great trees. Tristan had known, ever since his childhood, that art by which a man may sing the song of birds in the woods, and at his fancy, he would call as call the thrush, the blackbird and the nightingale, and all winged things; and sometimes in reply very many birds would come on to the branches of his hut and sing their song full-throated in the new light.

The lovers had ceased to wander through the forest, for none of the barons ran the risk of their pursuit knowing well that Tristan would have hanged them to the branches of a tree. One day, however, one of the four traitors, Guenelon, whom God blast! drawn by the heat of the hunt, dared enter the Morois. And that morning, on the forest edge in a ravine, Gorvenal, having unsaddled his horse, had let him graze on the new grass, while far off in their hut Tristan held the Queen, and they slept. Then suddenly Gorvenal heard the cry of the pack; the hounds pursued a deer, which fell into that ravine. And far on the heath the hunter showed – and Gorvenal knew him for the man whom his master hated above all. Alone, with bloody spurs, and striking his horse's mane, he galloped on; but Gorvenal watched him from ambush: he came fast, he would return more slowly. He passed and Gorvenal leapt from his ambush and seized the rein and, suddenly, remembering all the wrong that man had done, hewed him to death and carried off his head in his hands. And when the hunters found the body, as they followed, they thought Tristan came after and they fled in fear of death, and thereafter no man hunted in that wood. And far off, in the hut upon their couch of leaves, slept Tristan and the Queen.

There came Gorvenal, noiseless, the dead man's head in his hands that he might lift his master's heart at his awakening. He hung it by its hair outside the hut, and the leaves garlanded it about. Tristan woke and saw it, half hidden in the leaves, and staring at him as he gazed, and he became afraid. But Gorvenal said: "Fear not, he is dead. I killed him with this sword."

Then Tristan was glad, and henceforward from that day no one dared enter the wild wood, for terror guarded it and the lovers were lords of it all: and then it was that Tristan fashioned his bow "Failnaught" which struck home always, man or beast, whatever it aimed at.

My lords, upon a summer day, when mowing is, a little after Whitsuntide, as the birds sang dawn Tristan left his hut and girt his sword on him, and took his bow "Failnaught" and went off to hunt in the wood; but before evening, great evil was to fall on him, for no lovers ever loved so much or paid their love so dear.

When Tristan came back, broken by the heat, the Queen said:

"Friend, where have you been?"

"Hunting a hart," he said, "that wearied me. I would lie down and sleep."

So she lay down, and he, and between them Tristan put his naked sword, and on the Queen's finger was that ring of gold with emeralds set therein, which Mark had given her on her bridal day; but her hand was so wasted that the ring hardly held. And no wind blew, and no leaves stirred, but through a crevice in the branches a sunbeam fell upon the face of Iseult and it shone white like ice. Now a woodman found in the wood a place where the leaves were crushed, where the lovers had halted and slept, and he followed their track and found the hut, and saw them sleeping and fled off, fearing the terrible awakening of that lord. He fled to Tintagel, and going up the stairs of the palace, found the King as he held his pleas in hall amid the vassals assembled.

"Friend," said the King, "what came you hither to seek in haste and breathless, like a huntsman that has followed the dogs afoot? Have you some wrong to right, or has any man driven you?"

But the woodman took him aside and said low down:

"I have seen the Queen and Tristan, and I feared and fled."

"Where saw you them?"

"In a hut in Morois, they slept side by side. Come swiftly and take your vengeance."

"Go," said the King, "and await me at the forest edge where the red cross stands, and tell no man what you have seen. You shall have gold and silver at your will."

The King had saddled his horse and girt his sword and left the city alone, and as he rode alone he minded him of the night when he had seen Tristan under the great pine tree, and Iseult with her clear face, and he thought:

"If I find them I will avenge this awful wrong."

At the foot of the red cross he came to the woodman and said:

"Go first, and lead me straight and quickly."

The dark shade of the great trees wrapt them round, and as the King followed the spy he felt his sword, and trusted it for the great blows it had struck of old; and surely had Tristan wakened, one of the two had stayed there dead. Then the woodman said:

"King, we are near."

He held the stirrup, and tied the rein to a green apple tree, and saw in a sunlit glade the hut with its flowers and leaves. Then the King cast his cloak with its fine buckle of gold and drew his sword from its sheath and said again in his heart that they or he should die. And he signed to the woodman to be gone.

He came alone into the hut, sword bare, and watched them as they lay: but he saw that they were apart, and he wondered because between them was the naked blade.

Then he said to himself: "My God, I may not kill them. For all the time they have lived together in this wood, these two lovers, yet is the sword here between them, and throughout Christendom men know that sign. Therefore I will not slay, for that would be treason and wrong, but I will do so that when they wake they may know that I found them here, asleep, and spared them and that God had pity on them both."

And still the sunbeam fell upon the white face of Iseult, and the King took his ermined gloves and put them up against the crevice whence it shone.

Then in her sleep a vision came to Iseult. She seemed to be in a great wood and two lions near her fought for her, and she gave a cry and woke, and the gloves fell upon her breast; and at the cry Tristan woke, and made to seize his sword, and saw by the golden hilt that it was the King's. And the Queen saw on her finger the King's ring, and she cried:

"O, my lord, the King has found us here!"

And Tristan said:

"He has taken my sword; he was alone, but he will return, and will burn us before the people. Let us fly."

So by great marches with Gorvenal alone they fled towards Wales.

Ogrin the Hermit

AFTER THREE DAYS it happened that Tristan, in following a wounded deer far out into the wood, was caught by night fall, and took to thinking thus under the dark wood alone:

"It was not fear that moved the King ... he had my sword and I slept ... and had he wished to slay, why did he leave me his own blade? ... O, my father, my father, I know you now. There was pardon in your heart, and tenderness and pity ... yet how was that, for who could forgive in this matter without shame? ... It was not pardon it was understanding; the faggot and the chantry leap and the leper ambush have shown him God upon our side. Also I think he remembered the boy who long ago harped at his feet, and my land of Lyonesse which I left for him; the Morholt's spear and blood shed in his honour. He remembered how I made no avowal, but claimed a trial at arms, and the high nature of his heart has made him understand what men around him cannot; never can he know of the spell, yet he doubts and hopes and knows I have told no lie, and would have me prove my cause. O, but to win at arms by God's aid for him, and to enter his peace and to put on mail for him again ... but then he must take her back, and I must yield her ... it would have been much better had he killed me in my sleep. For till now I was hunted and I could hate and forget; he had thrown Iseult to the lepers, she was no more his, but mine; and now by his compassion he has wakened my heart and regained the Queen. For Queen she was at his side, but in this wood she lives a slave, and I waste her youth; and for rooms all hung with silk she has this savage place, and a hut for her splendid walls, and I am the cause that she treads this ugly road. So now I cry to God the Lord, who is King of the world, and beg Him to give me strength to yield back Iseult to King Mark; for she is indeed his wife, wed according to the laws of Rome before all the Barony of his land."

And as he thought thus, he leant upon his bow, and all through the night considered his sorrow.

Within the hollow of thorns that was their resting place Iseult the Fair awaited Tristan's return. The golden ring that King Mark had slipped there glistened on her finger in the moonlight, and she thought:

"He that put on this ring is not the man who threw me to his lepers in his wrath; he is rather that compassionate lord who, from the day I touched his shore, received me and protected. And he loved Tristan once, but I came, and see what I have done! He should have lived in the King's palace; he should have ridden through King's and baron's fees, finding adventure; but through me he has forgotten his knighthood, and is hunted and exiled from the court, leading a random life. ..."

Just then she heard the feet of Tristan coming over the dead leaves and twigs. She came to meet him, as was her wont, to relieve him of his arms, and she took from him his bow, "Failnaught," and his arrows, and she unbuckled his sword-straps. And, "Friend," said he, "it is the King's sword. It should have slain, but it spared us."

Iseult took the sword, and kissed the hilt of gold, and Tristan saw her weeping.

"Friend," said he, "if I could make my peace with the King; if he would allow me to sustain in arms that neither by act nor word have I loved you with a wrongful love, any knight from the Marshes of Ely right away to Dureaume that would gainsay me, would find me armed in the ring. Then if the King would keep you and drive me out I would cross to the Lowlands or to Brittany with Gorvenal alone. But wherever I went and always, Queen, I should be yours; nor would I have spoken thus, Iseult, but for the wretchedness you bear so long for my sake in this desert land."

"Tristan," she said, "there is the hermit Ogrin. Let us return to him, and cry mercy to the King of Heaven."

They wakened Gorvenal; Iseult mounted the steed, and Tristan led it by the bridle, and all night long they went for the last time through the woods of their love, and they did not speak a word. By morning they came to the Hermitage, where Ogrin read at the threshold, and seeing them, called them tenderly:

"Friends," he cried, "see how Love drives you still to further wretchedness. Will you not do penance at last for your madness?"

"Lord Ogrin," said Tristan, "hear us. Help us to offer peace to the King, and I will yield him the Queen, and will myself go far away into Brittany or the Lowlands, and if some day the King suffer me, I will return and serve as I should."

And at the hermit's feet Iseult said in her turn:

"Nor will I live longer so, for though I will not say one word of penance for my love, which is there and remains for ever, yet from now on I will be separate from him."

Then the hermit wept and praised God and cried: "High King, I praise Thy Name, for that Thou hast let me live so long as to give aid to these!"

And he gave them wise counsel, and took ink, and wrote a little writ offering the King what Tristan said.

That night Tristan took the road. Once more he saw the marble well and the tall pine tree, and he came beneath the window where the King slept, and called him gently, and Mark awoke and whispered:

"Who are you that call me in the night at such an hour?"

"Lord, I am Tristan: I bring you a writ, and lay it here."

Then the King cried: "Nephew! nephew! for God's sake wait awhile," but Tristan had fled and joined his squire, and mounted rapidly. Gorvenal said to him:

"O, Tristan, you are mad to have come. Fly hard with me by the nearest road."

So they came back to the Hermitage, and there they found Ogrin at prayer, but Iseult weeping silently.

The Ford

MARK HAD AWAKENED his chaplain and had given him the writ to read; the chaplain broke the seal, saluted in Tristan's name, and then, when he had cunningly made out the written words, told him what Tristan offered; and Mark heard without saying a word, but his heart was glad, for he still loved the Queen.

He summoned by name the choicest of his baronage, and when they were all assembled they were silent and the King spoke:

"My lords, here is a writ, just sent me. I am your King, and you my lieges. Hear what is offered me, and then counsel me, for you owe me counsel."

The chaplain rose, unfolded the writ, and said, upstanding:

"My lords, it is Tristan that first sends love and homage to the King and all his Barony, and he adds, 'O King, when I slew the dragon and conquered the King of Ireland's daughter it was to me they gave her. I was to ward her at will and I yielded her to you. Yet hardly had you wed her when felons made you accept their lies, and in your anger, fair uncle, my lord, you would have had us burnt without trial. But God took compassion on us; we prayed him and he saved the Queen, as justice was: and me also – though I leapt from a high rock, I was saved by the power of God. And since then what have I done blameworthy? The Queen was thrown to the lepers; I came to her succour and bore her away. Could I have done less for a woman, who all but died innocent through me? I fled through the woods. Nor could I have come down into the vale and yielded her, for there was a ban to take us dead or alive. But now, as then, I am ready, my lord, to sustain in arms against all comers that never had the Queen for me, nor I for her a love dishonourable to you. Publish the lists, and if I cannot prove my right in arms, burn me before your men. But if I conquer and you take back Iseult, no baron of yours will serve you as will I; and if you will not have me, I will offer myself to the King of Galloway, or to him of the Lowlands, and you will hear of me never again. Take counsel, King, for if you will make no terms I will take back Iseult to Ireland, and she shall be Queen in her own land.'"

When the barons of Cornwall heard how Tristan offered battle, they said to the King:

"Sire, take back the Queen. They were madmen that belied her to you. But as for Tristan, let him go and war it in Galloway, or in the Lowlands. Bid him bring back Iseult on such a day and that soon."

Then the King called thrice clearly:

"Will any man rise in accusation against Tristan?"

And as none replied, he said to his chaplain:

"Write me a writ in haste. You have heard what you shall write. Iseult has suffered enough in her youth. And let the writ be hung upon the arm of the red cross before evening. Write speedily."

Towards midnight Tristan crossed the Heath of Sand, and found the writ, and bore it sealed to Ogrin; and the hermit read the letter: "How Mark consented by the counsel of his barons to take back Iseult, but not to keep Tristan for his liege. Rather let him cross the sea, when, on the third day hence, at the Ford of Chances, he had given back the Queen into King Mark's hands." Then Tristan said to the Queen:

"O, my God! I must lose you, friend! But it must be, since I can thus spare you what you suffer for my sake. But when we part for ever I will give you a pledge of mine to keep, and from whatever unknown land I reach I will send some messenger, and he will bring back word of you, and at your call I will come from far away."

Iseult said, sighing:

"Tristan, leave me your dog, Toothold, and every time I see him I will remember you, and will be less sad. And, friend, I have here a ring of green jasper. Take it for the love of me, and put it on your finger; then if anyone come saying he is from you, I will not trust him at all till he show me this ring, but once I have seen it, there is no power or royal ban that can prevent me from doing what you bid – wisdom or folly."

"Friend," he said, "here give I you Toothold."

"Friend," she replied, "take you this ring in reward."

And they kissed each other on the lips.

Now Ogrin, having left the lovers in the Hermitage, hobbled upon his crutch to the place called the Mount, and he bought ermine there and fur and cloth of silk and purple and scarlet, and a palfrey harnessed in gold that went softly, and the folk laughed to see him spending upon these the small moneys he had amassed so long; but the old man put the rich stuffs upon the palfrey and came back to Iseult.

And "Queen," said he, "take these gifts of mine that you may seem the finer on the day when you come to the Ford."

Meanwhile the King had had cried through Cornwall the news that on the third day he would make his peace with the Queen at the Ford, and knights and ladies came in a crowd to the gathering, for all loved the Queen and would see her, save the three felons that yet survived.

On the day chosen for the meeting, the field shone far with the rich tents of the barons, and suddenly Tristan and Iseult came out at the forest's edge, and caught sight of King Mark far off among his Barony:

"Friend," said Tristan, "there is the King, your lord – his knights and his men; they are coming towards us, and very soon we may not speak to each other again. By the God of Power I conjure you, if ever I send you a word, do you my bidding."

"Friend," said Iseult, "on the day that I see the ring, nor tower, nor wall, nor stronghold will let me from doing the will of my friend."

"Why then," he said, "Iseult, may God reward you."

Their horses went abreast and he drew her towards him with his arm.

"Friend," said Iseult, "hear my last prayer: you will leave this land, but wait some days; hide till you know how the King may treat me, whether in wrath or kindness, for I am afraid. Friend, Orri the woodman will entertain you hidden. Go you by night to the abandoned cellar that you know and I will send Perinis there to say if anyone misuse me."

"Friend, none would dare. I will stay hidden with Orri, and if any misuse you let him fear me as the Enemy himself."

Now the two troops were near and they saluted, and the King rode a bow-shot before his men and with him Dinas of Lidan; and when the barons had come up, Tristan, holding Iseult's palfrey by the bridle, bowed to the King and said:

"O King, I yield you here Iseult the Fair, and I summon you, before the men of your land, that I may defend myself in your court, for I have had no judgment. Let me have trial at arms, and if I am conquered, burn me, but if I conquer, keep me by you, or, if you will not, I will be off to some far country."

But no one took up Tristan's wager, and the King, taking Iseult's palfrey by the bridle, gave it to Dinas, and went apart to take counsel.

Dinas, in his joy, gave all honour and courtesy to the Queen, but when the felons saw her so fair and honoured as of old, they were stirred and rode to the King, and said:

"King, hear our counsel. That the Queen was slandered we admit, but if she and Tristan re-enter your court together, rumour will revive again. Rather let Tristan go apart awhile. Doubtless some day you may recall him."

And so Mark did, and ordered Tristan by his barons to go off without delay.

Then Tristan came near the Queen for his farewell, and as they looked at one another the Queen in shame of that assembly blushed, but the King pitied her, and spoke his nephew thus for the first time:

"You cannot leave in these rags; take then from my treasury gold and silver and white fur and grey, as much as you will."

"King," said Tristan, "neither a penny nor a link of mail. I will go as I can, and serve with high heart the mighty King in the Lowlands."

And he turned rein and went down towards the sea, but Iseult followed him with her eyes, and so long as he could yet be seen a long way off she did not turn.

Now at the news of the peace, men, women, and children, great and small, ran out of the town in a crowd to meet Iseult, and while they mourned Tristan's exile they rejoiced at the Queen's return.

And to the noise of bells, and over pavings strewn with branches, the King and his counts and princes made her escort, and the gates of the palace were thrown open that rich and poor might enter and eat and drink at will.

And Mark freed a hundred of his slaves, and armed a score of squires that day with hauberk and with sword.

But Tristan that night hid with Orri, as the Queen had counselled him.

The Ordeal by Iron

ENOALEN, ANDRET, and Gondoin held themselves safe; Tristan was far over sea, far away in service of a distant king, and they beyond his power. Therefore, during a hunt one day, as the King rode apart in a glade where the pack would pass, and hearkening to the hounds, they all three rode towards him, and said:

"O King, we have somewhat to say. Once you condemned the Queen without judgment, and that was wrong; now you acquit her without judgment, and that is wrong. She is not quit by trial, and the barons of your land blame you both. Counsel her, then, to claim the ordeal in God's judgment, for since she is innocent, she may swear on the relics of the saints and hot iron will not hurt her. For so custom runs, and in this easy way are doubts dissolved."

But Mark answered:

"God strike you, my Cornish lords, how you hunt my shame! For you have I exiled my nephew, and now what would you now? Would you have me drive the Queen to Ireland too? What novel plaints have you to plead? Did not Tristan offer you battle in this matter? He offered battle to clear the Queen for ever: he offered and you heard him all. Where then were your lances and your shields?"

"Sire," they said, "we have counselled you loyal counsel as lieges and to your honour; henceforward we hold our peace. Put aside your anger and give us your safe-guard."

But Mark stood up in the stirrup and cried:

"Out of my land, and out of my peace, all of you! Tristan I exiled for you, and now go you in turn, out of my land!"

But they answered:

"Sire, it is well. Our keeps are strong and fenced, and stand on rocks not easy for men to climb."

And they rode off without a salutation.

But the King (not tarrying for huntsman or for hound but straight away) spurred his horse to Tintagel; and as he sprang up the stairs the Queen heard the jangle of his spurs upon the stones.

She rose to meet him and took his sword as she was wont, and bowed before him, as it was also her wont to do; but Mark raised her, holding her hands; and when Iseult looked up she saw his noble face in just that wrath she had seen before the faggot fire.

She thought that Tristan was found, and her heart grew cold, and without a word she fell at the King's feet.

He took her in his arms and kissed her gently till she could speak again, and then he said:

"Friend, friend, what evil tries you?"

"Sire, I am afraid, for I have seen your anger.

"Yes, I was angered at the hunt."

"My lord, should one take so deeply the mischances of a game?"

Mark smiled and said:

"No, friend; no chance of hunting vexed me, but those three felons whom you know; and I have driven them forth from my land."

"Sire, what did they say, or dare to say of me?"

"What matter? I have driven them forth."

"Sire, all living have this right: to say the word they have conceived. And I would ask a question, but from whom shall I learn save from you? I am alone in a foreign land, and have no one else to defend me."

"They would have it that you should quit yourself by solemn oath and by the ordeal of iron, saying 'that God was a true judge, and that as the Queen was innocent, she herself should seek such judgment as would clear her for ever.' This was their clamour and their demand incessantly. But let us leave it. I tell you, I have driven them forth."

Iseult trembled, but looking straight at the King, she said:

"Sire, call them back; I will clear myself by oath. But I bargain this: that on the appointed day you call King Arthur and Lord Gawain, Girflet, Kay the seneschal, and a hundred of his knights to ride to the Sandy Heath where your land marches with his, and a river flows between; for I will not swear before your barons alone, lest they should demand some new thing, and lest there should be no end to my trials. But if my warrantors, King Arthur and his knights, be there, the barons will not dare dispute the judgment."

But as the heralds rode to Carduel, Iseult sent to Tristan secretly her squire Perinis: and he ran through the underwood, avoiding paths, till he found the hut of Orri, the woodman, where Tristan for many days had awaited news. Perinis told him all: the ordeal, the place, and the time, and added:

"My lord, the Queen would have you on that day and place come dressed as a pilgrim, so that none may know you – unarmed, so that none may challenge – to the Sandy Heath. She must cross the river to the place appointed. Beyond it, where Arthur and his hundred knights will stand, be you also; for my lady fears the judgment, but she trusts in God."

Then Tristan answered:

"Go back, friend Perinis, return you to the Queen, and say that I will do her bidding."

And you must know that as Perinis went back to Tintagel he caught sight of that same woodman who had betrayed the lovers before, and the woodman, as he found him, had just dug a pitfall for wolves and for wild boars, and covered it with leafy branches to hide it, and as Perinis came near the woodman fled, but Perinis drove him, and caught him, and broke his staff and his head together, and pushed his body into the pitfall with his feet.

On the appointed day King Mark and Iseult, and the barons of Cornwall, stood by the river; and the knights of Arthur and all their host were arrayed beyond.

And just before them, sitting on the shore, was a poor pilgrim, wrapped in cloak and hood, who held his wooden platter and begged alms.

Now as the Cornish boats came to the shoal of the further bank, Iseult said to the knights:

"My lords, how shall I land without befouling my clothes in the river-mud? Fetch me a ferryman."

And one of the knights hailed the pilgrim, and said:

"Friend, truss your coat, and try the water; carry you the Queen to shore, unless you fear the burden."

But as he took the Queen in his arms she whispered to him:

"Friend."

And then she whispered to him, lower still:

"Stumble you upon the sand."

And as he touched shore, he stumbled, holding the Queen in his arms; and the squires and boatmen with their oars and boat-hooks drove the poor pilgrim away.

But the Queen said:

"Let him be; some great travail and journey has weakened him."

And she threw to the pilgrim a little clasp of gold.

Before the tent of King Arthur was spread a rich Nicean cloth upon the grass, and the holy relics were set on it, taken out of their covers and their shrines.

And round the holy relics on the sward stood a guard more than a king's guard, for Lord Gawain, Girflet, and Kay the seneschal kept ward over them.

The Queen having prayed God, took off the jewels from her neck and hands, and gave them to the beggars around; she took off her purple mantle, and her overdress, and her shoes with their precious stones, and gave them also to the poor that loved her.

She kept upon her only the sleeveless tunic, and then with arms and feet quite bare she came between the two kings, and all around the barons watched her in silence, and some wept, for near the holy relics was a brazier burning.

And trembling a little she stretched her right hand towards the bones and said: "Kings of Logres and of Cornwall; my lords Gawain, and Kay, and Girflet, and all of you that are my warrantors, by these holy things and all the holy things of earth, I swear that no man has held me in his arms saving King Mark, my lord, and that poor pilgrim. King Mark, will that oath stand?"

"Yes, Queen," he said, "and God see to it.

"Amen," said Iseult, and then she went near the brazier, pale and stumbling, and all were silent. The iron was red, but she thrust her bare arms among the coals and seized it, and bearing it took nine steps.

Then, as she cast it from her, she stretched her arms out in a cross, with the palms of her hands wide open, and all men saw them fresh and clean and cold. Seeing that great sight the kings and the barons and the people stood for a moment silent, then they stirred together and they praised God loudly all around.

Part the Third

The Little Fairy Bell

WHEN TRISTAN had come back to Orri's hut, and had loosened his heavy pilgrim's cape, he saw clearly in his heart that it was time to keep his oath to King Mark and to fly the land.

Three days yet he tarried, because he could not drag himself away from that earth, but on the fourth day he thanked the woodman, and said to Gorvenal:

"Master, the hour is come."

And he went into Wales, into the land of the great Duke Gilain, who was young, powerful, and frank in spirit, and welcomed him nobly as a God-sent guest.

And he did everything to give him honour and joy; but he found that neither adventure, nor feast could soothe what Tristan suffered.

One day, as he sat by the young Duke's side, his spirit weighed upon him, so that not knowing it he groaned, and the Duke, to soothe him, ordered into his private room a fairy thing, which pleased his eyes when he was sad and relieved his own heart; it was a dog, and the varlets brought it in to him, and they put it upon a table there. Now this dog was a fairy dog, and came from the Duke of Avalon; for a fairy had given it him as a love-gift, and no one can well describe its kind or beauty. And it bore at its neck, hung to a little chain of gold, a little bell; and that tinkled so gaily, and so clear and so soft, that as Tristan heard it, he was soothed, and his anguish melted away, and he forgot all that he had suffered for the Queen; for such was the virtue of the bell and such its property: that whosoever heard it, he lost all pain. And as Tristan stroked the little fairy thing, the dog that took away his sorrow, he saw how delicate it was and fine, and how it had soft hair like samite, and he thought how good a gift it would make for the Queen. But he dared not ask for it right out since he knew that the Duke loved this dog beyond everything in the world, and would yield it to no prayers, nor to wealth, nor to wile; so one day Tristan having made a plan in his mind said this:

"Lord, what would you give to the man who could rid your land of the hairy giant Urgan, that levies such a toll?"

"Truly, the victor might choose what he would, but none will dare."

Then said Tristan:

"Those are strange words, for good comes to no land save by risk and daring, and not for all the gold of Milan would I renounce my desire to find him in his wood and bring him down."

Then Tristan went out to find Urgan in his lair, and they fought hard and long, till courage conquered strength, and Tristan, having cut off the giant's hand, bore it back to the Duke.

And "Sire," said he, "since I may choose a reward according to your word, give me the little fairy dog. It was for that I conquered Urgan, and your promise stands."

"Friend," said the Duke, "take it, then, but in taking it you take away also all my joy."

Then Tristan took the little fairy dog and gave it in ward to a Welsh harper, who was cunning and who bore it to Cornwall till he came to Tintagel, and having come there put it secretly into Brangien's hands, and the Queen was so pleased that she gave ten marks of gold to the harper, but she put it about that the Queen of Ireland, her mother, had sent the beast. And she had a goldsmith work a little kennel for him, all jewelled, and encrusted with gold and enamel inlaid; and wherever she went she carried the dog with her in memory of her friend, and as she watched it sadness and anguish and regrets melted out of her heart.

At first she did not guess the marvel, but thought her consolation was because the gift was Tristan's, till one day she found that it was fairy, and that it was the little bell that charmed her soul; then she thought: "What have I to do with comfort since he is sorrowing? He could have kept it too and have forgotten his sorrow; but with high courtesy he sent it to me to give me his joy and to take up his pain again. Friend, while you suffer, so long will I suffer also."

And she took the magic bell and shook it just a little, and then by the open window she threw it into the sea.

Iseult of the White Hands

APART THE LOVERS could neither live nor die, for it was life and death together; and Tristan fled his sorrow through seas and islands and many lands.

He fled his sorrow still by seas and islands, till at last he came back to his land of Lyonesse, and there Rohalt, the keeper of faith, welcomed him with happy tears and called him son. But he could not live in the peace of his own land, and he turned again and rode through kingdoms and through baronies, seeking adventure. From the Lyonesse to the Lowlands, from the Lowlands on to the Germanies; through the Germanies and into Spain. And many lords he served, and many deeds did, but for two years no news came to him out of Cornwall, nor friend, nor messenger. Then he thought that Iseult had forgotten.

Now it happened one day that, riding with Gorvenal alone, he came into the land of Brittany. They rode through a wasted plain of ruined walls and empty hamlets and burnt fields everywhere, and the earth deserted of men; and Tristan thought:

"I am weary, and my deeds profit me nothing; my lady is far off and I shall never see her again. Or why for two years has she made no sign, or why has she sent no messenger to find me as I wandered? But in Tintagel Mark honours her and she gives him joy, and that little fairy bell has done a thorough work; for little she remembers or cares for the joys and the mourning of old, little for me, as I wander in this desert place. I, too, will forget."

On the third day, at the hour of noon, Tristan and Gorvenal came near a hill where an old chantry stood and close by a hermitage also;

and Tristan asked what wasted land that was, and the hermit answered:

"Lord, it is Breton land which Duke Hod holds, and once it was rich in pasture and ploughland, but Count Riol of Nantes has wasted it. For you must know that this Count Riol was the Duke's vassal. And the Duke has a daughter, fair among all King's daughters, and Count Riol would have taken her to wife; but her father refused her to a vassal, and Count Riol would have carried her away by force. Many men have died in that quarrel."

And Tristan asked:

"Can the Duke wage his war?"

And the hermit answered:

"Hardly, my lord; yet his last keep of Carhaix holds out still, for the walls are strong, and strong is the heart of the Duke's son Kaherdin, a very good knight and bold; but the enemy surrounds them on every side and starves them. Very hardly do they hold their castle."

Then Tristan asked:

"How far is this keep of Carhaix?"

"Sir," said the hermit, "it is but two miles further on this way."

Then Tristan and Gorvenal lay down, for it was evening.

In the morning, when they had slept, and when the hermit had chanted, and had shared his black bread with them, Tristan thanked him and rode hard to Carhaix. And as he halted beneath the fast high walls, he saw a little company of men behind the battlements, and he asked if the Duke were there with his son Kaherdin. Now Hod was among them; and when he cried "yes," Tristan called up to him and said:

"I am that Tristan, King of Lyonesse, and Mark of Cornwall is my uncle. I have heard that your vassals do you a wrong, and I have come to offer you my arms."

"Alas, lord Tristan, go you your way alone and God reward you, for here within we have no more food; no wheat, or meat, or any stores but only lentils and a little oats remaining."

But Tristan said:

"For two years I dwelt in a forest, eating nothing save roots and herbs; yet I found it a good life, so open you the door."

They welcomed him with honour, and Kaherdin showed him the wall and the dungeon keep with all their devices, and from the battlements he showed the plain where far away gleamed the tents of Duke Riol. And when they were down in the castle again he said to Tristan:

"Friend, let us go to the hall where my mother and sister sit."

So, holding each other's hands, they came into the women's room, where the mother and the daughter sat together weaving gold upon English cloth and singing a weaving song. They sang of Doette the fair who sits alone beneath the white-thorn, and round about her blows the wind. She waits for Doon, her friend, but he tarries long and does not come. This was the song they sang. And Tristan bowed to them, and they to him. Then Kaherdin, showing the work his mother did, said:

"See, friend Tristan, what a work-woman is here, and how marvellously she adorns stoles and chasubles for the poor minsters, and how my sister's hands run thread of gold upon this cloth. Of right, good sister, are you called, 'Iseult of the White Hands.'"

But Tristan, hearing her name, smiled and looked at her more gently.

And on the morrow, Tristan, Kaherdin, and twelve young knights left the castle and rode to a pinewood near the enemy's tents. And sprang from ambush and captured a waggon of Count Riol's food; and from that day, by escapade and ruse they would carry tents and convoys and kill off men, nor ever come back without some booty; so that Tristan and Kaherdin began to be brothers in arms, and kept faith and tenderness, as history tells. And as they came back from these rides, talking chivalry together, often did Kaherdin praise to his comrade his sister, Iseult of the White Hands, for her simplicity and beauty.

One day, as the dawn broke, a sentinel ran from the tower through the halls crying:

"Lords, you have slept too long; rise, for an assault is on."

And knights and burgesses armed, and ran to the walls, and saw helmets shining on the plain, and pennons streaming crimson, like flames, and all the host of Riol in its array. Then the Duke and Kaherdin deployed their horsemen before the gates, and from a bow-length off they stooped, and spurred and charged, and they put their lances down together and the arrows fell on them like April rain.

Now Tristan had armed himself among the last of those the sentinel had roused, and he laced his shoes of steel, and put on his mail, and his spurs of gold, his hauberk, and his helm over the gorget, and he mounted and spurred, with shield on breast, crying:

"Carhaix!"

And as he came, he saw Duke Riol charging, rein free, at Kaherdin, but Tristan came in between. So they met, Tristan and Duke Riol. And at the shock, Tristan's lance shivered, but Riol's lance struck Tristan's horse just where the breastpiece runs, and laid it on the field.

But Tristan, standing, drew his sword, his burnished sword, and said:

"Coward! Here is death ready for the man that strikes the horse before the rider."

But Riol answered:

"I think you have lied, my lord!"

And he charged him.

And as he passed, Tristan let fall his sword so heavily upon his helm that he carried away the crest and the nasal, but the sword slipped on the mailed shoulder, and glanced on the horse, and killed it, so that of force Duke Riol must slip the stirrup and leap and feel the ground. Then Riol too was on his feet, and they both fought hard in their broken mail, their 'scutcheons torn and their helmets loosened and lashing with their dented swords, till Tristan struck Riol just where the helmet buckles, and it yielded and the blow was struck so hard that the baron fell on hands and knees; but when he had risen again, Tristan struck him down once more with a blow that split the helm, and it split the headpiece too, and touched the skull; then Riol cried mercy and begged his life, and Tristan took his sword.

So he promised to enter Duke Hoël's keep and to swear homage again, and to restore what he had wasted; and by his order the battle ceased, and his host went off discomfited.

Now when the victors were returned Kaherdin said to his father:

"Sire, keep you Tristan. There is no better knight, and your land has need of such courage."

So when the Duke had taken counsel with his barons, he said to Tristan.

"Friend, I owe you my land, but I shall be quit with you if you will take my daughter, Iseult of the White Hands, who comes of kings and of queens, and of dukes before them in blood."

And Tristan answered:

"I will take her, Sire."

So the day was fixed, and the Duke came with his friends and Tristan with his, and before all, at the gate of the minster, Tristan wed Iseult of the White Hands, according to the Church's law.

But that same night, as Tristan's valets undressed him, it happened that in drawing his arm from the sleeve they drew off and let fall from his finger the ring of green jasper, the ring of Iseult the Fair. It sounded on the stones, and Tristan looked and saw it. Then his heart awoke and he knew that he had done wrong. For he remembered the day when Iseult the Fair had given him the ring. It was in that forest where, for his sake, she had led the hard life with him, and that night he saw again the hut in the wood of Morois, and he was bitter with himself that ever he had accused her of treason; for now it was he that had betrayed, and he was bitter with himself also in pity for this new wife and her simplicity and beauty. See how these two Iseults had met him in an evil hour, and to both had he broken faith!

Now Iseult of the White Hands said to him, hearing him sigh:

"Dear lord, have I hurt you in anything? Will you not speak me a single word?"

But Tristan answered: "Friend, do not be angry with me; for once in another land I fought a foul dragon and was near to death, and I thought of the Mother of God, and I made a vow to Her that, should I ever wed, I would spend the first holy nights of my wedding in prayer and in silence."

"Why," said Iseult, "that was a good vow."

And Tristan watched through the night.

The Madness of Tristan

WITHIN HER ROOM at Tintagel, Iseult the Fair sighed for the sake of Tristan, and named him, her desire, of whom for two years she had had no word, whether he lived or no.

Within her room at Tintagel Iseult the Fair sat singing a song she had made. She sang of Guron taken and killed for his love, and how by guile the Count gave Guron's heart to her to eat, and of her woe. The Queen sang softly, catching the harp's tone; her hands were cunning and her song good; she sang low down and softly.

Then came in Kariado, a rich count from a far-off island, that had fared to Tintagel to offer the Queen his service, and had spoken of love to her, though she disdained his folly. He found Iseult as she sang, and laughed to her:

"Lady, how sad a song! as sad as the Osprey's; do they not say he sings for death? and your song means that to me; I die for you."

And Iseult said: "So let it be and may it mean so; for never come you here but to stir in me anger or mourning. Ever were you the screech owl or the Osprey that boded ill when you spoke of Tristan; what news bear you now?"

And Kariado answered:

"You are angered, I know not why, but who heeds your words? Let the Osprey bode me death; here is the evil news the screech owl brings. Lady Iseult, Tristan, your friend is lost to you. He has wed in a far land. So seek you other where, for he mocks your love. He has wed in great pomp Iseult of the White Hands, the King of Brittany's daughter."

And Kariado went off in anger, but Iseult bowed her head and broke into tears.

Now far from Iseult, Tristan languished, till on a day he must needs see her again. Far from her, death came surely; and he had rather die at once than day by day. And he desired some death, but that the Queen might know it was in finding her; then would death come easily.

So he left Carhaix secretly, telling no man, neither his kindred nor even Kaherdin, his brother in arms. He went in rags afoot (for no one marks the beggar on the high road) till he came to the shore of the sea.

He found in a haven a great ship ready, the sail was up and the anchor-chain short at the bow.

"God save you, my lords," he said, "and send you a good journey. To what land sail you now?"

"To Tintagel," they said.

Then he cried out:

"Oh, my lords! take me with you thither!"

And he went aboard, and a fair wind filled the sail, and she ran five days and nights for Cornwall, till, on the sixth day, they dropped anchor in Tintagel Haven. The castle stood above, fenced all around. There was but the one armed gate, and two knights watched it night and day. So Tristan went ashore and sat upon the beach, and a man told him that Mark was there and had just held his court.

"But where," said he, "is Iseult, the Queen, and her fair maid, Brangien?"

"In Tintagel too," said the other, "and I saw them lately; the Queen sad, as she always is."

At the hearing of the name, Tristan suffered, and he thought that neither by guile nor courage could he see that friend, for Mark would kill him.

And he thought, "Let him kill me and let me die for her, since every day I die. But you, Iseult, even if you knew me here, would you not drive me out?" And he thought, "I will try guile. I will seem mad, but with a madness that shall be great wisdom. And many shall think me a fool that have less wit than I."

Just then a fisherman passed in a rough cloak and cape, and Tristan seeing him, took him aside, and said:

"Friend, will you not change clothes?"

And as the fisherman found it a very good bargain, he said in answer:

"Yes, friend, gladly."

And he changed and ran off at once for fear of losing his gain. Then Tristan shaved his wonderful hair; he shaved it close to his head and left a cross all bald, and he rubbed his face with magic herbs distilled in his own country, and it changed in colour and skin so that none could know him, and he made him a club from a young tree torn from a hedgerow and hung it to his neck, and went barefoot towards the castle.

The porter made sure that he had to do with a fool and said:

"Good morrow, fool, where have you been this long while?"

And he answered:

"At the Abbot of St. Michael's wedding, and he wed an abbess, large and veiled. And from the Alps to Mount St. Michael how they came, the priests and abbots, monks and regulars, all dancing on the green with croziers and with staves under the high trees' shade. But I left them all to come hither, for I serve at the King's board today."

Then the porter said:

"Come in, lord fool; the Hairy Urgan's son, I know, and like your father."

And when he was within the courts the serving men ran after him and cried:

"The fool! the fool!"

But he made play with them though they cast stones and struck him as they laughed, and in the midst of laughter and their cries, as the rout followed him, he came to that hall where, at the Queen's side, King Mark sat under his canopy.

And as he neared the door with his club at his neck, the King said:

"Here is a merry fellow, let him in."

And they brought him in, his club at his neck. And the King said:

"Friend, well come; what seek you here?"

"Iseult," said he, "whom I love so well; I bring my sister with me, Brunehild, the beautiful. Come, take her, you are weary of the Queen. Take you my sister and give me here Iseult, and I will hold her and serve you for her love."

The King said laughing:

"Fool, if I gave you the Queen, where would you take her, pray?"

"Oh! very high," he said, "between the clouds and heaven, into a fair chamber glazed. The beams of the sun shine through it, yet the winds do not trouble it at all. There would I bear the Queen into that crystal chamber of mine all compact of roses and the morning."

The King and his barons laughed and said:

"Here is a good fool at no loss for words."

But the fool as he sat at their feet gazed at Iseult most fixedly.

"Friend," said King Mark, "what warrant have you that the Queen would heed so foul a fool as you?"

"O! Sire," he answered gravely, "many deeds have I done for her, and my madness is from her alone."

"What is your name?" they said, and laughed.

"Tristan," said he, "that loved the Queen so well, and still till death will love her."

But at the name the Queen angered and weakened together, and said: "Get hence for an evil fool!"

But the fool, marking her anger, went on:

"Queen Iseult, do you mind the day, when, poisoned by the Morholt's spear, I took my harp to sea and fell upon your shore? Your mother healed me with strange drugs. Have you no memory, Queen?"

But Iseult answered:

"Out, fool, out! Your folly and you have passed the bounds!"

But the fool, still playing, pushed the barons out, crying:

"Out! madmen, out! Leave me to counsel with Iseult, since I come here for the love of her!"

And as the King laughed, Iseult blushed and said:

"King, drive me forth this fool!"

But the fool still laughed and cried:

"Queen, do you mind you of the dragon I slew in your land? I hid its tongue in my hose, and, burnt of its venom, I fell by the roadside. Ah! what a knight was I then, and it was you that succoured me."

Iseult replied:

"Silence! You wrong all knighthood by your words, for you are a fool from birth. Cursed be the seamen that brought you hither; rather should they have cast you into the sea!"

"Queen Iseult," he still said on, "do you mind you of your haste when you would have slain me with my own sword? And of the Hair of Gold? And of how I stood up to the seneschal?"

"Silence!" she said, "you drunkard. You were drunk last night, and so you dreamt these dreams."

"Drunk, and still so am I," said he, "but of such a draught that never can the influence fade. Queen Iseult, do you mind you of that hot and open day on the high seas? We thirsted and we drank together from the same cup, and since that day have I been drunk with an awful wine."

When the Queen heard these words which she alone could understand, she rose and would have gone.

But the King held her by her ermine cloak, and she sat down again.

And as the King had his fill of the fool he called for his falcons and went to hunt; and Iseult said to him:

"Sire, I am weak and sad; let me be go rest in my room; I am tired of these follies."

And she went to her room in thought and sat upon her bed and mourned, calling herself a slave and saying:

"Why was I born? Brangien, dear sister, life is so hard to me that death were better! There is a fool without, shaven criss-cross, and come in an evil hour, and he is warlock, for he knows in every part myself and my whole life; he knows what you and I and Tristan only know."

Then Brangien said: "It may be Tristan."

But – "No," said the Queen, "for he was the first of knights, but this fool is foul and made awry. Curse me his hour and the ship that brought him hither."

"My lady!" said Brangien, "soothe you. You curse over much these days. May be he comes from Tristan?"

"I cannot tell. I know him not. But go find him, friend, and see if you know him."

So Brangien went to the hall where the fool still sat alone. Tristan knew her and let fall his club and said:

"Brangien, dear Brangien, before God! have pity on me!"

"Foul fool," she answered, "what devil taught you my name?"

"Lady," he said, "I have known it long. By my head, that once was fair, if I am mad the blame is yours, for it was yours to watch over the wine we drank on the high seas. The cup was of silver and I held it to Iseult and she drank. Do you remember, lady?"

"No," she said, and as she trembled and left he called out: "Pity me!"

He followed and saw Iseult. He stretched out his arms, but in her shame, sweating agony she drew back, and Tristan angered and said:

"I have lived too long, for I have seen the day that Iseult will nothing of me. Iseult, how hard love dies! Iseult, a welling water that floods and runs large is a mighty thing; on the day that it fails it is nothing; so love that turns."

But she said:

"Brother, I look at you and doubt and tremble, and I know you not for Tristan."

"Queen Iseult, I am Tristan indeed that do love you; mind you for the last time of the dwarf, and of the flower, and of the blood I shed in my leap. Oh! and of that ring I took in kisses and in tears on the day we parted. I have kept that jasper ring and asked it counsel."

Then Iseult knew Tristan for what he was, and she said:

"Heart, you should have broken of sorrow not to have known the man who has suffered so much for you. Pardon, my master and my friend."

And her eyes darkened and she fell; but when the light returned she was held by him who kissed her eyes and her face.

So passed they three full days. But, on the third, two maids that watched them told the traitor Andret, and he put spies well-armed before the women's rooms. And when Tristan would enter they cried:

"Back, fool!"

But he brandished his club laughing, and said:

"What! May I not kiss the Queen who loves me and awaits me now?"

And they feared him for a mad fool, and he passed in through the door.

Then, being with the Queen for the last time, he held her in his arms and said:

"Friend, I must fly, for they are wondering. I must fly, and perhaps shall never see you more. My death is near, and far from you my death will come of desire."

"Oh friend," she said, "fold your arms round me close and strain me so that our hearts may break and our souls go free at last. Take me to that happy place of which you told me long ago. The fields whence none return, but where great singers sing their songs for ever. Take me now."

"I will take you to the Happy Palace of the living, Queen! The time is near. We have drunk all joy and sorrow. The time is near. When it is finished, if I call you, will you come, my friend?"

"Friend," said she, "call me and you know that I shall come."

"Friend," said he, "God send you His reward."

As he went out the spies would have held him; but he laughed aloud, and flourished his club, and cried:

"Peace, gentlemen, I go and will not stay. My lady sends me to prepare that shining house I vowed her, of crystal, and of rose shot through with morning."

And as they cursed and drave him, the fool went leaping on his way.

The Death of Tristan

WHEN HE WAS come back to Brittany, to Carhaix, it happened that Tristan, riding to the aid of Kaherdin his brother in arms, fell into ambush and was wounded by a poisoned spear; and many doctors came, but none could cure him of the ill. And Tristan weakened and paled, and his bones showed.

Then he knew that his life was going, and that he must die, and he had a desire to see once more Iseult the Fair, but he could not seek her, for the sea would have killed him in his weakness, and how could Iseult come to him? And sad, and suffering the poison, he awaited death.

He called Kaherdin secretly to tell him his pain, for they loved each other with a loyal love; and as he would have no one in the room save Kaherdin, nor even in the neighbouring rooms, Iseult of the White Hands began to wonder. She was afraid and wished to hear, and she came back and listened at the wall by Tristan's bed; and as she listened one of her maids kept watch for her.

Now, within, Tristan had gathered up his strength, and had half risen, leaning against the wall, and Kaherdin wept beside him. They wept their good comradeship, broken so soon, and their friendship: then Tristan told Kaherdin of his love for that other Iseult, and of the sorrow of his life.

"Fair friend and gentle," said Tristan, "I am in a foreign land where I have neither friend nor cousin, save you; and you alone in this place have given me comfort. My life is going, and I wish to see once more

Iseult the Fair. Ah, did I but know of a messenger who would go to her! For now I know that she will come to me. Kaherdin, my brother in arms, I beg it of your friendship; try this thing for me, and if you carry my word, I will become your liege, and I will cherish you beyond all other men."

And as Kaherdin saw Tristan broken down, his heart reproached him and he said:

"Fair comrade, do not weep; I will do what you desire, even if it were risk of death I would do it for you. Nor no distress nor anguish will let me from doing it according to my power. Give me the word you send, and I will make ready."

And Tristan answered:

"Thank you, friend; this is my prayer: take this ring, it is a sign between her and me; and when you come to her land pass yourself at court for a merchant, and show her silk and stuffs, but make so that she sees the ring, for then she will find some ruse by which to speak to you in secret. Then tell her that my heart salutes her; tell her that she alone can bring me comfort; tell her that if she does not come I shall die. Tell her to remember our past time, and our great sorrows, and all the joy there was in our loyal and tender love. And tell her to remember that draught we drank together on the high seas. For we drank our death together. Tell her to remember the oath I swore to serve a single love, for I have kept that oath."

But behind the wall, Iseult of the White Hands heard all these things; and Tristan continued:

"Hasten, my friend, and come back quickly, or you will not see me again. Take forty days for your term, but come back with Iseult the Fair. And tell your sister nothing, or tell her that you seek some doctor. Take my fine ship, and two sails with you, one white, one black. And as you return, if you bring Iseult, hoist the white sail; but if you bring her not, the black. Now I have nothing more to say, but God guide you and bring you back safe."

With the first fair wind Kaherdin took the open, weighed anchor and hoisted sail, and ran with a light air and broke the seas. They bore rich merchandise with them, dyed silks of rare colours, enamel of Touraine and wines of Poitou, for by this ruse Kaherdin thought to reach Iseult. Eight days and nights they ran full sail to Cornwall.

Now a woman's wrath is a fearful thing, and all men fear it, for according to her love, so will her vengeance be; and their love and their hate come quickly, but their hate lives longer than their love; and they will make play with love, but not with hate. So Iseult of the White Hands, who had heard every word, and who had so loved Tristan, waited her vengeance upon what she loved most in the world. But she hid it all; and when the doors were open again she came to Tristan's bed and served him with food as a lover should, and spoke him gently and kissed him on the lips, and asked him if Kaherdin would soon return with one to cure him ... but all day long she thought upon her vengeance.

And Kaherdin sailed and sailed till he dropped anchor in the haven of Tintagel. He landed and took with him a cloth of rare dye and a cup well chiselled and worked, and made a present of them to King Mark, and courteously begged of him his peace and safeguard that he might traffick in his land; and the King gave him his peace before all the men of his palace.

Then Kaherdin offered the Queen a buckle of fine gold; and "Queen," said he, "the gold is good."

Then taking from his finger Tristan's ring, he put it side by side with the jewel and said:

"See, O Queen, the gold of the buckle is the finer gold; yet that ring also has its worth."

When Iseult saw what ring that was, her heart trembled and her colour changed, and fearing what might next be said she drew Kaherdin apart near a window, as if to see and bargain the better; and Kaherdin said to her, low down:

"Lady, Tristan is wounded of a poisoned spear and is about to die. He sends you word that you alone can bring him comfort, and recalls to you the great sorrows that you bore together. Keep you the ring – it is yours."

But Iseult answered, weakening:

"Friend, I will follow you; get ready your ship tomorrow at dawn."

And on the morrow at dawn they raised anchor, stepped mast, and hoisted sail, and happily the barque left land.

But at Carhaix Tristan lay and longed for Iseult's coming. Nothing now filled him any more, and if he lived it was only as awaiting her; and day by day he sent watchers to the shore to see if some ship came, and to learn the colour of her sail. There was no other thing left in his heart.

He had himself carried to the cliff of the Penmarks, where it overlooks the sea, and all the daylight long he gazed far off over the water.

Hear now a tale most sad and pitiful to all who love. Already was Iseult near; already the cliff of the Penmarks showed far away, and the ship ran heartily, when a storm wind rose on a sudden and grew, and struck the sail, and turned the ship all round about, and the sailors bore away and sore against their will they ran before the wind. The wind raged and big seas ran, and the air grew thick with darkness, and the ocean itself turned dark, and the rain drove in gusts. The yard snapped, and the sheet; they struck their sail, and ran with wind and water. In an evil hour they had forgotten to haul their pinnace aboard; it leapt in their wake, and a great sea broke it away.

Then Iseult cried out: "God does not will that I should live to see him, my love, once – even one time more. God wills my drowning in this sea. O, Tristan, had I spoken to you but once again, it is little I should have cared for a death come afterwards. But now, my love, I cannot come to you; for God so wills it, and that is the core of my grief."

And thus the Queen complained so long as the storm endured; but after five days it died down. Kaherdin hoisted the sail, the white sail, right up to the very masthead with great joy; the white sail, that Tristan might know its colour from afar: and already Kaherdin saw Britanny far off like a cloud. Hardly were these things seen and done when a calm came, and the sea lay even and untroubled. The sail bellied no longer, and the sailors held the ship now up, now down, the tide, beating backwards and forwards in vain. They saw the shore afar off, but the storm had carried their boat away and they could not land. On the third night Iseult dreamt this dream: that she held in her lap a boar's head which befouled her skirts with blood; then she knew that she would never see her lover again alive.

Tristan was now too weak to keep his watch from the cliff of the Penmarks, and for many long days, within walls, far from the shore, he had mourned for Iseult because she did not come. Dolorous and alone, he mourned and sighed in restlessness: he was near death from desire.

At last the wind freshened and the white sail showed. Then it was that Iseult of the White Hands took her vengeance.

She came to where Tristan lay, and she said:

"Friend, Kaherdin is here. I have seen his ship upon the sea. She comes up hardly – yet I know her; may he bring that which shall heal thee, friend."

And Tristan trembled and said:

"Beautiful friend, you are sure that the ship is his indeed? Then tell me what is the manner of the sail?"

"I saw it plain and well. They have shaken it out and hoisted it very high, for they have little wind. For its colour, why, it is black."

And Tristan turned him to the wall, and said:

"I cannot keep this life of mine any longer." He said three times: "Iseult, my friend." And in saying it the fourth time, he died.

Then throughout the house, the knights and the comrades of Tristan wept out loud, and they took him from his bed and laid him on a rich cloth, and they covered his body with a shroud. But at sea the wind had risen; it struck the sail fair and full and drove the ship to shore, and Iseult the Fair set foot upon the land. She heard loud mourning in the streets, and the tolling of bells in the minsters and the chapel towers; she asked the people the meaning of the knell and of their tears. An old man said to her:

"Lady, we suffer a great grief. Tristan, that was so loyal and so right, is dead. He was open to the poor; he ministered to the suffering. It is the chief evil that has ever fallen on this land."

But Iseult, hearing them, could not answer them a word. She went up to the palace, following the way, and her cloak was random and wild. The Bretons marvelled as she went; nor had they ever seen woman of such a beauty, and they said:

"Who is she, or whence does she come?"

Near Tristan, Iseult of the White Hands crouched, maddened at the evil she had done, and calling and lamenting over the dead man. The other Iseult came in and said to her:

"Lady, rise and let me come by him; I have more right to mourn him than have you – believe me. I loved him more."

And when she had turned to the east and prayed God, she moved the body a little and lay down by the dead man, beside her friend. She kissed his mouth and his face, and clasped him closely; and so gave up her soul, and died beside him of grief for her lover.

When King Mark heard of the death of these lovers, he crossed the sea and came into Brittany; and he had two coffins hewn, for Tristan and Iseult, one of chalcedony for Iseult, and one of beryl for Tristan. And he took their beloved bodies away with him upon his ship to Tintagel, and by a chantry to the left and right of the apse he had their tombs built round. But in one night there sprang from the tomb of Tristan a green and leafy briar, strong in its branches and in the scent of its flowers. It climbed the chantry and fell to root again by Iseult's tomb. Thrice did the peasants cut it down, but thrice it grew again as flowered and as strong. They told the marvel to King Mark, and he forbade them to cut the briar any more.

The good singers of old time, Béroul and Thomas of Built, Gilbert and Gottfried told this tale for lovers and none other, and, by my pen, they beg you for your prayers. They greet those who are cast down, and those in heart, those troubled and those filled with desire. May all herein find strength against inconstancy and despite and loss and pain and all the bitterness of loving.

A Knightly Tristan

CHARLES MORRIS'S late-nineteenth-century version of the Tristan and Isolde legend, as told by the American writer Charles Morris, in the sections relating to 'Arthur' in his multi-volume *Historical Tales: The Romance of Reality* as presented here, is adapted from Thomas Malory's *Tale of Sir Tristram of Lyonesse*. This *Tale* is found in the middle of Malory's fifteenth-century *Le Morte Darthur*, which in turn took a lot of material from the French Prose *Tristan*. Morris's version of the tale clearly positions Tristram as a chivalric knight, well within the orbit of Arthurian mythology. Great attention is paid to Tristram's knightly adventures, as well as to his friendship with the other great knight of Arthur's court, Sir Lancelot du Lac. In this version King Mark is depicted very clearly as a villain of bad intent. His cruelty and vengeful plotting against Tristram is placed as a counterpoint to King Arthur's honourable behaviour. As a result of the text's primary concern with chivalric reputation, the love affair itself is somewhat neglected at times. Isolde too is replaced at Tristram's side by his new knightly companions.

Sir Tristram here is a paragon of knightly behaviour, always ready to join in a noble fight to save damsels and fellow knights alike. He has a longstanding feud with the Saracen Palamides, who we are told loved La Belle Isolde back in Ireland. Their relationship is certainly one that goes back and forth from friends to enemies, until eventually they are reconciled and Tristram takes Palamides finally to be baptised as a Christian.

The death scene itself is somewhat underwhelming compared to the dramatic Love-Death of so many other versions, taking up only a few lines at the end of Morris's text. This reflects Malory's own anticlimactic conclusion to his narrative of Tristram's life. There we only hear of the fate of the lovers through a few retrospective comments regarding the villainy of King Mark, the killer of Sir Tristram.

Morris's text serves as a good example of the Arthurian strand of the Tristan and Isolde legend. It gives insight into the ways in which that legend was manipulated for different purposes, incorporated into other pseudo-historical myths and moulded to fit new and evolving narrative styles, both in the Middle Ages and in later periods.

Book VI
Tristram of Lyonesse and the Fair Isolde

Chapter I
How Tristram Was Knighted

S AD WAS THE DAY when the renowned knight, Tristram of Lyonesse, was born, for on that day his mother died, and his father lay in prison through the arts of an enchantress. Therefore he was called Tristram, which signifies one of a sorrowful birth.

It happened that when he was seven years of age his father, King Meliodas, of the country of Lyonesse, married again. His first wife had been Elizabeth, sister of King Mark of Cornwall. He now married the daughter of King Howell of Brittany, a woman who proved of evil soul.

For after the new queen had children of her own she grew to hate the boy who stood between her son and the throne of Lyonesse, and so bitter grew her hatred that in the end she laid a foul plot for his murder. She put poison in a silver cup in the chamber where the young princes were used to play together, with the hope that Tristram when thirsty would drink from that cup. But fate so willed that the queen's own son drank of the poisoned cup, when thirsty from play, and died of it.

This fatal error filled the queen with deep anguish, but it added doubly to her hate, and with murderous intent she again put the poisoned cup into the chamber. But God protected the boy, for this time King Meliodas, being thirsty, saw the envenomed cup of wine, and took it up with purpose to drink. Before he could do so the queen, who was nearby, ran hastily forward, snatched the deadly cup from his hand, and threw its contents on the floor.

This hasty act filled the king with suspicion, for the sudden death of his young son had seemed to him like the work of poison. In a burst of passion he caught the guilty woman fiercely by the hand, drew his sword, and swore a mighty oath that he would kill her on the spot, unless she told him what had been in the cup and why it was put there.

At this threat the queen, trembling and weeping with fright, acknowledged that it had been her design to kill Tristram, in order that her son should inherit the kingdom of Lyonesse.

"Thou false traitress and murderess!" cried the king in redoubled passion. "By my royal soul, you shall have the fate you designed for my son. A worse one you shall have, for you shall be burned at the stake as a poisoner."

Then he called a council of his barons, who confirmed this sentence on learning the dark crime of the queen, and by the order of the court a fire of execution was prepared, and the murderess bound to the stake, while fagots were heaped about her drooping form.

The flames were already kindled, and were crawling like deadly serpents through the dry wood, but before they could reach the condemned queen young Tristram kneeled before his father and begged him a boon.

"You shall have it, my son. What would you ask?"

"Grant me the life of the queen. I cannot bear to see her die so terrible a death."

"Ask not that," said the king. "You should hate her who would have poisoned you. I have condemned her more for your sake than my own."

"Yet I beseech you to be merciful to her. I have forgiven her, and pray God to do so. You granted me my boon for God's love, and I hold you to your promise."

"If you will have it so, I cannot withdraw my word," said the king. "I give her to you. Go to the fire and take her, and do with her what you will."

This gladdened the boy's heart, which had been full of horror at the dreadful spectacle, and he hastened to release the victim from the flames.

But after that Meliodas would have nothing to do with her until after years had passed, when Tristram reconciled them with each other. And he sent his son from the court, being afraid the pardoned murderess might devise some new scheme for his destruction. The noble-hearted lad was therefore given as tutor a learned gentleman named Gouvernail, who took him to France, that he might learn the language and be taught the use of arms. There he remained seven years, learning not only the language, but the art of minstrelsy, till he became so skilful that few could equal him in the use of the harp and other instruments of music. And as he grew older he practised much in hunting and hawking, and in time became famous also for his skill in this noble art. He in afterlife devised many terms used in hunting, and bugle calls of the chase, so that from him the book of venery, or of hunting and hawking, came to be called the "Book of Sir Tristram."

Thus Tristram grew in accomplishments and nobleness till he attained the age of nineteen years, when he had become a youth of handsome face and powerful form, being large of size and vigorous of limb. The king, his father, had great joy in his promise of lusty manhood, and so had the queen, whose heart had been won to Tristram when he saved her from the flames, and who loved him ever afterwards as much as she had hated him in his childhood. Everyone loved him, indeed, for he proved himself a noble and gentle-hearted youth, loyal and kind to all he met, and with a heart free from evil thoughts or selfish desires.

He had learned the use of arms, and knew well how to wield the shield and sword, though as yet he had not sought knighthood by deeds of battle; but events were preparing that would bring him soon from youth to manhood. For it so happened that King Anguish of Ireland sent to King Mark of Cornwall, demanding from him tribute which he said was due, but had not been paid for many years. King Mark sent word back that he owed and would pay no tribute; and that if the King of Ireland wished to prove his claim, he must send a knight who could overcome King Mark's champion.

King Anguish was very angry at this answer, but accepted the challenge, and sent as his champion Sir Marhaus, brother to his wife, that valiant knight who had gone with Gawaine and Uwaine to the country of strange adventures, and had afterwards been made a Knight of the Round Table.

Marhaus accepted the championship, and hastened to Cornwall, where he sent his challenge to King Mark; but the latter had taken no steps to provide himself with a worthy champion. Marhaus thereupon encamped near the castle of Tintagil, whither he daily sent a demand to King Mark either to pay the tribute or to find a knight to fight his battle.

Anxious efforts were now made by the Cornish monarch to find a champion, some of the barons advising him to send to King Arthur's court for Lancelot du Lac. But others dissuaded the king from this, saying that neither Lancelot nor any Knight of the Round Table would fight against their fellow-knight Marhaus. Thus the King of Cornwall was sore put to it to find a champion fit to hold the field against such a knight as Marhaus.

Word of this soon spread over the country and quickly reached the castle of Meliodas, to which young Tristram had long before returned. The heart of the ardent youth filled with anger when he learned that not a knight could be found in all Cornwall able and willing to do battle with the Irish champion.

In fervent haste he sought his father, and asked him what was to be done to save Cornwall from this disgrace.

"I know not," answered the king. "Marhaus is one of the best knights of the Round Table, and there is no knight in this country fit to cope with him."

"I wish heartily that I were a knight," cried Tristram hotly. "If I were, Sir Marhaus should never depart to Ireland and boast that all Cornwall could not furnish a knight ready to break a spear with him. I pray you, dear father, to let me ride to King Mark's court, and beg of him to make me a knight and choose me as his champion."

"Your spirit honors you, my son," said Meliodas. "You have it in you to become an able knight, and I give you full leave to do as your courage prompts you."

Tristram thanked his father warmly for this assent, and, taking horse, rode without delay to the castle of his uncle King Mark. When he reached there he found the king depressed in spirit and the whole court deep in gloom, for it seemed as if no champion could be found, and that the tribute must be paid. Tristram went at once to his uncle and said with modest ardor:

"Sir, it is a shame and disgrace that Cornwall has no champion. I am but an untried youth, yet, if you will give me the order of knighthood, I stand ready to do battle for you with Sir Marhaus."

"Who are you, and whence come you?" asked the king.

"I come from King Meliodas, who wedded your sister, and I am a gentleman born."

Hope came into the king's eyes when he saw how large and strongly built was his youthful visitor, and marked the spirit of battle in his eyes, but he again demanded his name and place of birth.

"My name is Tristram and I was born in the country of Lyonesse," answered the youth.

"You speak with spirit, and look like the making of a good warrior," said the king. "If you agree to do this battle, I will grant you knighthood."

"It is that, and that alone, brings me here," answered Tristram.

Then the king knighted him, and at once sent word to Sir Marhaus that he had a champion ready to do battle with him to the uttermost.

"That may well be," answered Marhaus, "but I fight not with every springal. Tell King Mark that I shall fight with none but one of royal blood. His champion must be son either of a king or a queen."

This answer King Mark gave to Tristram, and said, gloomily:

"I fear this rules out your championship."

"Not so," said Tristram. "I came not here to boast, but if I must tell my lineage, you may let him know that I am of as noble blood as he. My father is King Meliodas, and my mother was Elizabeth, your own sister. I am the heir of Lyonesse."

"Is it so?" cried the king, clasping the youth's hands gladly. "Then I bid you warmly welcome, my fair nephew, and I could ask no better nor nobler champion."

He sent word in all haste to Marhaus that a better born man than himself should fight with him, the son of King Meliodas, and his own nephew. And while he waited an answer he took care to find for his nephew the best horse and the finest suit of armor that gold could procure. By the time he was thus provided word came back from Marhaus that he would be glad and blithe to fight with a gentleman of such noble birth. And he requested that the combat should take place in an island near which lay his ships. This being accepted, Tristram was sent thither in a vessel, with his horse and armor, but attended only by his tutor Gouvernail, whom he now made his squire.

On reaching the island Tristram saw on the further shore six ships, but he saw no knight. Then he bade Gouvernail to bring his horse ashore and arm him. This done, he mounted and took his shield, and then said:

"Where is this knight with whom I have to fight? I see him not."

"Yonder he hovers," answered Gouvernail, "under the shadow of the ships. He waits you on horseback, and fully armed."

"True enough. I see him now. All is well. Do you take the vessel and go back to my uncle Mark, and tell him that if I be slain it will not be through cowardice, and pray him, if I die in fair fight, to see that I be interred honorably; but if I should prove recreant then he shall give me no Christian burial. And come you not near the island, on your life, till you see me overcome or slain, or till I give you the signal of victory."

Then Gouvernail departed, weeping, for his young master had spoken so resolutely that he dared not disobey. Tristram now rode boldly towards Sir Marhaus, who came forward to meet him. Much courteous conversation passed between the two knights, Tristram at the end saying:

"I trust, Sir Marhaus, to win honor and renown from you, and to deliver Cornwall from tribute for ever, and to this end I shall do my best in all valor and honor."

"Fair sir," answered Marhaus, "your spirit pleases me; but as for gaining honor from me, you will lose none if you keep back three strokes beyond my reach, for King Arthur made me not Knight of the Round Table except for good cause."

"That may well be," answered Tristram; "but if I show the white feather in my first battle may I never bear arms again."

Then they put their spears in rest and rode so furiously together that both were hurled to the earth, horse and man alike. But Tristram had the ill fortune to receive a severe wound in the side from the spear of his adversary.

Heedless of this, he drew his sword and met Marhaus boldly and bravely. Then they began a fierce and desperate fight, striking and foining, rushing together in furious onset, and drawing back in cautious heed, while the ring of sword on armor was like that of hammer on anvil. Hours passed in the fight, and the blood flowed freely from the wounds which each had received, yet still they stood boldly up to the combat. But Tristram proved a stronger and better-winded man than Marhaus, and was still fresh when his enemy was growing weary and faint. At the end he threw all his strength into his right arm, and smote Marhaus so mighty a blow on the helm that it cut down through the steel covering and deep into his head, the sword sticking so fast that Tristram could hardly pull it out.

When he did so the edge of the sword was left in the skull, and the wounded knight fell heavily on his knees. But in a minute he rose and, flinging his sword and shield away, fled hastily to his ships.

"Why do you withdraw, Knight of the Round Table?" cried Tristram. "I am but a young knight, but before I would fly from an adversary I would abide to be cut into a thousand pieces."

Marhaus answered only with deep groans of pain and distress.

"Go thy way then, sir knight," said Tristram. "I promise you your sword and shield shall be mine, and I will wear your shield in the sight of King Arthur and all the Round Table, to let them see that Cornwall is not a land of cowards."

While he stood thus, hot with anger, the sails of the ships were spread, and the fleet sailed away, leaving the victor alone on the island. He was deeply wounded and had bled profusely, and when he grew cold from rest could hardly move his limbs. So he seated himself upon a little hillock, while his wounds still bled freely. But Gouvernail, who had kept within sight in the vessel, and had seen the end of the combat, now hastened gladly to the island, where he bound up the young knight's wounds, and then brought him to the main land. Here King Mark and his barons came in procession to meet him, their hearts full of joy and triumph, and the victor was borne in glad procession to the castle of Tintagil. When King

Mark saw his deep and perilous wounds he wept heartily, and cried:

"God help me, I would not for all my lands that my nephew should die!"

But Tristram lay in groaning pain for more than a month, ever in danger of death from the spear-wound he had received from Sir Marhaus. For the spearhead was poisoned, and no leech in the land, with his most healing remedy, could overcome the deadly effect of that venom. The king sent far and wide for skilled doctors, but none could be found whose skill was of any avail. At length there came a learned woman to the court, who told them plainly that the wounded man could never be cured except in the country from which the venom came. He might be helped there, but nowhere else.

When King Mark heard this he had a good vessel prepared, in which Tristram was placed, under charge of Gouvernail, and so set sail for Ireland, though all were strictly warned not to tell who they were or whence they came.

Long before this the fleet of Marhaus had arrived on the Irish coast, and the wounded knight been borne to the king's court, where all was done that could be to save his life, but in vain.

He died soon of his deep wound, and when his head was examined by the surgeons they found therein a piece of Tristram's sword, which had sunk deep into his skull. This piece the queen, his sister, kept, for she was full of revengeful thoughts, and she hoped by its aid to find the man to whom he owed his death.

Chapter II
La Belle Isolde

WHEN TRISTRAM ARRIVED in Ireland, chance so provided that he landed near a castle in which the king and queen, with all their court, then were. He had brought his harp with him, and on his arrival sat up in his bed and played a merry lay, which gave joy to all that heard it.

Word was quickly brought to the king that a harper of wonderful skill had reached his shores, and he at once sent to have him brought to the castle, where he asked him his name and whence he came.

"My name," replied the wounded knight, "is Tramtrist; I am of the country of Lyonesse, and the wound from which I suffer was received in a battle I fought for a lady who had been wronged."

"You shall have all the help here we can give you," said King Anguish. "I have just met with a sad loss myself, for the best knight in my kingdom has been slain."

Then he told Tristram of the battle with King Mark's champion, little dreaming that the knight to whom he spoke knew far more about it than he did himself.

"As for your wound," said the king, "my daughter, La Belle Isolde, is a leech of wonderful skill, and as you seem so worthy a man I shall put you under her care."

This said, he departed, and sent his daughter to the knight; but no sooner did Tristram behold her than he received a deeper wound from love than he had yet had from sword or spear. For La Belle Isolde was the most beautiful lady in the world, a maiden of such wondrous charm and grace that no land held her equal.

When she examined the young knight's wound she quickly saw that he was suffering from poison, but it was a venom with which she knew well how to deal, and she was not long in healing his deep hurt. In return for this great service, he taught her the art of harping, while the love he felt for her soon left some reflection of its warm presence in her soul.

But she already had a lover in the court, a worthy and valiant Saracen knight named Palamides, who sought her day after day, and made her many gifts, for his love for her was deep. He was well esteemed by the king and queen, and had declared his willingness to be made a Christian for the sake of La Belle Isolde. In consequence there soon arose hot blood between Tristram and Palamides, for each feared that the other was a favored rival.

And now it happened that King Anguish announced a tournament to be held in honor of a cousin of his called the Lady of the Lawns, it being declared that the grand prize of the tournament should be the hand of the lady and the lordship of her lands. The report of this tournament spread through England, Wales and Scotland, reaching even to Brittany and France, and many knights came to try their fortune in the lists.

When the day drew near the fair Isolde told Tristram of the tournament, and expressed a warm desire that he would take part in it.

"Fair lady," he answered, "I am as yet but feeble, and only for your generous care might be dead. I should be glad to obey any wish of yours, but you know that I am not in condition for the lists."

"Ah, Tramtrist," she replied, "I trust that you may be able to take part in this friendly joust. Palamides will be there, and I hoped that you would meet him, for I fear that otherwise he will not find his equal."

"You do me great honor," he replied. "You forget that I am but a young knight, and that in the only battle I have fought I was wounded nearly unto death. But for the love I have for you I shall attend the tournament, and jeopard my poor person for your sake, if you will only keep my counsel and let no person know that I have entered the lists."

"That shall I," she replied, gladly. "Horse and armor shall be ready for you, and I but ask you to do your best. I am sure your best must win."

"With Isolde's eyes upon me I can do no less," answered Tristram, with a glad heart. "I am at your command in all things, and for your love would dare tenfold this risk."

When the day of the tournament came, Palamides appeared in the lists with a black shield, and so many knights fell before him that all the people marvelled at his prowess. Throughout the first day's fight he held his own against all comers, bearing off the honors of the lists. As for Tristram, he sat among the spectators, and when King Anguish asked him why he did not joust, replied that he was still too weak from his wound.

On the morning of the next day Palamides came early into the field, and began the same career of conquest as on the day before. But in the midst of his good fortune there rode into the lists an unknown knight, who seemed to the spectators like an angel, for his horse and his armor were of the whiteness of snow.

No sooner had Palamides espied this stranger than he put his spear in rest and rode against him at furious speed. But there came a sudden change in his fortunes, for the white knight struck him with such force as to hurl him from his horse to the ground.

Then there arose a great noise and uproar among the people, for they had grown to think that no knight could face the Saracen, and Gawaine and others whom he had overthrown marvelled who this stranger knight could be. But Isolde was glad at heart, for the love of Palamides was a burden to her, and well she knew the knight of the white arms.

As for the Palamides, he was so ashamed and disconcerted by his fall that, on mounting his horse again, he sought privately to withdraw from the field. But the white knight rode hastily after him and bade him turn, saying that he should not leave the lists so lightly. At these words Palamides turned and struck a fierce sword-blow at the white champion. But the latter put the stroke aside, and returned it with so mighty a buffet on the Saracen's head that he fell from his horse to the earth.

Then Tristram – for he was the white knight – bade him yield and consent to do his command, or he would slay him. To this Palamides agreed, for he was hurt past defence.

"This, then, is my command," said Tristram. "First, upon pain of your life, you shall cease your suit of the lady La Belle Isolde, and come not near her. Second, for a year and a day you shall wear no armor or weapons of war. Promise me this, or you shall die."

"This is a bitter penance," cried Palamides. "You shame me before the world. For nothing less than life would I consent."

But he took the oath as Tristram commanded, and then in anger and despite threw off his armor and cut it into pieces, flinging the fragments away. Then he departed, weighed down with sadness and shame.

This done, Tristram left the lists, where he could find no knight willing to fight with him, and rode to the private postern of the castle whence he had come to the field. Here he found the fair Isolde awaiting him with a joyous face and a voice of thanks, praising him so highly that the knight was abashed with modest shame, though gladness filled his heart. And when she had told the king and queen that it was Tramtrist who had vanquished the Saracen, they treated him as if he had been of royal blood, for he had shown such prowess as Lancelot himself could not exceed.

After this Tristram dwelt long in the castle, highly esteemed by the king and queen, and loved by La Belle Isolde, whose heart he had fully won by his prowess in the tournament. Those were days of joy and gladness, too soon, alas to end, for he loved her with all his soul, and saw his heaven in her eyes, while for all his love she gave him the warm devotion of a true heart in return.

But fate at length brought this dream of happiness to an end. For on a day when Tristram was in the bath, attended by his squire Gouvernail, chance brought the queen and Isolde into the chamber of the knight. On the bed lay his sword, and this the queen picked up and held it out for Isolde's admiration, as the blade which had done such noble work in the tournament.

But as she held it so she saw that there was a gap in the edge, a piece being broken out about a foot from the point. At sight of this she let the weapon fall, while her heart gave a great bound of pain and anger.

"Liar and traitor, have I found you at last!" she cried, in an outbreak of rage. "It is this false villain that slew my brother Marhaus!"

With these words she ran in haste from the chamber, leaving Isolde trembling with dread for her lover, for though she knew not the cause of the queen's rage, she knew well how cruel she could be in her passion.

Quickly the queen returned, bringing with her the fragment of steel that had been found in Marhaus's skull, and, snatching up the sword, she fitted this into the broken place. It fitted so closely that the blade seemed whole. Then with a cry of passionate rage the furious woman ran to where Tristram was in the bath, and would have run him through had not Gouvernail caught her in his arms and wrested the sword from her hand.

Failing in this deadly intent, she tore herself from the squire's grasp and flew to the king, throwing herself on her knees before him and crying:

"Oh, my lord and husband! you have here in your house that murderous wretch who killed my brother, the noble Sir Marhaus!"

"Ha! can that be?" said the king. "Where is he?"

"It is Tramtrist," she replied. "It is that villanous knight whom our daughter healed, and who has shamefully abused our hospitality." And she told him by what strange chance she had made this discovery.

"Alas!" said the king, "what you tell me grieves me to the heart. I never saw a nobler knight than he, and I would give my crown not to have learned this. I charge you to leave him to me. I will deal with him as honor and justice demand."

Then the king sought Tristram in his chamber, and found him there fully armed and ready to mount his horse.

"So, Tramtrist, you are ready for the field," he said. "I tell you this, that it will not avail·you to match your strength against my power. But I honor you for your nobility and prowess, and it would shame me to slay my guest in my court; therefore, I will let you depart in safety, on condition that you tell me your name and that of your father, and if it was truly you that slew my brother, Sir Marhaus."

"Truly it was so," said Tristram. "But what I did was done in honor and justice, as you well know. He came as a champion and defied all the knights of Cornwall to battle, and I fought him for the honor of Cornwall. It was my first battle, for I was made a knight that very day. And no man living can say that I struck him foully."

"I doubt me not that you acted in all knightly honor," answered the king. "But you cannot stay in my country against the ill-will of my barons, my wife and her kindred."

"As for who I am," continued the knight, "my father is King Meliodas of Lyonesse, and my uncle King Mark of Cornwall. My name is Tristram; but when I was sent to your country to be cured of my wound I called myself Tramtrist, for I feared your anger. I thank you deeply for the kind welcome you have given me, and the goodness my lady, your daughter, has shown me. It may happen that you will win more by my life than by my death, for in England I may yet do you some knightly service. This I promise you, as I am a true knight, that in all places I shall hold myself the servant and knight of my lady, your daughter, and shall never fail to do in her honor and service all that a knight may. Also I beseech you that I may take leave of your barons and knights, and pray you to grant me leave to bid adieu to your daughter."

"I cannot well refuse you this," said the king.

With this permission, Tristram sought La Belle Isolde, and sadly bade her farewell, telling her who he was, why he had changed his name, and for what purpose he had come to Ireland.

"Had it not been for your care and skill I should now have been dead," he said.

"Gentle sir," she sadly replied, "I am woeful indeed that you should go, for I never saw man to whom I felt such good will as to you."

And she wept bitterly as she held out her hand in adieu. But Tristram took her in his arms and kissed away her tears.

"I love you, Isolde, as my soul," he said. "If this despite of fate shall stand between you and me, this I promise, to be your knight while life is left to me."

"And this I promise," answered Isolde, "that if I am married within these seven years it shall only be by your assent! If they stand between me and my love, at least they shall not force me to wed against your will."

Then she gave Tristram a ring and received one from him in return, and he departed from her with a pain as if the parting wrenched their hearts asunder, while she beheld him go with such tears and lamentation that it seemed as if her faithful heart would break.

Tristram next sought the great hall of the court, where were assembled the barons of King Anguish, and took his leave of them all, saying:

"Fair lords, fortune wills that I must leave you. If there be any man here whom I have offended or aggrieved let him make complaint now, and I shall amend the wrong so far as it is in my power. If there be any who may incline to say a wrongful thing of me behind my back, let him speak now, and I will make it good with him, body against body."

But no man spoke in reply. There were knights there of the blood of Sir Marhaus and the queen, but none that cared to have to do in the field against Sir Tristram.

So bidding them all adieu, he departed, and took ship for Tintagil, in Cornwall.

Chapter III
The Wager of Battle

WHEN TIDINGS CAME to King Mark that Tristram had returned to Cornwall, cured of his wounds, the king and all his barons were glad, and on the arrival of the knight he was treated with the greatest honor. No long time passed before he rode to the castle of his father, King Meliodas, who received him with fatherly love and pride, while the queen greeted him with the warmest joy. And that their knightly son should have wherewithal to make a fair show in the world, they parted with much of their lands and wealth to him, endowing him with broad estates and lordly castles.

Afterwards, at his father's desire, who wished his son to gain all honor, Tristram returned to the court of Cornwall, where he was gladly welcomed. And here, though his love for La Belle Isolde lay deep in his heart, it was dimmed by later feelings, for there were many fair ladies at the court, and the young knight was at that age when the heart is soft and tender.

In the end it happened that a jealousy and unfriendliness arose between King Mark and him. This grew with time, and in the end the king, who was base and treacherous of soul, waylaid Tristram, aided by two knights of his counsel, and sought to slay him. But so valiantly did he defend himself that he hurled the three to the earth, wounding the king so deeply that he was long in recovering.

The king now grew to hate his young guest bitterly, and laid plans to destroy him. Finally, it occurred to him to send Tristram to Ireland for La Belle Isolde, whose beauty and goodness the young knight had praised so warmly that King Mark had it in his heart to wed her. But his main purpose in sending Tristram to Ireland was to compass his destruction, for he knew how he was hated there.

Tristram was not blind to the danger into which this mission might bring him, and suspected the purpose of the king, but his love of adventure was so great that for it he was ready to dare any risk.

As for Isolde, absence and affection for other ladies had dimmed his passion for her, so that for the time his love was forgotten, and he came to look upon it as a youthful episode not knowing how deeply it still lay under all these later feelings. He, therefore, accepted the mission, and made ready to go in royal state.

He selected for his companions a number of the ablest knights of the court, and saw that they were richly arrayed and appointed, with the hope that such a noble train might win him favor at the Irish court. With this array he departed, and set sail for the coast of Ireland.

But when they had reached the mid-channel a tempest arose that blew the fleet back towards the coast of England, and, as chance had it, they came ashore near Camelot. Here they were forced to land, for their ships were no longer seaworthy. Tristram, therefore, set up his pavilion upon the coast of Camelot, and hung his shield before it.

That same day two knights of Arthur's court, Sir Morganor and Sir Hector de Maris, chanced to ride that way, and, seeing the shield, they touched it with their spears, bidding the knight of the pavilion to come out and joust, if he had an inclination to do so.

"I hold myself ready alike for sport or battle," answered Tristram. "If you tarry a little while, you will find me ready to meet you."

This said, he armed himself, and mounting his horse rode against his two challengers with such fortune that he first smote Sir Hector to the earth, and then Sir Morganor, felling them both with one spear. Rising painfully to their feet, the disconcerted knights asked Tristram who he was and of what country.

"My noble sirs, I am a knight of Cornwall," he answered. "You have been in the habit of scorning the warriors of my country, but you see we have some good blood there."

"A Cornish knight!" cried Hector. "That I should be overcome by a knight from that land! I am not fit to wear armor more." And in despite he put off his armor and left the place on foot, too full of shame to ride.

As it turned out, fortune had worked more favorably for Tristram than he supposed. For King Anguish was then on his way to Camelot, whither he had been summoned by King Arthur as his vassal, for a purpose which he was not told.

It happened that when he reached Camelot neither King Arthur nor Lancelot was there to give judgment on the charge against him, but the kings of Carados and of Scotland were left as judges. And when King Anguish demanded why he had been summoned, Blamor de Ganis, a Knight of the Round Table, accused him of treason, declaring that he had treacherously slain a cousin of his at his court in Ireland.

This accusation threw King Anguish into great trouble, for he did not dream that he had been brought for such a purpose, and knew well that there was but one answer to make to such a charge. For the custom in those days was that any man who was accused of murder or treason should decide the case by the Wager of Battle, fighting his accuser to the death, or finding a knight who would take up his quarrel. And murders of all kinds in those days were called treason.

King Anguish was thrown into a sorrowful frame of mind, for he knew that Blamor de Ganis was a knight of prowess beyond his own strength, nor had he a suitable champion in his train. He therefore withheld his answer, and the judges gave him three days for his decision.

All this was told to Tristram by his squire Gouvernail, who had heard it from people of the country.

"Truly," said Tristram, "no man in England could bring me better tidings, for the king of Ireland will be glad of my aid, since no knight of this country not of Arthur's court will dare fight with Blamor. As I wish to win the good will of King Anguish, I will take on myself his battle. So, Gouvernail, go to the king for me, and tell him there is a champion ready to assume his cause."

Gouvernail thereupon went to Camelot, and greeted King Anguish, who returned his greeting and asked his errand.

"There is a knight near at hand who desires to speak with you," was the reply. "He bade me say that he was ready to do you knightly service."

"What knight may he be?" asked the king.

"Sir, it is Tristram of Lyonesse. For the grace you showed him in your country he is ready to repay you here, and to take the field as your champion."

"God be praised for this welcome news!" cried the king. "Come, good fellow, show me the way to Sir Tristram. Blamor will find he has no boy to handle."

He mounted a hackney, and with few followers rode under Gouvernail's guidance till they came to Tristram's pavilion. The knight, when he saw his visitor, ran to him and would have held his stirrup, but this the king would not permit. He leaped lightly from his horse and took Tristram warmly in his arms.

"My gracious lord," said Tristram, "I have not forgot the goodness which you formerly showed me, and which at that time I promised to requite by knightly service if it should ever be in my power."

"I have great need of you, indeed, gentle sir," answered the king. "Never before was I in such deep necessity of knightly aid."

"How so, my noble lord?" asked Tristram.

"I shall tell you. I am held answerable for the death of a knight who was akin to Lancelot, and for which I must fight his relative, Blamor de Ganis, or find a knight in my stead. And well you know the knights of King Ban's blood are hard men to overcome in battle."

"That may be," said Tristram, "yet I dread not to meet them. For the honor which you showed me in Ireland, and for the sake of your gracious daughter La Belle Isolde, I will take the battle on two conditions: first, that you swear that you are in the right, and had no hand in the knight's death; second, that if I win in this fight you grant me the reward I may ask, if you deem it reasonable."

"Truly, I am innocent, and you shall have whatever you ask," said the king.

"Then I accept the combat," said Tristram. "You may return to Camelot and make answer that your champion is ready, for I shall die in your quarrel rather than be recreant. Blamor is said to be a hardy knight, but I would meet him were he the best warrior that now bears shield and spear."

King Anguish then departed and told the judges that he had his champion ready, and was prepared for the wager of battle at any time that pleased them. In consequence, Blamor and Tristram were sent for to hear the charge. But when the knights of the court learned that the champion was he who had vanquished Marhaus and Palamides, there was much debate and shaking of the head, and many who had felt sure of the issue now grew full of doubt, the more so when they learned the story of Hector de Maris and his companion.

But the combatants took their charge in all due dignity, and then withdrew to make ready for the battle. Blamor was attended by his brother Sir Bleoberis, who said to him, feelingly:

"Remember, dear brother, of what kin we are, being cousins to Lancelot du Lac, and that there has never been a man of our blood but would rather die than be shamed in battle."

"Have no doubt of me," answered Blamor. "I know well this knight's record; but if he should strike me down through his great might, he shall slay me before I will yield as recreant."

"You will find him the strongest knight you have ever had to do with. I know that well, for I had once a bout with him at King Mark's court. So God speed you!"

"In God and my cause I trust," answered Blamor.

Then he took his horse and rode to one end of the lists, and Tristram to the other, where, putting their spears in rest, they spurred their gallant steeds and rushed together with the speed of lightning. The result was that Blamor and his horse together were hurled to the earth, while Tristram kept his seat. Then Blamor drew his sword and threw his shield before him, bidding Tristram to alight.

"Though a horse has failed me," he said, "I trust that the earth will stand me in good stead."

Without hesitation Tristram consented, springing to the ground, sword in hand, and the combatants broke at once into fierce battle, fighting like madmen, till all who saw them marvelled at their courage and strength. Never had knights been seen to fight more fiercely, for Blamor was so furious and incessant in his attacks, and Tristram so active in his defence, that it was a wonder they had breath to stand. But at last Tristram smote his antagonist such a blow on the helm that he fell upon his side, while his victor stood looking grimly down upon him.

When Blamor could gain breath to speak, he said:

"Sir Tristram de Lyonesse, I require thee, as thou art a true knight, to slay me, for I would not live in shame, though I might be lord of the earth. You must slay me, indeed, if you would win the field, for I shall never speak the hateful word of surrender."

When Tristram heard this knightly defiance he knew not what to do. The thought of slaying one of Lancelot's blood hurt him sorely, but his duty as a champion required him to force his antagonist to yield, or else to slay him. In deep distress of mind he went to the kingly judges and kneeled before them, beseeching them for the sake of King Arthur and Lancelot, and for their own credit, to take this matter out of his hands.

"It were a pity and shame that the noble knight who lies yonder should be slain," he said, "yet he refuses to yield. As for the king I fight for, I shall require him, as I am his true knight and champion, to have mercy on the vanquished."

"That yield I freely," said King Anguish. "And I heartily pray the judges to deal with him mercifully."

Then the judges called Bleoberis to them and asked his advice.

"My lords," he replied, "my brother is beaten, I acknowledge, yet, though Sir Tristram has vanquished his body, he has not conquered his heart, and I thank God he is not shamed by his defeat. And rather than he should be shamed I require you to bid Tristram to slay him."

"That shall not be," replied the judges. "Both his adversaries, the king and his champion, have pity on him, and you should have no less."

"I leave his fate to you," said Bleoberis. "Do what seems to you well."

Then, after further consultation, the judges gave their verdict that the vanquished knight should live, and by their advice Tristram and Bleoberis took him up and brought him to King Anguish, who forgave and made friends with him. Then Blamor and Tristram kissed each other and the two brothers took oath that neither of them would ever fight with their noble antagonist, who took the same oath. And from the day of that battle there was peace and love between Tristram and all the kindred of Lancelot for ever.

The happy close of this contest made great rejoicing in Arthur's court, King Anguish and his champion being treated with all the honor that could be laid upon them, and for many days thereafter feasting and merry making prevailed. In the end the king and his champion sailed for Ireland with great state and ceremony, while many noble knights attended to bid them farewell.

When they reached Ireland, King Anguish spread far and wide the story of what Tristram had done for him, and he was everywhere greeted with honor and delight. Even the queen forgot her anger, and did all that lay in her power to give her lord's champion a glad welcome to the court.

As for La Belle Isolde, she met Tristram with the greatest joy and gladness. Absence had dimmed the love in both their hearts, and it no longer burned as of yore, yet only time and opportunity were needed to make it as warm as ever.

Chapter IV
The Draught of Love

AT LENGTH there came a day, after Tristram had dwelt long at King Anguish's court, that the king asked him why he had not demanded his boon, since the royal word had been passed that whatever he asked should be his without fail.

"I asked you not," said Tristram, "since it is a boon that will give me no pleasure, but so much pain that with every day that passes I grow less inclined to ask it."

"Then why ask it at all?"

"That I must, for I have passed my word of honor, and the word of a knight is his best possession. What I am forced to demand, then, is that you will give me the hand of La Belle Isolde, not for myself, and that is what makes my heart so sore, but for my uncle, King Mark, who desires to wed her, and for whom I have promised to demand her."

"Alas!" cried the king, "that you should ask me so despiteful a boon. I had rather than all King Mark's dominions that you should wed her yourself."

"I never saw woman whom I would rather wed," he replied. "But if I should do so I would be the shame of the world for ever, as a false knight, recreant to his promise. Therefore, I must stand by my word, and hold you to your boon, that you will give me La Belle Isolde to go with me to Cornwall, there to be wedded to King Mark, my uncle."

"As for that, I cannot deny you. She shall go with you, but as to what may happen thereafter, I leave that for you to decide. If you choose to wed her yourself, that will give me the greatest joy. But if you determine to give her to King Mark, the right rests with you. I have passed my word, though I wish now that I had not."

Then Isolde was told of what had passed, and bade to make ready to go with Tristram, a lady named Bragwaine going with her as chief gentlewoman, while many others were selected as her attendants. When the preparations were fully made, the queen, Isolde's mother, gave to Dame Bragwaine and Gouvernail a golden flask containing a drink, and charged them that on the day of Isolde's wedding they should give King Mark that drink, bidding him to quaff it to the health of La Belle Isolde, and her to quaff his health in return.

"It is a love draught," continued the queen, "and if they shall drink it I undertake to say that each shall love the other for all the days of their life."

Not many days passed before Tristram took to the sea, with the fair maiden who had been committed to his charge, and they sailed away on a mission that had for them both far more of sadness than of joy, for their love grew as the miles passed.

One day, as they sat together in the cabin, it happened that they became thirsty, and by chance they saw on a shelf near them a little golden flask, filled with what by the color seemed to be a noble wine. Tristram took it down and said, with a laugh:

"Madam Isolde, here is the best drink that ever you drank, a precious draught which Dame Bragwaine, your maiden, and Gouvernail, my servant, are keeping for themselves. Let us drink from their private store."

Then with laughter and merriment they drank freely from the flask, and both thought that they had never tasted draught so sweet and delicious in their lives before. But when the magic wine got into their blood, they looked upon each other with new eyes, for their hearts were suddenly filled with such passionate love as they had not dreamed that heart could feel. Tristram thought that never had mortal eyes gazed upon a maiden of such heavenly charms, and Isolde that there was never man born so grand and graceful as the knight of her love.

Then all at once she fell into bitter weeping as the thought of her destiny came upon her, and Tristram took her in his arms and kissed her sweet lips again and again, speaking words of love that brought some comfort to her lovesick heart. And thus it was between them day by day to the end of their voyage, for a love had grown between them of such fervent depth that it could never leave them while blood flowed in their veins.

Such magic power had the draught which the queen had prepared for King Mark, and which the unthinking lovers drank in fate's strange error. It was the bittersweet of love; for it was destined to bring them the deepest joy and sorrow in the years to come.

Many days passed before the lovers reached Cornwall, and strange adventures met them by the way, of which we have but little space to speak. For chance brought them to land near a castle named Pleure, or the weeping castle. It was the custom of the lord of that castle, when any knight passed by with a lady, to take them prisoners. Then, when the knight's lady was compared with the lady of the castle, whichever was the least lovely of the two was put to death, and the knight was made to fight with the lord of the castle for the other, and was put to death if vanquished. Through this cruel custom many a noble knight and fair lady had been slain, for the castle lord was of great prowess and his lady of striking beauty.

It chanced that Tristram and Isolde demanded shelter at this castle, and that they were made prisoners under its cruel custom. At this outrage Tristram grew bitterly indignant, and demanded passionately what it meant, as honor demanded that those who sought harbor should be received hospitably as guests, and not despitefully as prisoners. In answer he was told the custom of the castle, and that he must fight for his lady and his liberty.

"It is a foul and shameful custom," he replied. "I do not fear that your lord's lady will surpass mine in beauty, nor that I cannot hold my own in the field, but I like to have a voice in my own doings. Tell him, however, if he is so hot for battle, that I shall be ready for the test tomorrow morning, and may heaven be on the side of truth and justice."

When morning came the test of beauty was made, and the loveliness of Isolde shone so far beyond that of the castle lady that Breunor, the lord, was forced to admit it. And now Tristram grew stern and pitiless, for he said that this lady had consented to the death of many innocent rivals, and richly deserved death as a punishment for the ruthless deeds done in her behalf, and to gratify her cruel vanity. Thereupon her head was struck off without mercy.

Full of anger at this, Breunor attacked Tristram with all his strength and fury, and a long and fiery combat took place, yet in the end he fell dead beneath the sword of the knight of Cornwall.

But, as it happened, the castle lord had a valiant son, named Sir Galahad the high prince, a knight who in after years was to do deeds of great emprise. Word was brought to him of the death of his father and mother, and he rode in all haste to the castle, having with him that renowned warrior known as the king with the hundred knights.

Reaching the castle, Galahad fiercely challenged Tristram to battle, and a mighty combat ensued. But at the last Galahad was forced to give way before the deadly strokes of his antagonist, whose strength seemed to grow with his labor.

When the king with the hundred knights saw this, he rushed upon Tristram with many of his followers, attacking him in such force as no single knight could hope to endure.

"This is no knightly deed," cried Tristram to Galahad. "I deemed you a noble knight, but it is a shameful act to let all your men set on me at once."

"However that be," said Galahad, "you have done me a great wrong, and must yield or die."

"Then I must yield, since you treat me so unfairly. I accepted your challenge, not that of all your followers. To yield thus puts me to no dishonor."

And he took his sword by the point and put the pommel in the hand of his opponent. But despite this action the king and his knights came on, and made a second attack on the unarmed warrior.

"Let him be," cried Sir Galahad. "I have given him his life, and no man shall harm him."

"Shame is it in you to say so!" cried the king. "Has he not slain your father and mother?"

"For that I cannot blame him greatly. My father held him in prison, and forced him to fight to the death. The custom was a wicked and cruel one, and could have but one end. Long ago, it drove me from my father's castle, for I could not favor it by any presence."

"It was a sinful custom, truly," said the king.

"So I deem it, and it would be a pity that this brave knight should die in such a cause, for I know no one save Lancelot du Lac who is his equal. Now, fair knight, will you tell me your name?"

"My name is Tristram of Lyonesse, and I am on my way to the court of King Mark of Cornwall, taking to him La Belle Isolde, the daughter of King Anguish of Ireland, whom he desires to wed."

"Then you are welcome to these marches, and all that I demand of you is that you promise to go to Lancelot du Lac, and become his fellow. I shall promise that no such custom shall ever be used in this castle again."

"You will do well," said Tristram. "I would have you know that when I began to fight with you I fancied you were Lancelot. And I promise, as soon as I may, to seek him, for of all the knights in the world I most desire his fellowship."

Soon afterwards Tristram and his fair companion resumed their journey, and in due time reached Cornwall. But as they came near Tintagil their hearts were ready to break, for that magic draught was still in their veins, and they loved each other with a love that was past all telling.

Thoughts came into Tristram's heart to marry the maiden in despite of custom and his plighted word, and gladly would she have consented thereto. But strong as was his love, his honor was stronger, and Isolde, deeply as she grieved, could not ask him to break his word. And thus for many long miles they journeyed onward side by side in silence, their eyes alone speaking, but they telling a story of love and grief to which they dared not give words, lest their hearts' desire should burst all boundaries of faith and honor, and men's condemnation come to them both.

So they came with drooping hearts to the court of King Mark, where the king and his barons received them with state and ceremony. Quickly thereafter the wedding took place, for the king looked with eyes of warm approval upon the beautiful maiden, and prepared richly and nobly for the ceremony, at which many noble knights and lords were present, but from which Tristram withdrew in the deepest anguish, as he could not endure the sight. And so his knightly word was kept, though to keep it almost broke his heart.

Chapter V
The Perils of True Love

THE MARRIAGE of King Mark with La Belle Isolde was celebrated with rich feasts and royal tournaments, and for many days pleasure ruled supreme at Tintagil Castle, whither noble guests came and went. Among those who came was Palamides the Saracen, drawn thither by his love of Isolde,

which his overthrow by Tristram had not banished from his heart.

Strange events soon followed. Two ladies of Isolde's train, who envied and hated Dame Bragwaine, laid a plot for her destruction. She was sent into the forest to obtain herbs, and there was met by men sent by her enemies, who bound her hand and foot to a tree, where she remained for three days. By good fortune, at the end of that time, she was found by Palamides, who saved her from death, and took her to a nunnery that she might recover from her pain and exhaustion.

The disappearance of Dame Bragwaine troubled the queen greatly, for she loved her most of all women, and as the days went by and she returned not, the grief of Isolde grew deep. She wandered into the forest, which had been searched in vain for the lost lady, and, plunged in sad thought, seated herself by a woodland spring, where she moaned bitterly for her favorite.

As she sat there Palamides appeared, and, after listening awhile to her sad complaining, said:

"Queen Isolde, I know well the cause of your grief, and if you will grant the boon I shall ask, I promise to bring you Dame Bragwaine, safe and sound."

The queen was so glad to hear this, that without thought she agreed to grant his wish, thinking more of the lost lady than of what he might demand.

"I trust to your promise," said Palamides. "Remain here half an hour and you shall see her."

"I shall remain," said the queen.

Palamides then rode away, and within the time mentioned returned with the maiden, whom Isolde clasped to her heart with happy tears.

"Now, madam, I have kept my word," said Palamides; "you must keep yours."

"I promised you hastily," answered the queen; "and I warn you now that I will grant you nothing evil; so beware of your asking."

"My boon will keep till I meet you before the king," said Palamides. "What it is I shall not tell you now."

Then the queen rode home with her maiden, and Palamides followed close after, entering the court while Isolde was telling the king of what had happened.

"Sir King," said the knight, "your lady has told you of the boon she proffered me. The honor of knighthood requires that you shall make her word good."

"Why made you this promise, my lady?" asked the king.

"I did so for grief at the loss of Dame Bragwaine, and for joy to recover her."

"Then what you have hastily proffered you must truly perform. The word of king and queen is not to be lightly spoken or lightly broken."

"What I demand is this," said Palamides, "that you deliver to me your queen, to lead her where I wish and govern her as I will."

At this bold request the king frowned deeply, and anger leaped to his lips. But his word had been passed, and the thought came to him that he could trust to Tristram quickly to rescue the queen, and punish this bold adventurer.

"Take her if you will," he cried. "But I tell you this, you will not keep her long, and that you are asking a dangerous gift."

"As for that, I shall dare the risk."

Then he took Isolde by the hand, and led her from the court, and from the presence of the king and his barons, not one of whom moved, though the queen looked round with suppliant eyes. Leading her to his war-horse, he set her behind him on the saddle, and rode proudly away.

No sooner had they gone than the king sent for Tristram, but he was nowhere to be found, for he was in the forest hunting, as was always his custom when not engaged in feats of arms.

"What shall be done?" cried the king. "Can no one find Tristram? My honor will be shamed if the Saracen be not met and overcome."

"I shall follow him, and seek to rescue the queen," said a knight named Lambegus, one of Tristram's followers.

"I thank you, Sir Lambegus. If I live, I will remember the service."

So Lambegus got to horse and followed Palamides hotly, but to his own sorrow, as it proved, for he was no match for the Saracen, who soon laid him upon the earth wounded nearly to death.

But while the battle went on, Isolde, who had been set upon the earth pending the combat, ran into the forest, and continued to fly till she came to a deep spring, where in her grief she sought to drown herself. But good fortune brought thither a knight named Sir Adtherp, who had a castle nearby. Seeing the despair of the queen, he led her to his castle, and then, learning her story, took upon himself her battle, and rode forth to meet the Saracen.

But he, too, fared badly, for Palamides wounded him severely, and made him tell what he had done with the queen, and where his castle might be found.

Palamides, leaving him bleeding on the ground, rode in all haste to the castle. But as he approached, Isolde saw him from a window, and gave orders that the gate should be shut and the drawbridge raised. When Palamides came up and saw that the castle was closed against him, and entrance denied, he took the saddle and bridle from his horse and put him to pasture, while he seated himself before the gate like a man who cared not what became of him.

Meanwhile, Tristram had returned from the hunt, and when he learned what had happened, he was half beside himself with anger.

"Lambegus is no match for the Saracen," he said. "Would I had been here in his stead. The unchristianed villain shall answer for this outrage if he can be found."

Then he armed himself in all haste, and rode into the forest. Not far had he gone when he found Lambegus, sorely wounded, and had him borne to a place of shelter. Somewhat farther on he found Adtherp, also hurt and bleeding, and from him he learned what had taken place.

"Where is my lady now?" he asked.

"Safe in my castle," said the knight. "And there she can hold herself secure against the Saracen."

"Then I owe you much," said Tristram. "Trust me to see that some of your men be sent to your aid."

He continued his journey till he came to the castle, and here he saw Palamides sitting by the gate fast asleep, with his horse grazing beside him.

"The misbegotten rogue takes life easy," said Tristram. "Go rouse him, Gouvernail. Bid him make ready to answer for his outrage."

But he was in such deep slumber that Gouvernail called to him in vain. He returned and told Tristram that the knight was either asleep or mad.

"Go again and tell him that I, his mortal foe, am here."

Gouvernail now prodded him with the butt of his spear, and cried:

"Arise, Sir Palamides, and make ready, for yonder is Sir Tristram, and he sends you word that he is your mortal foe."

Then Palamides rose without a word of answer, and saddled and bridled his horse, upon which he sprang, putting his spear in rest. But he remained not long in his saddle, for when they met in mid-channel, Tristram smote him so hard a blow as to thrust him over his horse's tail to the ground.

Then they drew their swords and fought with all their strength, for the lady whom they both loved looked upon them from the walls, and well-nigh swooned for grief and distress on seeing how sorely each was hurt.

"Alas!" she cried, "one of them I love, and the other loves me. It would be a great pity to see Sir Palamides slain, much as he has troubled me, and slain he will be if this fight goes on."

Then, moved by her tender heart, she went down and besought Tristram to fight no more.

"What mean you?" he asked. "Would you have me shamed?"

"I desire not your dishonor; but for my sake I would have you spare this unhappy knight, whose love for me has made him mad."

"As you wish," he replied. "The fight shall end, since you desire it."

"As for you, Sir Palamides," she said, "I command that you shall go out of this country while I am in it."

"If it must be, it must," he answered, in bitter anguish; "but it is sorely against my will, for not to see you is not to live."

"Take your way to the court of King Arthur," she said, "and there recommend me to Queen Guenever. Tell her that Isolde says that in all the land there are but four lovers, and that these are Lancelot du Lac and Queen Guenever, and Tristram de Lyonesse and Queen Isolde."

This message filled Palamides with the greatest heaviness of heart, and mounting his steed he rode away moaning bitterly. But Isolde was full of gladness in being well rid of her troublesome lover, and Tristram in having rescued her from his rival. So he brought her back to King

Mark, and there was great joy over her homecoming, while the king and all the court showered honors on the successful champion. Sir Lambegus was brought back to the court and put under the care of skilful leeches, and for a long time joy and good will reigned.

But Tristram had in King Mark's court a bitter foe, who sought to work him injury, though he was his near cousin. This traitor, Sir Andred by name, knew well of the love between Tristram and Isolde, and that they had secret meetings and tender conversations, so he lay in wait to spy upon them and slander them before the court.

A day came at length when Andred observed Tristram in secret parley with Isolde at a window, and he hastened to the king and poisoned his mind with a false report of what he had seen. King Mark, on hearing this, burst into a fury of passion, and seizing a sword, ran to where Tristram stood. Here he violently berated him as a traitor, and struck at him a furious blow.

But Tristram took the sword-point under his arm, and ran in on the king, wresting the weapon from his hand.

"Where are my knights and men?" cried the enraged king. "I charge you to kill this traitor!"

But of those present not a man would move. When Tristram saw this, he shook the sword threateningly against the king, and took a step forward as if he would have slain him. At this movement King Mark fled, while Tristram followed, and struck him so strong a blow with the flat of the sword on his neck that he was flung prostrate on his nose. Then Tristram hastened to his room and armed himself, after which he took his horse and his squire and rode into the forest.

Here the valorous champion killed some of the knights whom the king had sent against him and put to flight thirty more, so that King Mark in fear and fury called a council of his lords, and asked what was to be done with his rebellious subject.

"Our counsel is," said the barons, "that you send for Sir Tristram and make friends with him, for you well know that if you push him hard many of your men will join him. He is peerless and matchless among Christian knights except Sir Lancelot, and if you drive him to seek King Arthur's court he will find such friends there that he may defy your power. Therefore we counsel you to beg him to return to the court, under assurance of safety."

"You may send for him, then," said the king, though his heart burned with secret fury. The barons now sent for Tristram under a safe conduct, and he returned to the court, where he was welcomed by the king, and all that had passed seemed to be forgotten.

Shortly after this the king and queen went hunting, accompanied by Tristram and many knights and gentlemen of the court. Entering the forest, they set up their pavilions and tents beside a river, where they hunted and jousted daily, for King Mark had with him thirty knights who stood ready to meet all comers.

Fortune brought thither two knights-errant, one being Lamorak de Galis, who of all knights was counted next to Lancelot and Tristram. The other was Sir Driant, both being Knights of the Round Table.

Driant jousted first with the Cornish knights, and, after unhorsing some of them, got a stunning fall. Then Lamorak offered to meet them, and of the thirty knights not one kept his seat before him, while some were sorely hurt.

"What knight is this who fights so well?" asked the king.

"Sir," said Tristram, "it is Lamorak de Galis, one of the best knights who ever put spear in rest."

"Then, Sir Tristram, you must meet him. It were a shame to us all to let him go away victor."

"It were a greater shame to overthrow a noble knight when he and his horse are worn out with over-labor."

"He shall not leave here and boast of how he vanquished King Mark's knights. I charge you, as you love me and my lady La Belle Isolde, to take your arms and joust with this Lamorak."

"You charge me to do what is against knighthood, for it is no honor for a fresh man and horse to master spent and weary ones. Since you command it I must do it, but it is sorely against my will."

Then he armed himself and took his horse, and in the joust easily overthrew Lamorak and his weary steed. The knight lightly sprang from the falling charger and drew his sword, boldly challenging Tristram to meet him on foot. But this Tristram would by no means do, though Lamorak hotly renewed the challenge.

"You are great of heart, Sir Lamorak," said Tristram, "but no knight nor horse was ever made that could for ever endure. Therefore I will not meet you, and I am sorry for having jousted with you."

"You have done me an evil turn," said Lamorak, angrily, "for which I shall repay you when an opportunity comes."

Lamorak soon got his revenge. For as he rode with Sir Driant towards Camelot he met by the way a boy who had been sent by Morgan le Fay to King Arthur. For the false enchantress still held to her hatred against her noble brother, and by all means sought his harm. So by magic art she had made a drinking-horn of such strange virtue that if any lady drank of it who had been false to her husband all the wine would be spilled, but if she had been true to him, she might drink in peace and safety.

This horn she sent to Arthur's court, hoping that Guenever might drink thereof and be dishonored, for her love for Lancelot was known to all but the king.

Lamorak, learning from the boy his errand, bade him bear the horn to King Mark's court, and tell the king that it was sent to prove the falseness of his lady, who loved Sir Tristram more than she did her wedded lord.

Soon afterwards, therefore, the boy appeared at Tintagil Castle, and presented King Mark the magic horn, telling him of its virtues, and all that Sir Lamorak had bidden him say.

"By my royal faith we shall try it, then!" said the king. "Not only my queen, but all the ladies of the court, shall drink of it, and we shall learn who among them has other lovers than their liege lords."

Much to their unwillingness, Queen Isolde and a hundred ladies of the court were made to drink from the magic horn, and of them all only four drank without spilling the wine.

"Now, by my knightly honor, all these false dames shall be burnt!" cried the king. "My court shall be purged of this vile stain."

"That shall they not," cried the barons. "We shall never consent that the queen and all these ladies shall be destroyed for a horn wrought by sorcery, and sent here to make mischief by as foul a sorceress and witch as the earth holds. She has always been an enemy to all true lovers and sought to do them harm, and if we meet with Morgan le Fay she will get but scant courtesy at our hands. We would much rather believe the horn false than all our ladies untrue."

But Tristram's anger was turned towards Lamorak for this affront, for he knew well what had been his purpose. And he vowed in his heart that he would yet repay him for this treacherous act.

His affection for Queen Isolde kept as warm as though the love-draught still flowed in his veins, and he sought her at every opportunity, for the two greatest joys that life held for him were to tell her of his love and hear from her lips that her love for him had never dimmed.

But his treacherous cousin Andred watched his every movement, and kept the king advised that Tristram continued his secret interviews with the queen. So an ambush of twelve knights was set, and one day, when Tristram had just paid a stolen visit to the queen, and sat in loving converse by her side, these ambushed knights broke suddenly upon him, took him prisoner, and bound him hand and foot.

Then, by order of the king, he was borne to a chapel that stood on a rocky height above the sea, where Andred and some others of the barons who were his enemies came together to pass judgment upon him.

Tristram in all his life had never stood in such peril, for his hands were bound fast to two knights, and forty others surrounded him, everyone a foe. Care had been taken to get rid of his friends among the barons by sending them away from the court on various pretexts. Like a lion surrounded by jackals he chafed in his bonds, while his great heart swelled as if it would break. No escape seemed possible, but with a reproachful voice he said:

"Fair lords, I have in my time done something for Cornwall, and taken upon myself great peril for your benefit. Who among you all was ready to meet Sir Marhaus, or to cope with Palamides? Is this shameful death my reward for my services to your country? You know well that I never met a knight but that I was his match or his better."

"Boast not, false traitor," cried Andred. "For all thy vaunting, thou shalt die this day."

"O Andred, Andred, that you my kinsman should treat me thus!" said Tristram sorrowfully. "You can be bold when I am bound, but if there were none here but you and me, you would crouch like a cur at my feet."

"Would I so?" cried Andred, angrily. "You shall see what I would do."

And as he spoke he drew his sword, and advanced upon his cousin with intent to slay him on the spot. But Tristram, when he saw him coming with murderous looks, suddenly drew inwards with all his strength the two knights to whom he was bound, and with a mighty wrench broke the strong cords asunder. Then with the leap of a tiger he sprang upon his treacherous cousin, wrested the sword from his hand, and smote him a blow that hurled him insensible to the earth. This done, he rushed with the fury of a madman on his enemies, striking mighty blows to right and left, till in a few minutes ten of them lay dead and wounded on the earth.

But seeing that they were pressing on him in too great force, he retreated into the chapel, in whose doorway he stood, sword in hand, holding it against all their assaults.

Soon, however, the cry went forth that the prisoner had escaped, and had felled Andred and killed many of the barons, and others of his foes hastened up, till more than a hundred beleaguered him in the chapel.

Tristram now looked despairingly on his unarmed form, and saw that many of his assailants wore armor of proof. Death was sure unless he could find some means of escape. He knew that the chapel stood on the brow of the cliff, and here seemed his only hope of safety, though it was a perilous one. Quickly retreating, he shut and barred the door, and then with hand and sword wrenched and tore the iron bars from a window over the cliff, out of which he desperately leaped.

The descent was a deep one, but he fortunately reached the sea below without striking any of the rocks in his descent. Here he drew himself into a crevice at the foot of the cliff.

Those above rushed to the rocky edge and looked down into the boiling waters far below, but they saw nothing of the daring knight, and after a long and vain effort to see him, went away to report to the king that his enemy was drowned.

But while King Mark and Tristram's enemies were congratulating one another upon this, there came to the top of the cliff, Gouvernail, Lambegus and others of Tristram's men, who, looking down, saw him creeping up from the water to a safer place of shelter among the rocks.

Hailing him, they bade him to be of good heart, and, letting down a rope which they quickly procured, they managed to draw him up to the summit, where they congratulated him warmly on his escape. Without delay, however, he left that spot, for fear of his foes returning, and sought a place of shelter in the forest.

Here he abode for some time, but the news of his escape got abroad, to the discomfiture of his foes. And on a day when he had fallen asleep, a man to whom he had done some injury crept up and shot him in the shoulder with an arrow. Tristram sprang up and killed the man, but the wound pained him day by day. And on news of it being brought to La Belle Isolde she sent him word by Dame Bragwaine that the arrow had been poisoned, and with a venom that no leech in England could cure. "My lady, La Belle Isolde, bids you haste into Brittany to King Howell," said Dame Bragwaine, "for she knows no one who can help you but his daughter, Isolde la Blanche Mains."

Hearing this, the wounded knight sent a sad farewell to his lady love, and took ship with Gouvernail his squire, and sailed to Brittany, where he was warmly welcomed by King Howell.

And when Isolde of the White Hands heard of the errand of the knight, she applied to his wound healing herbs of such virtue that in a little while he was whole again.

Afterwards Tristram dwelt long in Brittany, and helped King Howell much in his wars.

Chapter VI
The Madness of Sir Tristram

OF THE VISIT of Sir Tristram to Brittany, and the healing of his wound, with the great deeds he did there, and how he overthrew the giant knight Nabon le Noire, we shall not further speak. Letters at length came to him from La Belle Isolde, in which she spoke pitifully of tales that had been brought her,

saying that he had been false to her, and had married Isolde the White Handed, daughter of King Howell of Brittany.

On receiving these letters, Tristram set out in all haste for Cornwall, bringing with him Kehydius, King Howell's son. On his way there he had many adventures, and rescued King Arthur from an enchantress, who had brought him near to death in the forest perilous. When at length he came to Cornwall he sought the castle of Dinas the seneschal, his warmest friend, and sent him to tell Queen Isolde that he had secretly returned.

At this longed-for news the queen swooned from pure joy. When she recovered and was able to speak, she said, in pitiful accents:

"Gentle seneschal, I pray you bring him where I may speak with him, or my heart will break."

"Trust me for that," answered Dinas.

Then he and Dame Bragwaine brought Tristram and Kehydius privately to the court, and to a chamber which Isolde had assigned for them. But to tell the joy of the meeting between Tristram and La Belle Isolde we shall not endeavor, for no tongue could tell it, nor heart think it, nor pen write it.

Yet misfortune still pursued these true lovers, and this time it came from friends instead of foes, for the presence of Kehydius in the castle led to the most doleful and melancholy misfortune which the world ever knew. For, as the chronicles make mention, no sooner had Kehydius seen La Belle Isolde, than he became so enamoured of her that his heart might never more be free. And at last, as we are told, he died from pure love of this beautiful queen, but with that we are not here concerned. But privately he wrote her letters which were full of moving tales of his love, and composed love poems to her which no minstrel of those days might surpass.

All these he managed to put into the queen's hands privately, and at length, when she saw how deeply he was enamoured, she was moved by such pity for his hopeless love that, out of the pure kindness of her heart, she unwisely wrote him a letter, seeking to comfort him in his distress.

Sad was it that pity should bring such sorrow and pain to two loving hearts as came from that fatal letter. For on a day when King Mark sat playing chess at a chamber window, it chanced that La Belle Isolde and Kehydius were in the chamber above, where they awaited the coming of Tristram from the turret-room in which he was secretly accommodated. But as ill luck would have it, there fell into Tristram's hands the last letter which Kehydius had written to the queen, and her answer, which was so worded that it seemed as if she returned his love.

These the young lover had carelessly left in Tristram's chamber, where he found them and thoughtlessly began reading them. But not far had he read when his heart sank deep in woe, and then leaped high in anger. He hurried in all haste to the chamber where Isolde and Kehydius were, the letters in his hand.

"Isolde," he cried, pitifully, "what mean these letters – this which Kehydius has written you, and this, your answer, with its vile tale of love? Alas! is this my repayment for the love I have lavished on you, that you thus treacherously desert me for the viper that I have brought hither? As for you, Kehydius, you have foully repaid my trust in you and all my services. But bear you well in mind that I shall be amply revenged for your falsehood and treason."

Then he drew his sword with such a fierce and threatening countenance that Isolde swooned out of pure fear; and Kehydius, when he saw him advancing with murder in his face, saw but one chance for life, and leaped out of a bay window immediately over that where King Mark sat playing at chess.

When the king saw the body of a man hurtling down over his head, so close that he almost touched him as he sat at the window, he sprang up in alarm and cried:

"What the foul fiend is this? Who are you, fellow? and where in the wide world have you come from?"

Kehydius, who had fallen on his feet, answered the king with ready wit.

"My lord, the king," he said, "blame me not, for I fell in my sleep. I was seated in the window above you, and slumbered there, and you see what has come of it."

"The next time you are sleepy, good fellow, hunt a safer couch," laughed the king, and turned again to his chess.

But Tristram was sure that his presence in the castle would now be known to the king, and hastened to arm himself with such armor as he could find, in dread of an assault in force. But as no one came against him, he sent Gouvernail for his horse and spear, and rode in knightly guise openly from the gates of Tintagil.

At the gate it chanced that he met with Gingalin, the son of Gawaine, who had just arrived; and the young knight, being full of ardor, and having a fancy to tilt with a Cornish warrior, put his spear in rest and rode against Tristram, breaking his spear on him.

Tristram had yet no spear, but he drew his sword and put all his grief and anger into the blow he gave the bold young knight. So hard he struck that Gingalin was flung from his saddle, and the sword, slipping down, cut through the horse's neck, leaving the knight with a headless charger.

Then Tristram rode on until he disappeared in the forest. All this was seen by King Mark, who sent a squire to the hurt knight and asked him who he was. When he knew it was Sir Gingalin, he welcomed him, and proffered him another horse, asking what knight it was he had encountered.

"That I know not," said Gingalin, "but he has a mighty wrist, whoever he is. And he sighed and moaned as if some great disaster had happened him. I shall beware of weeping knights hereafter, if they all strike like this."

As Tristram rode on he met Sir Fergus, one of his own knights, but by this time his grief and pain of heart had grown so bitter that he fell from his horse in a swoon, and lay thus for three days and nights.

When at length he came to himself, he sent Fergus, who had remained with him, to the court, to bring him what tidings he might learn. As Fergus rode forward he met a damsel whom Palamides had sent to inquire about Sir Tristram. Fergus told her how he had met him, and that he was almost out of his mind.

"Where shall I find him?" asked the damsel.

"In such a place," explained Fergus, and rode on to the court, where he learned that Queen Isolde was sick in bed, moaning pitifully, though no one knew the source of her pain.

The damsel meanwhile sought Tristram, whom she found in such grief as she had never before seen, and the more she tried to console him the more he moaned and bewailed. At the last he took his horse and rode deeply into the forest, as if he would be away from all human company.

The damsel now sought him diligently, but it was three days before she could find him, in a miserable woodland hut. Here she brought him meat and drink, but he would eat nothing, and seemed as if he wished to starve himself.

A few days afterwards he fled from her again, and on this occasion it chanced that he rode by the castle before which he and Palamides had fought for La Belle Isolde. Here the damsel found him again, moaning dismally, and quite beside himself with grief. In despair what to do, she went to the lady of the castle and told her of the misfortune of the knight.

"It grieves me to learn this," said the lady. "Where is he?"

"Here, nearby your castle."

"I am glad he is so near. He shall have meat and drink of the best, and a harp which I have of his, and on which he taught me to play. For in harping he has no peer in the world."

So they took him meat and drink, but had much ado to get him to eat. And during the night his madness so increased that he drove his horse from him, and unlaced his armor and threw it wildly away. For days afterwards he roamed like a wild man about the wilderness; now in a mad frenzy breaking boughs from the trees, and even tearing young trees up by the roots, and now for hours playing on the harp which the lady had given him, while tears flowed in rivulets from his eyes.

Sometimes, again, when the lady knew not where he was, she would sit down in the wood and play upon the harp, which he had left hanging on a bough. Then Tristram would come like a tamed fawn and listen to her, hiding in the bushes; and in the end would come out and take the harp from her hand and play on it himself, in mournful strains that brought the tears to her eyes.

Thus for a quarter of a year the demented lover roamed the forest near the castle. But at length he wandered deeper into the wilderness, and the lady knew not whither he had gone. Finally, his clothes torn into tatters by the thorns, and he fallen away till he was lean as a hound, he fell into the fellowship of herdsmen and shepherds, who gave him daily a share of their food, and made him do servile tasks. And when he did any deed not to their liking they would beat him with rods. In the end, as they looked upon him as witless, they clipped his hair and beard, and made him look like a fool.

To such a vile extremity had love, jealousy, and despair brought the brave knight Tristram de Lyonesse, that from being the fellow of lords and nobles he became the butt of churls and cowherds. About this time it happened that Dagonet, the fool and merry-maker of King Arthur, rode into Cornwall with two squires, and chance brought them to a well in the forest which was much haunted by the demented knight. The weather was hot, and they alighted and stooped to drink at the well, while their horses ran loose. As they bent over the well in their thirst, Tristram suddenly appeared, and, moved by a mad freak, he seized Dagonet and soused him headforemost in the well, and the two squires after him. The dripping victims crawled miserably from the water, amid the mocking laughter of the shepherds, while Tristram ran after the stray horses. These being brought, he forced the fool and the squires to mount, soaked as they were, and ride away.

But after Tristram had departed, Dagonet and the squires returned, and accusing the shepherds of having set that madman on to assail them, they rode upon the keepers of beasts and beat them shrewdly. Tristram, as it chanced, was not so far off but that he saw this ill-treatment of those who had fed him, and he ran back, pulled Dagonet from the saddle, and gave him a stunning fall to the earth. Then he wrested the sword from his hand and with it smote off the head of one of the squires, while the other fled in terror. Tristram followed him, brandishing the sword wildly, and leaping like a madman as he rushed into the forest.

When Dagonet had recovered from his swoon, he rode to King Mark's court, and there told what had happened to him in the wildwood.

"Let all beware," he said, "how they come near that forest well. For it is haunted by a naked madman, and that fool soused me, King Arthur's fool, and had nearly slain me."

"That must be Sir Matto le Breune," said King Mark, "who lost his wit because Sir Gaheris robbed him of his lady."

Meanwhile, Kehydius had been ordered out of Cornwall by Queen Isolde, who blamed him for all that had happened, and with a dolorous heart he obeyed. By chance he met Palamides, to whom the damsel had reported the sad condition of the insane knight, and for days they sought him together, but in vain.

But at Tintagil a foul scheme was laid by Andred, Tristram's cousin and foe, to gain possession of his estates. This villain got a lady to declare that she had nursed Tristram in a fatal illness, that he had died in her care, and had been buried by her near a forest well; and she further said that before his death he had left a request that King Mark would make Andred king of Lyonesse, of which country Tristram now was lord.

On hearing these tidings, King Mark made a great show of grief, weeping and lamenting as if he had lost his best friend in the world. But when the news came to La Belle Isolde, so deep a weight of woe fell upon her that she nearly went out of her mind. So deeply did she grieve, indeed, that she vowed to destroy herself, declaring bitterly that she would not live if Tristram was dead.

So she secretly got a sword and went with it into her garden, where she forced the hilt into a crevice in a plum tree so that the naked point stood out breast high. Then she kneeled down and prayed piteously: "Sweet Lord Jesus, have pity on me, for I may not live after the death of Sir Tristram. My first love he was, and he shall be my last."

All this had been seen by King Mark, who had followed her privily, and as she rose and was about to cast herself on the sword he came behind and caught her in his arms. Then he tore the sword from the tree, and bore her away, struggling and moaning, to a strong tower, where he set guards upon her, bidding them to watch her closely. After that she lay long sick, and came nigh to the point of death.

Meanwhile, Tristram ran wildly through the forest, with Dagonet's sword in his hand, till he came to a hermitage, where he lay down and slept. While he slumbered, the hermit, who knew of his madness, stole the sword from him and laid meat beside him. Here he remained ten days, and afterwards departed and returned to the herdsmen.

And now another adventure happened. There was in that country a giant named Tauleas, brother to that Taulard whom Sir Marhaus had killed. For fear of Tristram he had for seven years kept close in his castle, daring not to go at large and commit depredations as of old. But now, hearing the rumor that Tristram was dead, he resumed his old evil courses. And one day he came to where the herdsmen were engaged, and seated himself to rest among them. By chance there passed along the road nearby a Cornish knight named Sir Dinant, with whom rode a lady.

When the giant saw them coming, he left the herdsmen and hid himself under a tree near a well, deeming that the knight would stop there to drink. This he did, but no sooner had he sought the well than the giant slipped from his covert and leaped upon the horse. Then he rode up to Sir Dinant, took him by the collar, and pulled him before him upon the horse, reaching for his dagger to strike off his head.

At this moment the herdsmen called to Tristram, who had just come from the forest depths: "Help the knight."

"Help him yourselves," said Tristram.

"We dare not," they replied.

Then Tristram ran up and seized the sword of the knight, which had fallen to the ground, and with one broad sweep struck off the head of Tauleas clean from the shoulders. This done he dropped the sword as if he had done but a trifle and went back to the herdsmen.

Shortly after this, Sir Dinant appeared at Tintagil, bearing with him the giant's head, and there told what had happened to him and how he had been rescued.

"Where had you this adventure?" asked the king.

"At the herdsmen's fountain in the forest," said Dinant. "There where so many knights-errant meet. They say this madman haunts that spot."

"He cannot be Matto le Breune, as I fancied," said the king. "It was a man of no small might who made that stroke. I shall seek this wild man myself."

On the next day King Mark, with a following of knights and hunters, rode into the forest, where they continued their course till they came to the well. Lying beside it they saw a gaunt, naked man, with a sword beside him. Who he was they knew not, for madness and exposure had so changed Tristram's face that no one knew it.

By the king's command he was picked up slumbering and covered with mantles, and thus borne in a litter to Tintagil. Here they bathed and washed him, and gave him warm food and gentle care, till his madness passed away and his wits came back to him. But no one knew him, so much had he changed, while all deemed Tristram dead, and had no thought of him.

Word of what had happened came to Isolde where she lay sick, and with a sudden whim she rose from her bed and bade Bragwaine come with her, as she had a fancy to see the forest madman.

Asking where he was, she was told that he was in the garden, resting in an arbor, in a light slumber. Hither they sought him and looked down upon him, knowing him not.

But as they stood there Tristram woke, and when he saw the queen he turned away his head, while tears ran from his eyes. It happened that the queen had with her a little brachet, which Tristram had given her when she first came to Cornwall, and which always remembered and loved its old master.

When this little creature came near the sick man, she leaped upon him and licked his cheeks and hands, and whined about him, showing great joy and excitement.

"The dog is wiser than us all," cried Dame Bragwaine. "She knows her master. They spoke falsely who said he was dead. It is Sir Tristram."

But Isolde fell to the ground in a swoon, and lay there long insensible. When at length she recovered, she said:

"My dear lord and knight, I thank God deeply that you still live, for the story of your death had nearly caused mine. Your life is in dread danger, for when King Mark knows you he will either banish or destroy you. Therefore I beg you to fly from this court and seek that of King Arthur where you are beloved. This you may trust, that at all times, early and late, my love for you will keep fresh in my heart."

"I pray you leave me, Isolde," answered the knight. "It is not well that you should be seen here. Fear not that I will forget what you have said."

Then the queen departed, but do what she would the brachet would not follow her, but kept with the sick knight. Soon afterwards King Mark visited him, and to his surprise the brachet sat upon the prostrate man and bayed at the king.

"What does this mean?" he asked.

"I can tell you," answered a knight. "That dog was Sir Tristram's before it was the queen's. The brachet is wiser than us all. It knows its master."

"That I cannot believe," said the king. "Tell me your name, my good man."

"My name is Tristram of Lyonesse," answered the knight. "I am in your power. Do with me what you will."

The king looked at him long and strangely, with anger in his eyes.

"Truly," he said, "you had better have died while you were about it. It would have saved me the need of dealing with you as you deserve."

Then he returned to the castle, and called his barons hastily to council, sternly demanding that the penalty of death should be adjudged against the knight. Happily for Tristram, the barons would not consent to this, and proposed instead that the accused knight should be banished.

So in the end the sentence was passed that Tristram should be banished for ten years from the country of Cornwall, not to return under pain of death. To this the knight assented, taking an oath before the king and his barons that he would abide by the decision of the court.

Many barons accompanied him to the ship in which he was to set sail. And as he was going, there arrived at Tintagil a knight of King Arthur's court named Dinadan, who had been sent to seek Sir Tristram and request him to come to Camelot.

On being shown the banished knight, he went to him and told his errand.

"You come in good season," said Tristram, "for to Camelot am I now bound."

"Then I would go with you in fellowship."

"You are right welcome, Sir Dinadan." Then Tristram turned to the others and said:

"Greet King Mark from me, and all my enemies as well, and tell them that I shall come again in my own good time. I am well rewarded for all I have done for him, but revenge has a long life, as he may yet learn."

Then he took ship and put to sea, a banished man. And with him went Dinadan to cheer him in his woe, for, of all the knights of the Round Table, Dinadan was the merriest soul.

Book VII
How Tristram Came to Camelot

Chapter I
Tristram and Dinadan

AND NOW IT BEHOOVES us to follow the banished knight in his adventures, for they were many and various, and arduous were the labors with which he won his right to a seat at the Round Table. We have told the tale of his love and madness, and now must relate the marvellous exploits of his banishment.

Hardly, indeed, had Tristram and Dinadan landed in Arthur's realms when they met two knights of his court, Hector de Maris and Bors de Ganis. This encounter took place upon a bridge, where Hector and Dinadan jousted, and Dinadan and his horse were overthrown. But Bors refused to fight with Tristram, through the contempt he felt for Cornish knights. Yet the honor of Cornwall was soon retrieved, for Sir Bleoberis and Sir Driant now came up, and Bleoberis proffered to joust with Tristram, who quickly smote him to the earth.

This done, Tristram and Dinadan departed, leaving their opponents in surprise that such valor and might could come out of Cornwall. But not far had the two knights-errant gone when they entered a forest, where they met a damsel, who was in search of some noble knights to rescue Sir Lancelot. Morgan le Fay, who hated him bitterly since his escape from her castle, had laid an ambush of thirty knights at a point which Lancelot was approaching, thinking to attack him unawares and so slay him.

The damsel, who had learned of this plot, had already met the four knights whom Tristram and Dinadan had encountered, and obtained their promise to come to the rescue.

She now told her story of crime and treachery to the two wanderers, with the same request.

"Fair damsel," said Tristram, "you could set me no more welcome task. Guide me to the place where those dastards lie in ambush for Lancelot."

"What would you do?" cried Dinadan. "We cannot match thirty knights. Two or three are enough for any one knight, if they be men. I hope you don't fancy that I will take fifteen to my share!"

"Come, come, good comrade," said Tristram. "Do not show the white feather."

"I would rather wear the white feather than the fool's cap," said Dinadan. "Lend me your shield if you will; for I had sooner carry a Cornish shield, which all men say only cowards bear, than try any such foolhardy adventure."

"Nay; I will keep my shield for the sake of her who gave it to me," answered Tristram. "But this I warn you, if you will not abide with me I shall slay you before we part, for a coward has no right to cumber the earth. I ask no more of you than to fight one knight. If your heart is too faint for that, then stand by and see me meet the whole crew."

"Very well," said Dinadan, "you can trust me to look on bravely, and mayhap to do something to save my head from hard knocks; but I would give my helmet if I had not met you. Folks say you are cured of your mad fit, but I vow if I have much faith in your sound sense."

Tristram smiled grimly at Dinadan's scolding, and kept on after the damsel. Not far had they gone before they met the thirty knights. These had already passed the four knights of Arthur's court, without a combat, and they now rode in the same way past Tristram and Dinadan, with no show of hostility.

But Tristram was of different mettle. Turning towards them he cried with a voice of thunder: "Lo! sir villains. I have heard of your plot to murder Lancelot. Turn and defend yourselves. Here is a knight ready to fight you all for the love of Lancelot du Lac!"

Then, spurring his good war-steed, he rode upon them with the fury of a lion, slaying two with his spear. He then drew his mighty blade, and attacked them with such fierce spirit and giant strength that ten more soon fell dead beneath his furious blows. Nor did Dinadan stand and look on, as he had grumblingly threatened, but rode in and aided Tristram nobly, more than one of the villains falling before his blows. When, at length, the murderous crew took to flight, there were but ten of them alive.

Sir Bors and his companions had seen this battle at a distance, but it was all over before they could reach the scene of fray. High was their praise of the valor and prowess of the victor, who, they said, had done such a deed as they had deemed only Lancelot could perform.

They invited him with knightly warmth and courtesy to go with them to their lodging.

"Many thanks, fair sirs," said Tristram, "but I cannot go with you."

"Then tell us your name, that we may remember it as that of one of the best of knights, and give you the honor which is your due."

"Nor that either," answered Tristram. "In good time you shall know my name, but not now."

Leaving them with the dead knights, Tristram and Dinadan rode forward, and in time found themselves near a party of shepherds and herdsmen, whom they asked if any lodging was to be had nearby.

"That there is," said the herdsmen, "and good lodging, in a castle close at hand. But it is not to be had for the asking. The custom of that castle is that no knight shall lodge there except he fight with two knights of the castle. But as you are two, you can fight your battle man for man, if you seek lodging there."

"That is rough pay for a night's rest," said Dinadan. "Lodge where you will, I will not rest in that castle. I have done enough today to spoil my appetite for fighting."

"Come, come," said Tristram, "and you a Knight of the Round Table! You cannot refuse to win your lodging in knightly fashion."

"Win it you must if you want it," said the herdsmen; "for if you have the worse of the battle no lodging will you gain in these quarters, except it be in the wild wood."

"Be it so, if it must," said Dinadan. "In flat English, I will not go to the castle."

"Are you a man?" demanded Tristram, scornfully. "Come, Dinadan, I know you are no coward. On your knighthood, come."

Growling in his throat, Dinadan followed his comrade, sorely against his will, and together they rode into the castle court. Here they found, as they had been told, two armed knights ready to meet them.

To make a long story short, Tristram and Dinadan smote them both down, and afterwards entered the castle, where the best of good cheer was served them. But when they had disarmed, and were having a merry time at the well-filled table, word was brought them that two other knights, Palamides and Gaheris, had entered the gates, and demanded a joust according to the castle custom.

"The foul fiend take them!" cried Dinadan. "Fight I will not; I am here for rest."

"We are now the lords of the castle, and must defend its custom," said Tristram. "Make ready, therefore, for fight you must."

"Why, in the devil's name, came I here in your company?" cried Dinadan. "You will wear all the flesh off my bones."

But there was nothing to do but arm themselves and meet the two knights in the courtyard. Of these Gaheris encountered Tristram, and got a fall for his pains; but Palamides hurled Dinadan from his horse. So far, then, it was fall for fall, and the contest could be decided only by a fight on foot. But Dinadan was bruised from his fall and refused to fight. Tristram unlaced his helmet to give him air, and prayed him for his aid.

"Fight them yourself, if you will; two such knights are but a morsel to you," said Dinadan. "As for me, I am sore wounded from our little skirmish with the thirty knights, and have no valor left in me. Sir Tristram, you are a madman yet, and I curse the time that ever I saw you. In all the world there are no two such mad freaks as Lancelot and you. Once I fell into fellowship with Lancelot as I have now with you, and what followed? Why, he set me a task that kept me a quarter of a year in bed. Defend me from such head-splitters, and save me from your fellowship."

"Then if you will not fight I must face them both," said Tristram. "Come forth, both of you, I am ready for you."

At this challenge Palamides and Gaheris advanced and struck at the two knights. But after a stroke or two at Gaheris, Dinadan withdrew from the fray.

"This is not fair, two to one," said Palamides. "Stand aside, Gaheris, with that knight who declines to fight, and let us two finish the combat."

Then he and Tristram fought long and fiercely, Tristram in the end driving him back three paces. At this Gaheris and Dinadan pushed between them and bade them cease fighting, as both had done enough for honor.

"So be it," said Tristram, "and these brave knights are welcome to lodge with us in the castle if they will."

"With you, not with us," said Dinadan, dryly. "When I lodge in that devil's den may I sell my sword for a herring. We will be called up every hour of the night to fight for our bedding. And as for you, good friend, when I ride with you again, it will be when you have grown older and wiser, or I younger and more foolish."

With these words he mounted his horse and rode in an ill-humor out of the castle gates.

"Come, good sirs, we must after him," said Tristram, with a laugh. "He is a prime good fellow, if he has taken himself off in a pet; it is likely I gave him an overdose of fighting."

So, asking a man of the castle to guide them to a lodging, they rode after Dinadan, whom they soon overtook, though he gave them no hearty welcome. Two miles farther brought them to a priory, where they spent the night in comfort.

Early the next day Tristram mounted and rode away, leaving Dinadan at the priory, for he was too much bruised to mount his horse. There remained at the priory with him a knight named Pellinore, who sought earnestly to learn Tristram's name, and at last said angrily to Dinadan,—

"Since you will not tell me his name, I will ride after him and make him tell it himself, or leave him on the ground to repent."

"Beware, my good sir," said Dinadan, "or the repentance will be yours instead of his. No wise man is he who thrusts his own hand in the fire."

"Good faith, I fear him not," said Pellinore, haughtily, and rode on his way.

But he paid dearly for his hardiness, for a half-hour afterwards he lay on the earth with a spear wound in his shoulder, while Tristram rode unscathed on his way.

On the day following Tristram met with pursuivants, who were spreading far and wide the news of a great tournament that was to be held between King Carados and the king of North Wales, at the Castle of Maidens. They were seeking for good knights to take part in that tournament, and in particular King Carados had bidden them to seek Lancelot, and the king of Northgalis to seek Tristram de Lyonesse.

"Lancelot is not far away," said Tristram. "As for me, I will be there, and do my best to win honor in the fray."

And so he rode away, and soon after met with Sir Kay and Sir Sagramore, with whom he refused to joust, as he wished to keep himself fresh for the tournament.

But as Kay twitted him with being a cowardly knight of Cornwall, he turned on him and smote him from his horse. Then, to complete the tale, he served Sagramore with the same sauce, and serenely rode on his way, leaving them to heal their bruises with repentance.

Chapter II
On the Road to the Tournament

TRISTRAM NOW RODE far alone through a country strange to him, and void of knightly adventures. At length, however, chance brought to him a damsel, who told him disconsolately that she sought a champion to cope with a villanous knight, who was playing the tyrant over a wide district, and who defied all errant knights.

"If you would win great honor come with me," she said.

"To win honor is the breath of my life," said Tristram. "Lead on, fair maiden."

Then he rode with her a matter of six miles, when good fortune brought them in contact with Sir Gawaine, who recognized the damsel as one of Morgan le Fay's. On seeing her with an unknown knight he at once surmised that there was some mischief afoot.

"Fair sir," said Gawaine, "whither ride you with that damsel?"

"Whither she may lead me," said Tristram. "That is all I know of the matter."

"Then, by my good blade, you shall ride no farther with her, for she has a breeder of ill for mistress, and means you a mischief."

He drew his sword as he spoke, and said in stern accents to the damsel:

"Tell me wherefore and whither you lead this knight, or you shall die on the spot. I know you, minx, and the false-hearted witch who sends you."

"Mercy, Sir Gawaine!" she cried, trembling in mortal fear. "Harm me not, and I will tell you all I know."

"Say on, then. I crave not your worthless life, but will have it if you tell me not the truth."

"Good and valiant sir," she answered, "Queen Morgan le Fay, my lady, has sent me and thirty ladies more, in search of Sir Lancelot or Sir Tristram. Whoever of us shall first meet either of these knights is to lead him to her castle, with a tale of worshipful deeds to be done and wrongs to be righted. But thirty knights lie in wait in a tower ready to sally forth and destroy them."

"Foul shame is this," cried Gawaine, "that such treachery should ever be devised by a queen's daughter and the sister of the worshipful King Arthur. Sir knight, will you stand with me, and unmask the malice of these thirty ambushed rogues?"

"That shall I willingly," said Tristram. "Trust me to do my share to punish these dogs. Not long since I and a fellow met with thirty of that lady's knights, who were in ambush for Lancelot, and we gave them something else to think of. If there be another thirty on the same vile quest, I am for them."

Then they rode together towards the queen's castle, Gawaine with a shrewd fancy that he knew his Cornish companion, for he had heard the story of how two knights had beaten thirty. When they reached the castle, Gawaine called in a loud voice:

"Queen Morgan le Fay, send out the knights whom you hold in ambush against Lancelot and Tristram. I know your treason, and will tell of it wherever I ride. I, Sir Gawaine, and my fellow here, dare your thirty knights to come out and meet us like men."

"You bluster bravely, friend Gawaine," answered the knights. "But we well know that your pride and valor come from the knight who is there with you. Some of us have tried conclusions with that head-splitter who wears the arms of Cornwall, and have had enough of him. You alone would not keep us long in the castle, but we have no fancy to measure swords with him. So ride your way; you will get no glory here."

In vain did Gawaine berate them as dastards and villains; say what he would, not a soul of them would set foot beyond the walls, and in time the two knights rode away in a rage, cursing all cowards in their beards.

For several days they rode together without adventure. Then they beheld a shameful sight, that roused their souls to anger. For they saw a villanous knight, known in those parts as Breuse Sans Pitié, who chased a lady with intent to kill her, having slain her lover before. Many dastardly deeds of this kind had he done, yet so far had escaped all retribution for his crimes.

"Let me ride alone against him," said Gawaine. "I know his tricks. He will stand to face one man, but if he sees us both, he will fly, and he always rides so swift a horse that none can overtake him."

Then he rode at full speed between the lady and her pursuer, and cried loudly:

"False knight and murderer, leave that lady and try your tricks on me."

Sir Breuse, seeing but one, put his spear in rest and rode furiously against Gawaine, whom he struck so strong a blow that he flung him prostrate to the ground. Then, with deadly intent, he forced his horse to trample over him twenty times backward and forward, thinking to destroy him. But when Tristram saw this villany he broke from his covert and rushed in fury upon the murderous wretch.

But Breuse Sans Pitié had met with Tristram before, and knew him by his arms. Therefore he turned his horse and fled at full speed, hotly pursued by the furious knight. Long he chased him, full of thirst for revenge, but the well-horsed villain rode at such a pace that he left him in the distance. At length Tristram, despairing of overtaking him, and seeing an inviting forest spring, drew up his horse and rode thither for rest and refreshment.

Dismounting and tying his horse to a tree, he washed his face and hands and took a deep and grateful draught of the cool water. Then laying himself to rest by the spring side, he fell sound asleep.

While he lay there good fortune brought to that forest spring a lady who had sought him far and wide. This was Dame Bragwaine, the lady companion of La Belle Isolde, who bore him letters from the queen. She failed to recognize the sleeping knight, but at first sight knew his noble charger, Passe Brewel, which Tristram had ridden for years. So she seated herself gladly by the knight, and waited patiently till he awoke. Then she saluted him, and he her, for he failed not to recognize his old acquaintance.

"What of my dear lady, La Belle Isolde?" he asked, eagerly.

"She is well, and has sent me to seek you. Far and wide have I sought for you through the land, and glad enough am I to hand you the letters I bear."

"Not so glad as I am to receive them," said Tristram, joyfully, taking them from her hand and opening them with eager haste, while his soul overflowed with joy as he read Isolde's words of love and constancy, though with them was mingled many a piteous complaint.

"Come with me, Dame Bragwaine," he said. "I am riding to the tournament to be held at the Castle of Maidens. There will I answer these letters, and to have you there, to tell the tale of my doings to my Lady Isolde, will give me double strength and valor."

To this Dame Bragwaine willingly agreed, and mounting they rode till they came to the castle of a hospitable old knight, near where the tournament was to be held. Here they were given shelter and entertainment.

As they sat at supper with Sir Pellounes, their ancient host, he told them much of the great tournament that was at hand, among other things that Lancelot would be there, with thirty-two knights of his kindred, each of whom would bear a shield with the arms of Cornwall.

In the midst of their conversation a messenger entered, who told Pellounes that his son, Persides de Bloise, had come home, whereupon the old knight held up his hands and thanked God, telling Tristram that he had not seen his son for two years.

"I know him," said Tristram, "and a good and worthy knight he is."

On the next morning, when Tristram came into the castle hall clad in his house attire, he met with Persides, similarly unarmed, and they saluted each other courteously.

"My father tells me that you are of Cornwall," said Persides. "I jousted there once before King Mark, and fortune helped me to overthrow ten knights. But Tristram de Lyonesse overthrew me and took my lady from me. This I have not forgotten, and I will repay him for it yet."

"You hate Sir Tristram, then? Do you think that will trouble him much, and that he is not able to withstand your malice?"

"He is a better knight than I, that I admit. But for all that I owe him no good will."

As thus they stood talking at a bay window of the castle, they saw many knights ride by on their way to the tournament. Among these Tristram marked a strongly-built warrior mounted on a great black horse, and bearing a black shield.

"What knight is that?" he asked. "He looks like a strong and able one."

"He is one of the best in the world," said Persides. "I know him well."

"Is it Sir Lancelot?"

"No, no. It is Palamides, an unchristened Saracen, but a noble man."

"Palamides! I should know him too, but his arms deceived me."

As they continued to look they saw many of the country people salute the black knight. Some time afterwards a squire came to Pellounes, the lord of the castle, and told him that a fierce combat had taken place in the road some distance in advance, and that a knight with a black shield had smitten down thirteen others. He was still there, ready for any who might wish to meet him, and holding a tournament of his own in the highway.

"On my faith, that is Palamides!" said Tristram. "The worthy fellow must be brimful of fight. Fair brother, let us cast on our cloaks and see the play."

"Not I," said Persides. "Let us not go like courtiers there, but like men ready to withstand their enemies."

"As you will. To fight or to look on is all one to me."

Then they armed and rode to the spot where so many knights had tried their fortune before the tournament. When Palamides saw them approach, he said to his squire:

"Go to yonder knight with a green shield and in it a lion of gold. Tell him that I request a passage-at-arms with him, and that my name is Palamides."

Persides, who wore the shield thus described, did not hesitate to accept the challenge, and rode against Palamides, but quickly found himself felled to the earth by his powerful antagonist. Then Tristram made ready to avenge his comrade, but before he could put his spear in rest Palamides rode upon him like a thunderbolt, taking him at advantage, and hurling him over his horse's tail.

At this Tristram sprang up in furious anger and sore shame, and leaped into his saddle.

Then he sent Gouvernail to Palamides, accusing him of treachery, and demanding a joust on equal terms.

"Not so," answered Palamides. "I know that knight better than he fancies, and will not meet him now. But if he wants satisfaction he may have it tomorrow at the Castle of Maidens, where I will be ready to meet him in the lists."

As Tristram stood fretting and fuming in wrathful spite, Dinadan, who had seen the affair, came up, and seeing the anger of the Cornish knight, restrained his inclination to jest.

"Here it is proved," he said, "that a man can never be so strong but he may meet his equal. Never was man so wise but that his brain might fail him, and a passing good rider is he that never had a fall."

"Let be," cried Tristram, angrily. "You are readier with your tongue than with your sword, friend Dinadan. I will revenge myself, and you shall see it."

As they stood thus talking there came by them a likely knight, who rode soberly and heavily, bearing a black shield.

"What knight is that?" asked Tristram.

"It is Sir Briant of North Wales," answered Persides. "I know him well."

Just behind him came a knight who bore a shield with the arms of Cornwall, and as he rode up he sent a squire to Sir Briant, whom he required to joust with him.

"Let it be so, if he will have it so," said Briant. "Bid him make ready."

Then they rode together, and the Welsh knight got a severe fall.

"What Cornish knight is this?" asked Tristram.

"None, as I fancy," said Dinadan. "I warrant he is of King Ban's blood, which counts the noblest knights of the world."

Then two other knights came up and challenged him with the Cornish shield, and in a trice he smote them both down with one spear.

"By my faith," said Tristram, "he is a good knight, whoever he be, and I never saw one yet that rode so well."

Then the king of Northgalis rode to Palamides, and prayed him for his sake to joust with that knight who had just overturned two Welsh knights.

"I beg you ask me not," said Palamides. "I have had my full share of jousting already, and wish to keep fresh for the tournament tomorrow."

"One ride only, for the honor of North Wales," beseeched the king.

"Well, if you will have it so; but I have seen many a man have a fall at his own request."

Then he sent a squire to the victor knight, and challenged him to a joust.

"Fair fellow," said the knight, "tell me your lord's name."

"It is Sir Palamides."

"He is well met, then. I have seen no knight in seven years with whom I would rather tilt."

Then the two knights took spears from their squires, and rode apart.

"Now," said Dinadan, "you will see Palamides come off the victor."

"I doubt it," answered Tristram. "I wager the knight with the Cornish shield will give him a fall."

"That I do not believe," said Dinadan.

As they spoke, the two knights put spears in rest, and spurred their horses, riding hotly together. Palamides broke a spear on his antagonist, without moving him in his saddle; but on his side he received such a blow that it broke through his shield and hauberk, and would have slain him outright had he not fallen.

"How now?" cried Tristram. "Am I not right? I knew by the way those knights ride which would fall."

The unknown knight now rode away and sought a well in the forest edge, for he was hot and thirsty with the fray. This was seen by the king of Northgalis, who sent twelve knights after him to do him a mischief, so that he would not be able to appear at the tournament and win the victory.

They came upon him so suddenly that he had scarcely time to put on his helm and spring to his horse's back before they assailed him in mass.

"Ye villains!" he cried, "twelve to one! And taking a man unawares! You want a lesson, and by my faith you shall have it."

Then spurring his horse he rode on them so fiercely that he smote one knight through the body, breaking his spear in doing so. Now he drew his sword and smote stoutly to right and left, killing three others and wounding more.

"Dogs and dastards! know you me not?" he cried in a voice of thunder. "My name is Lancelot du Lac. Here's for you, cowards and traitors!"

But the name he had shouted was enough. Those who were still able, fled, followed by the angry knight. By hard riding they escaped his wrath, and he, hot and furious, turned aside to a lodging where he designed to spend the night. In consequence of his hard labor in this encounter Lancelot fought not on the first day of the tournament, but sat beside King Arthur, who had come hither from Camelot to witness the passage-at-arms.

Chapter III
At the Castle of Maidens

WHEN CAME THE DAWN of the first day of the tournament, many ladies and gentlemen of the court took their seats on a high gallery, shaded by a rich canopy of parti-colored

silk, while in the centre of the gallery sat King Arthur and Queen Guenever, and, by the side of the king, Lancelot du Lac. Many other noble lords and ladies of the surrounding country occupied the adjoining seats, while round the circle that closed in the lists sat hosts of citizens and country people, all eager for the warlike sports.

Knights in glittering armor stood in warlike groups outside the entrance gates, where rose many pavilions of red and white silk, each with its fluttering pennon, and great war-horses that impatiently champed the bit, while the bright steel heads of the lances shone like star-points in the sun.

Within the lists the heralds and pursuivants busied themselves, while cheery calls, and bugle-blasts, and the lively chat of the assembled multitude filled the air with joyous sound.

Tristram de Lyonesse still dwelt with the old knight Sir Pellounes, in company with Sir Persides, whom he yet kept in ignorance of his name. And as it was his purpose to fight that day unknown, he ordered Gouvernail, his squire, to procure him a black-faced shield, without emblem or device of any kind.

So accoutred, he and Persides mounted in the early morn and rode together to the lists, where the parties of King Carados and the king of Northgalis were already being formed. Tristram and his companion joined the side of Carados, the Scottish king, and hardly had they ridden to their place when King Arthur gave the signal for the onset, the bugles loudly sounded, and the two long lines of knights rode together with a crash as of two thunder clouds meeting in mid-air.

Many knights and horses went to the earth in that mad onset, and many others who had broken their spears drew their swords and so kept up the fray. The part of the line where Tristram and Persides was drove back the king of Northgalis and his men, with many noble knights who fought on the side of the Welsh king. But through the rush and roar of the onset there pushed forward Bleoberis de Ganis and Gaheris, who hurled Persides to the earth, where he was almost slain, for as he lay there helpless more than forty horsemen rode over him in the fray.

Seeing this, and what valiant deeds the two knights did, Tristram marvelled who they were. But perceiving the danger in which his comrade Persides lay, he rushed to the rescue with such force that Gaheris was hurled headlong from his horse. Then Bleoberis in a rage put his spear in rest and rode furiously against Tristram, but he was met in mid-career, and flung from his saddle by the resistless spear of the Cornish knight.

The king with the hundred knights now rode angrily forward, pressed back the struggling line, and horsed Gaheris and Bleoberis. Then began a fierce struggle, in which Bleoberis and Tristram did many deeds of knightly skill and valor.

As the violent combat continued, Dinadan, who was on the other side, rode against Tristram, not knowing him, and got such a buffet that he swooned in his saddle. He recovered in a minute, however, and, riding to his late companion, said in a low voice:

"Sir knight, is this the way you serve an old comrade, masking under a black shield? I know you now better than you deem. I will not reveal your disguise, but by my troth I vow I will never try buffets with you again, and, if I keep my wits, sword of yours shall never come near my headpiece."

As Dinadan withdrew to repair damages, Bleoberis rode against Tristram, who gave him such a furious sword-blow on the helm that he bowed his head to the saddle. Then Tristram caught him by the helm, jerked him from his horse, and flung him down under the feet of the steed.

This ended the fray, for at that moment Arthur bade the heralds to blow to lodging, and the knights who still held saddle sheathed their swords. Tristram thereupon departed to his pavilion and Dinadan with him.

But Arthur, and many of those with him, wondered who was the knight with the black shield, who had with sword and spear done such wondrous deeds. Many opinions were given, and some suspected him of being Tristram, but held their peace. To him the judges awarded the prize of the day's combat, though they named him only the knight of the black shield, not knowing by what other name to call him.

When the second day of the tournament dawned, and the knights prepared for the combat, Palamides, who had fought under Northgalis, now joined King Arthur's party, that led by Carados, and sent to Tristram to know his name.

"As to that," answered Tristram, "tell Sir Palamides that he shall not know till I have broken two spears with him. But you may tell him that I am the same knight that he smote down unfairly the day before the tournament, and that I owe him as shrewd a turn. So whichever side he takes I will take the opposite."

"Sir," said the messenger, "he will be on King Arthur's side, in company with the noblest knights."

"Then I will fight for Northgalis, though yesterday I held with Carados."

When King Arthur blew to field and the fray began, King Carados opened the day by a joust with the king with the hundred knights, who gave him a sore fall. Around him there grew up a fierce combat, till a troop of Arthur's knights pushed briskly in and bore back the opposite party, rescuing Carados from under the horses' feet. While the fight went on thus in one part of the field, Tristram, in jet-black armor, pressed resistlessly forward in another part, and dealt so roughly and grimly with Arthur's knights that not a man of them could withstand him.

At length he fell among the fellowship of King Ban, all of whom bore Cornish shields, and here he smote right and left with such fury and might that cries of admiration for his gallant bearing went up from lords and ladies, citizens and churls. But he would have had the worse through force of numbers had not the king with the hundred knights come to his rescue, and borne him away from the press of his assailants, who were crowding upon him in irresistible strength.

Hardly had Tristram escaped from this peril than he saw another group of about forty knights, with Kay the seneschal at their head. On them he rode like a fury, smote Kay from his horse, and fared among them all like a greyhound among conies.

At this juncture Lancelot, who had hitherto taken little part, met a knight retiring from the lists with a sore wound in the head.

"Who hurt you so badly?" he asked.

"That knight with the black shield, who is making havoc wherever he goes," was the answer. "I may curse the time I ever faced him, for he is more devil than mortal man."

Lancelot at these words drew his sword and advanced to meet Tristram, and as he rode forward saw the Cornish champion hurtling through a press of foes, bringing down one with nearly every stroke of his sword.

"A fellow of marvellous prowess he, whoever he be," said Lancelot. "If I set upon this knight after all his heavy labor, I will shame myself more than him." And he put up his sword.

Then the king with the hundred knights, with his following, and a hundred more of the Welsh party, set upon the twenty of Lancelot's kin, and a fearful fray began, for the twenty held together like wild boars, none failing the others, and faced the odds against them without yielding a step.

When Tristram, who had for the moment withdrawn, beheld their noble bearing, he marvelled at their valor, for he saw by their steadfastness that they would die together rather than leave the field.

"Valiant and noble must be he who has such knights for his kin," he said, meaning Lancelot; "and likely to be a worthy man is he who leads such knights as these."

Then he rode to the king with the hundred knights and said:

"Sir, leave off fighting with these twenty knights. You can win no honor from them, you being so many and they so few. I can see by their bearing that they will die rather than leave the field, and that will bring you no glory. If this one sided fray goes on I will join them and give them what help I can."

"You shall not do so," said the king. "You speak in knightly courtesy, and I will withdraw my men at your request. I know how courage favors courage, and like draws to like."

Then the king called off his knights, and withdrew from the combat with Lancelot's kindred.

Meanwhile Lancelot was watching for an opportunity to meet Tristram and hail him as a fellow in heart and hand, but before he could do so Tristram, Dinadan and Gouvernail suddenly left the lists and rode into the forest, no man perceiving whither they had gone.

Then Arthur blew to lodging, and gave the prize of the day to the king of Northgalis, as the true champion of the tournament was on his side and had vanished. Lancelot rode hither and thither, vainly seeking him, while a cry that might have been heard two miles off went up: "The knight with the black shield has won the day!"

"Alas, where has that knight gone!" said Arthur. "It is a shame that those in the field have let him thus vanish. With gentleness and courtesy they might have brought him to me at the Castle of Maidens, where I should have been glad to show him the highest honor."

Then he went to the knights of his party and comforted them for their discomfiture.

"Be not dismayed, my fair fellows," he said, "though you have lost the field, and many of you are the worst in body and mind. Be of good cheer, for tomorrow we fight again. How the day will go I cannot say, but I will be in the lists with you, and lend you what aid is in my arm."

During that day's fight Dame Bragwaine had sat near Queen Guenever, observing Tristram's valorous deeds. But when the queen asked her why she had come thither, she would not tell the real reason, but said only:

"Madam, I came for no other cause than that my lady, La Belle Isolde, sent me to inquire after your welfare."

After the fray was done she took leave of the queen and rode into the forest in search of Sir Tristram. As she went onward she heard a great cry, and sent her squire to learn what it might mean. He quickly came to a forest fountain, and here he found a knight bound to a tree, crying out like a madman, while his horse and harness stood by. When he saw the squire, he started so furiously that he broke his bonds, and then ran after him, sword in hand, as if to slay him. The squire at this spurred his horse and rode swiftly back to Dame Bragwaine, whom he told of his adventure.

Soon afterwards she found Tristram, who had set up his pavilion in the forest, and told him of the incident.

"Then, on my head, there is mischief here afloat," said Tristram; "some good knight has gone distracted."

Taking his horse and sword he rode to the place, and there he found the knight complaining woefully.

"What misfortune has befallen me?" he lamented; "I, woeful Palamides, who am defiled with falsehood and treason through Sir Bors and Sir Hector! Alas, why live I so long?"

Then he took his sword in his hands, and with many strange signs and movements flung it into the fountain. This done, he wailed bitterly and wrung his hands, but at the end he ran to his middle in the water and sought again for his sword. Tristram, seeing this, ran upon him and clasped him in his arms, fearing he would kill himself.

"Who are you that holds me so tightly?" said Palamides.

"I am a man of this forest, and mean you no harm, but would save you from injury."

"Alas!" said the knight, "I shall never win honor where Sir Tristram is. Where he is not, only Lancelot or Lamorak can win from me the prize. More than once he has put me to the worse."

"What would you do if you had him?"

"I would fight him and ease my heart. And yet, sooth to say, he is a gentle and noble knight."

"Will you go with me to my lodging?"

"No; I will go to the king with the hundred knights. He rescued me from Bors and Hector, or they had slain me treacherously."

But by kind words Tristram got him to his pavilion, where he did what he could to cheer him. But Palamides could not sleep for anguish of soul, and rose before dawn and secretly left the tent, making his way to the pavilions of Gaheris and Sagramour le Desirous, who had been his companions in the tournament.

Not far had the next day's sun risen in the eastern sky, when King Arthur bade the heralds blow the call to the lists, and with warlike haste the knights came crowding in to the last day of the well-fought tournament.

Fiercely began the fray, King Carados and his ally, the king of Ireland, being smitten from their horses early in the day. Then came in Palamides full of fury, and made sad work among his foes, being known to all by his indented shield.

But this day King Arthur, as he had promised, rode in shining armor into the field, and fought so valorously that the king of Northgalis and his party had much the worse of the combat.

While the fight thus went on in all its fury, Tristram rode in, still bearing his black shield. Encountering Palamides, he gave him such a thrust that he was driven over his horse's croup. Then King Arthur cried:

"Knight with the black shield, make ready for me!"

But the king met with the same fate from Tristram's spear that Palamides had done, and was hurled to the earth. Seeing this, a rush of the knights of his party drove back the foe, and Arthur and Palamides were helped to their saddles again.

And now the king, his heart burning with warlike fury, rushed fiercely on Tristram, and struck him so furious a blow that he was hurled from his horse. As he lay there Palamides spurred upon him in a violent rage, and sought to override him as he was rising to his feet. But Tristram saw his purpose and sprang aside. As Palamides rode past he wrathfully caught him by the arm and pulled him from his horse.

"Sword to sword let it be!" cried Tristram.

Palamides, nothing loath, drew his weapon, and so fierce a combat began in the midst of the arena that lords and ladies alike stood in their seats in eagerness to behold it. But at the last Tristram struck Palamides three mighty strokes on the helm, crying with each stroke, "Take this for Sir Tristram's sake!"

So fierce were the blows that Palamides was felled to the earth. Then the king with the hundred knights dashed forward and brought Tristram his horse. Palamides was horsed at the same time, and with burning ire he rushed upon Tristram, spear in rest, before he could make ready to meet him. But Tristram lightly avoided the spear, and, enraged at his repeated treachery, he caught him with both hands by the neck as his horse bore him past, tore him clean from the saddle, and carried him thus ten spears' length across the field before he let him fall.

At that moment King Arthur spurred upon the Cornish champion, sword in hand, and Tristram fixed his spear to meet him, but with a sword-blow Arthur cut the spear in two, and then dealt him three or four vigorous strokes before he could draw. But at the last Tristram drew his sword and assailed the king with equal energy.

This battle continued not long, for the press of battling knights forced the combatants asunder. Then Tristram rode hither and thither, striking and parrying, so that that day he smote down in all eleven of the good knights of King Ban's blood, while all in seats and gallery shouted in loud acclaim for the mighty warrior with the black shield.

This cry met the ears of Lancelot, who was engaged in another part of the field. Then he got a spear and came towards the cry. Seeing Tristram standing without an antagonist, he cried out:

"Knight with the black shield, well and worthily have you done; now make ready to joust with me."

When Tristram heard this he put his spear in rest, and both with lowered heads rode together with lightning speed. Tristram's spear broke into fragments on Lancelot's shield; but Lancelot, by ill-fortune, smote him in the side, wounding him deeply. He kept his saddle, however, and, drawing his sword, rushed upon Lancelot and gave him three such strokes that fire flew from his helm, and he was forced to lower his head towards his saddle-bow. This done, Tristram left the field, for he felt as if he would die. But Dinadan espied him and followed him into the forest.

After Tristram left the lists, Lancelot fought like a man beside himself, many a noble knight going down before his spear and sword. King Arthur, seeing against what odds he fought, came quickly to his aid, with the knights of his own kindred, and in the end they won the day against the king of Northgalis and his followers. So the prize was adjudged to Lancelot.

But neither for king, queen nor knights would he accept it, and when the cry was raised by the heralds:

"Sir Lancelot, Sir Lancelot has won the field this day!" he bade them change, and cry instead:

"The knight with the black shield has won the day."

But the estates and the commonalty cried out together:

"Sir Lancelot has won the field, whoever say nay!"

This filled Lancelot with shame and anger, and he rode with a lowering brow to King Arthur, to whom he cried:

"The knight with the black shield is the hero of the lists. For three days he held against all, till he got that unlucky wound. The prize, I say, is his."

"Sir Tristram it is," said the king. "I heard him shout his name three times when he gave those mighty strokes to Palamides. Never better nor nobler knight took spear or sword in hand. He was hurt indeed; but when two noble warriors encounter one must have the worst."

"Had I known him I would not have hurt him for all my father's lands," said Lancelot. "Only lately he risked his life for me, when he fought with thirty knights, with no help but Dinadan. This is poor requital for his noble service."

Then they sought Tristram in the forest, but in vain. They found the place where his pavilion had been pitched, but it was gone and all trace of its owner vanished. Thereupon they returned to the Castle of Maidens, where for three days was held high feast and frolic, and where all who came were warmly welcomed by King Arthur and Queen Guenever.

Chapter IV
The Quest of the Ten Knights

WHEN TRISTRAM was well within the forest shades, he alighted and unlaced his armor and sought to stanch his wound. But so pale did he become that Dinadan thought he was like to die.

"Never dread thee, Dinadan," said Tristram, cheerily, "for I am heart whole, and of this wound I shall soon be healed, by God's mercy."

As they sat conversing Dinadan saw at a distance Sir Palamides, who was riding straight upon them, with seeming evil intent. Dinadan hastily bid Tristram to withdraw, and offered himself to meet the Saracen and take the chance of life and death with him.

"I thank you, Sir Dinadan, for your good will," said Tristram, "but you shall see that I am able to handle him."

He thereupon hastily armed himself, and, mounting his horse, rode to meet Palamides. Then a challenge to joust passed between them, and they rode together. But Tristram kept his seat and Palamides got a grievous fall, and lay on the earth like one dead.

Leaving him there with a comrade, Tristram and Dinadan rode on, and obtained lodging for that night at the castle of an old knight, who had five sons at the tournament.

As for Palamides, when he recovered from his swoon, he well-nigh lost his wits through sheer vexation. He rode headlong forward, wild with rage, and meeting a deep stream sought to make his horse leap it. But the horse fell in and was drowned, and the knight himself reached shore only by the barest chance.

Now, mad with chagrin, he flung off his armor, and sat roaring and crying like a man distracted. As he sat there, a damsel passed by, who on seeing his distressful state sought to comfort him, but in vain. Then she rode on till she came to the old knight's castle, where Tristram was, and told how she had met a mad knight in the forest.

"What shield did he bear?" asked Tristram.

"It was indented with black and white," answered the damsel.

"That was Palamides. The poor fellow has lost his wits through his bad luck. I beg that you bring him to your castle, Sir Darras."

This the old knight did, for the frenzy of the Saracen had now passed, and he readily accompanied him. On reaching the castle he looked curiously at Tristram, whom he felt sure he had seen before, but could not place him in his mind. But his anger against his fortunate rival continued, and he boasted proudly to Dinadan of what he would do when he met that fellow Tristram.

"It seems to me," answered Dinadan, "that you met him not long since, and got little good of him. Why did you not hold him when you had him in your hands? You were too easy with the fellow not to pummel him when you had so fine an opportunity."

This scornful reply silenced the boastful Saracen, who fell into an angry moodiness.

Meanwhile King Arthur was sore at heart at the disappearance of Tristram, and spoke in reproach to Lancelot as being the cause of his loss.

"My liege Arthur," answered Lancelot, "you do me ill justice in this. When men are hot in battle they may well hurt their friends as well as their foes. As for Tristram, there is no man living whom I would rather help. If you desire, I will make one of ten knights who will go in search of him, and not rest two nights in the same place for a year until we find him."

This offer pleased the king, who quickly chose nine other knights for the quest, and made them all swear upon the Scriptures to do as Lancelot had proposed.

With dawn of the next day these ten knights armed themselves, and rode from the Castle of Maidens, continuing in company until they came to a roadside cross, from which ran out four highways. Here they separated into four parties, each of which followed one of the highways. And far and wide they rode through field and forest for many days in quest of the brave knight of Cornwall.

Of them all, Sir Lucan, the butler, came nearest to good fortune, for chance brought him to the castle of the old knight, Sir Darras. Here he asked harbor, sending in his name by the porter.

"He shall not rest here unless he first joust with me," cried Sir Daname, the old knight's nephew. "Bid him make ready, for he must earn his lodging."

But better had Daname held his peace, for Lucan smote him over his horse's croup, and followed him hotly when he fled into the castle.

"This is a shame to our host," said Dinadan. "Let me try conclusions with our doughty butler. It will not do to let him take our castle by storm."

He thereupon rode against Lucan, and fared still worse, for he got for his pains a spear thrust through the thigh. Then Tristram, in anger, armed and followed Lucan, who had ridden on, in search of a more peaceful place of shelter. Within a mile he overtook him and bade him turn and joust. Nothing loath, Lucan did so, and in his turn got a sore fall, though he little dreamed that he had been overthrown by the knight of his quest. At this juncture another of the ten knights, Sir Uwaine, came up, and seeing Sir Lucan's misfortune, rode furiously against the victor. His luck was no better, for he was hurled to the ground with a sorely wounded side. Having thus revenged his comrades, Tristram returned to the castle.

Meanwhile a damsel from the Castle of Maidens had come thither, and told Sir Darras a woeful story. Of his five sons, three had been slain at the tournament, and the other two were dangerously wounded, all this having been done by the knight of the black shield. Deep grief filled the old knight's heart at this sad tale. But his sorrow turned to rage when the damsel was shown Tristram's shield and recognized it as that of the champion of the tournament.

"So," cried the old knight in a hot passion. "I am harboring here my sons' murderer, and troubling myself to give him noble cheer. By my father's grave, I will revenge my boys' death on him and his companions."

Then in grief and rage he ordered his knights and servants to seize Tristram, Dinadan, and Palamides, and put them in a strong dungeon he had in the keep of his castle.

This was done before the three knights could defend themselves, and for many days they lay in this dismal cell, until Tristram grew so sick from his wound and confinement that he came near to dying. While they lay thus in durance vile some knights of Darras's kindred came to the castle, and on hearing the story wished to kill the captives, but this the old knight would not permit, though he determined to hold them close prisoners. So deep in time grew Tristram's sickness that his mind nearly failed him, and he was ready to slay himself for pain and grief. Palamides gave him what aid he could, though all the time he spoke of his hatred to Tristram, the Cornishman, and of the revenge he yet hoped to have. To this Tristram made no reply, but smiled quietly.

Meanwhile the ten knights continued their fruitless search, some here, some there, while one of them, Gaheris, nephew to King Arthur, made his way to King Mark's court, where he was well received.

As they sat at table together the king asked his guest what tidings he brought from Arthur's realm of Logris.

"Sir," he answered, "King Arthur still reigns nobly, and he lately presided at a grand tournament where fought many of the noblest knights of the kingdom. But best of them all was a valiant knight who bore a black shield, and who kept the lordship of the lists for three days."

"Then by my crown it must have been Lancelot, or Palamides the Pagan."

"Not so. These knights were against him of the black shield."

"Was it Sir Tristram?" asked the king.

"In sooth you have it now."

The king held down his head at this, but La Belle Isolde, who was at the feast, heard it with great secret joy, and her love for Tristram grew warmer in her soul.

But King Mark nourished treason in his heart, and sought within his brain some device to do dishonor to Tristram and to Arthur's knights. Soon afterward Uwaine came to his court and challenged any knight of Cornwall to meet him in the lists. Two of these, Andred, and Dinas the seneschal, accepted the challenge, but both were overthrown. Then King Mark in a fury cried out against his knights, and Gaheris, as his guest, proffered to meet the champion. But when Uwaine saw his shield, he knew him for his own cousin, and refused to joust with him, reproving him for breaking his oath of fellowship as a Knight of the Round Table.

This reproof cut Gaheris deeply, and returning to King Mark he took his leave of him and his court, saying:

"Sir king, this I must say, that you did a foul shame to yourself and your kingdom when you banished Sir Tristram. Had he stayed here you would not have wanted a champion."

All this added to the king's rage, and arming himself he waylaid Uwaine at a secret place as he was passing unawares, and ran him through the body. But before he could kill him as he designed, Kay the seneschal came that way and flew to the aid of the wounded knight, while King Mark rode in dastardly haste away. Kay sought to learn from Uwaine who had hurt him, but this he was not able to tell.

He then bore him to a neighboring abbey of the black cross, where he left him in the care of the monks. Not far had he ridden from there when he met King Mark, who accosted him courteously, and bade him, if he sought an adventure, to ride into the forest of Morris, where he would find one to try his prowess.

"I will prove what it is worth," said Kay, and bade adieu to the king.

A mile or two further on he met Gaheris, who, learning his errand, warned him against doing anything at the suggestion of King Mark, who meant but treachery and harm.

"Come with me, then," said Kay. "Adventures are not so abundant, and we two should be able to match the wiles of this dastard king."

"I shall not fail you," said Gaheris.

Into the forest they then rode till they came to the edge of a little lake, known as the Perilous Lake, and here they waited under the woodland shadows.

It was now night, but the moon rode high in the skies, and flung its silvery rays wide over the forest glade. As they stood thus, there rode into the moonlit opening a knight all in black armor and on a great black horse, who tilted against Sir Kay. The seneschal's horse was smaller than that of the stranger, and was overthrown by the shock, falling upon its rider, whom it bruised severely.

During this encounter Gaheris had remained hidden under the woodland shadows. He now cried sternly:

"Knight, sit thou fast in thy saddle, for I will revenge my fellow;" and rode against the black knight with such fury that he was flung from his horse. Then he turned to a companion of the black knight, who now appeared, and hurled him to the earth so violently that he came near to breaking his neck in the fall.

Leaping from his horse and helping Kay to his feet, Gaheris sternly bade his antagonists to tell their names or they should die.

"Beware what you do," said the second knight. "This is King Mark of Cornwall, and I am his cousin Andred."

"You are traitors both," cried Gaheris, in a fury, "and have laid this ambush for us. It were a pity to let such craven rascals live."

"Spare my life," prayed the king, "and I will make full amends."

"You a king; and dealing in treachery!" cried Gaheris. "You have lived long enough."

With this he struck fiercely at King Mark with his sword, while the dastard king cowered under his shield. Kay attacked Andred at the same time.

King Mark now flung himself on his knees before Gaheris and swore on the cross of his sword never while he lived to do aught against errant knights. And he also swore to be a friend unto Sir Tristram if he should come into Cornwall.

With this they let them go, though Kay was eager to slay Andred, for his deeds of treachery against his cousin Tristram. The two knights now rode out of the kingdom of Cornwall, and soon after met Lancelot, who asked them what tidings they brought from King Mark's country, and if they had learned aught of Tristram. They answered that they had not, and told him of their adventure, at which Lancelot smiled.

"You will find it hard to take out of the flesh that which is bred in the bone," he said.

Then Lancelot, Kay, and Gaheris rode together to seek Tristram in the country of Surluse, not dreaming that he lay in prison not many miles from the Castle of Maidens.

Leaving them to pursue their useless journey, we must return to the three prisoners. Tristram still continued sick almost unto death, while Palamides, while giving him daily care, continued to rail loudly against him and to boast of how he would yet deal with him. Of this idle boasting Dinadan in time had more than he could bear, and broke out angrily on the Saracen.

"I doubt if you would do him harm if he were here before you," he said; "for if a wolf and a sheep were together in prison the wolf would leave the sheep in peace. As for Sir Tristram, against whom you rail like a scold, here he lies before you. Now do your worst upon him, Sir Saracen, while he is too sick to defend himself."

Surprise and shame overcame Palamides at this announcement, and he dropped his head in confusion.

"I have heard somewhat too much of your ill will against me;" said Tristram, "but shall let it pass at present, for we are in more danger here from the lord of this place than from each other."

As they spoke, a damsel brought them their noontide meal, and said as she gave it them:

"Be of good cheer, sir knights, for you are in no peril of your lives. So much I heard my lord, Sir Darras, say this morning."

"So far your news is good," cried Dinadan. "Good for two of us at least, for this good knight promises to die without waiting for the executioner."

The damsel looked upon Tristram, and observing the thinness of his face and hands, went and told Sir Darras of what she had heard and seen.

"That must not be," cried the knight. "God defend that I should suffer those who came to me for succor to die in my prison. Bring them hither."

Then Tristram was brought to the castle hall on his couch, with the other two knights beside him.

"Sir knight," said the castle lord, "I am sorry for your sickness, and would not have so noble a knight as you die in prison, though I owe to you the death of three of my sons."

"As for that," said Tristram, "it was in fair fight, and if they were my next of kin I could not have done otherwise. If I had slain them by treachery, I would have deserved death at your hands."

"You acted knightly, and for that reason I could not put you to death," said Sir Darras. "You and your fellows shall go at full liberty, with your horses and armor, on this covenant, that you will be a good friend to my two sons who are still living, and that you tell me your name."

"My name is Tristram de Lyonesse. I was born in Cornwall, and am nephew to King Mark. And I promise you by the faith of my body that while I live I shall be a friend to you and your sons, for what you have done to us was but by force of nature."

"If you be the good knight Sir Tristram, I am sorry to have held you in durance, and thank you for your proffer of service. But you must stay with me still till you are well and strong."

To this Tristram agreed, and staid many more days with the old knight, growing well rapidly under the healing influence of hope and liberty.

Chapter V
The Knight with the Covered Shield

WHEN TRISTRAM'S strength had all come back again he took his leave of Sir Darras, and rode away with Palamides and Dinadan. Soon they came to a cross-way, and here Tristram said:

"Good sirs, let us here take each his own road, and many fair adventures may come to us all."

To this they agreed, and Tristram rode on along the main highway, chance bringing him that night to a castle in which was Queen Morgan le Fay. Here he was given lodging and good cheer, but when he was ready to depart the next day the queen said to him,—

"Sir knight, it is one thing to enter this castle and another to leave it. You will not depart so easily as you came. Know that you are a prisoner."

"God forfend," said Tristram. "I am just released from prison, and have had enough of that regimen."

"You shall stay here, nevertheless, till I learn who you are and whence you came, but I promise you no hard quarters."

She set him, therefore, by her side at table, and made so much of him that a knight who loved her clutched his sword-hilt in jealous rage, half disposed to rush upon Tristram and run him through unawares.

"Tell me your name," said the queen, at the end of the repast, "and you shall depart when you will."

"Thanks for your promise, fair lady. My name is Tristram de Lyonesse."

"Then I am sorry I made so hasty a promise. But I will hold to my word if you will engage to bear a shield which I shall give you to the Castle of the Hard Rock, where King Arthur has announced that a tournament is to be held. I have heard of your deeds of arms at the Castle of Maidens, and hope you will do as much for me at this new tournament."

"Let me see the shield that you wish me to bear," asked Tristram.

So the shield was brought. It was golden on its face, and on it was painted a king and queen, with a knight standing above them with a foot on the head of each.

"This is a fair shield," said Tristram; "but what signifies the device?"

"It signifies King Arthur and Queen Guenever," said Morgan, "and a knight that holds them both in bondage."

"And who is the knight?"

"That you shall not know at present."

So Tristram took the shield, not dreaming that it was intended as a rebuke to Sir Lancelot, and promised to bear it at the tournament.

But as he rode away he was followed by Sir Hemison, the knight who loved Morgan le Fay, and whose jealous anger had been roused. Overtaking Tristram before he had gone far, he rushed upon him at the speed of his horse, crying, in a voice of thunder:

"Sir knight, defend yourself!"

This Tristram did with good effect, for his assailant's spear broke upon his body, while he thrust him through and hurled him to the earth with a mortal wound.

"Fool, you have brought it on yourself," said Tristram. "It is not my fault if you got what you designed for me."

Then he rode on, and left the wounded knight to the care of his squire, who removed his helmet, and asked if his life was in any danger.

"There is little life in me," said the knight, "and that is ebbing fast. Therefore help me to my saddle, and mount behind me and hold me on so that I shall not fall, and so bring me to Queen Morgan le Fay. For deep draughts of death draw to my heart, and I would fain speak to her before I die."

The squire did as commanded, and brought his bleeding master to the castle, but he died as he entered the hall, falling lifeless at the feet of the lady of his love. Much she wept and great lamentation she made for his untimely fate, and buried him in a stately tomb, on which was written, "Here lieth Sir Hemison, slain by the hands of Tristram de Lyonesse".

On the next day Tristram arrived at the castle of Roche-dure, where he saw the lists prepared for the tournament, with gay pennons flying, while full five hundred tents were pitched in a fair meadow by the gates. Over the seats of honor were silken canopies, that shaded noble lords and beautiful ladies clad in gay apparel. Within the lists the kings of Scotland and Ireland held out strongly against King Arthur's knights, and dread was the noise and turmoil within.

Tristram at once joined in the fray, and smote down many knights; King Arthur marvelling the while at the device on his shield, while Guenever grew heavy at heart, for well she guessed its meaning.

Ever King Arthur's eye was on that shield, and much he wondered who the knight could be, for he had heard that Tristram was in Brittany, and he knew that Lancelot was in quest of him, while he knew no other knight of equal prowess.

As the combat went on, Arthur's knights drove back their antagonists, who began to withdraw from the field. On seeing this the king determined that the knight with the strange shield should not escape, so he armed and called Sir Uwaine, entering the lists with him and riding up to confront the unknown knight.

"Sir stranger," said the king, "before we fight, I require you to tell me where you got that shield."

"I had it from Morgan le Fay, sister to King Arthur," answered Tristram.

"Then, if you are worthy to bear it, you are able to tell me its meaning."

"That I cannot," answered the knight. "It was given me by Queen Morgan, not through any asking of mine. She told me not what it signified, nor do I know, but I promised to bear it worthily."

"In truth," said Arthur, "no knight should bear arms he cannot understand. But at least you will tell me your name."

"To what intent?" asked Tristram.

"Simply that I wish to know."

"That is small reason. I decline to tell you."

"If not, we must do battle together."

"What!" cried Tristram; "you will fight me on so small a cause? My name is my own, to be given or withheld as I will. It is not honorable for a fresh knight to challenge me to battle, after all I have done this day. But if you think you have me at advantage, you may find that I am able to hold my own."

Then they put their spears in rest and furiously dashed together across the lists. But King Arthur's spear shivered to splinters on Tristram's shield, while he himself got such a blow from the Cornish knight that horse and man fell headlong to the earth, the king with a dangerous wound in the side.

When Uwaine saw this he reined back his horse in haste, and crying loudly, "Knight, defend thyself!" he rode furiously on Tristram. But man fared no better than master. Uwaine was borne out of his saddle to the earth, while Tristram sat unmoved.

Then Tristram wheeled his horse and said:

"Fair sirs, I had no need to joust with you, for I have done enough today; but you forced me to it."

"We have had what we deserved," answered Arthur. "Yet I would fain know your name, and would further learn if that device on your shield is intended as an insult to King Arthur."

"That you must ask Morgan le Fay: she alone knows. But report says she does not love her royal brother over much. Yet she told me not what it means, and I have borne it at her command. As for my name, it shall be known when I will."

So Tristram departed, and rode far over hill and dale, everywhere seeking for Lancelot, with whom he in his heart wished to make fellowship. As he went on he came by a forest, on the edge of which stood a tall tower, and in front of it a fair level meadow. And here he saw one knight fighting against ten, and bearing himself so well that it seemed marvellous that a single man could hold his own so bravely against such odds. He had slain half their horses, and unhorsed the remaining knights, so that their chargers ran free in the field. The ten had then assailed him on foot, and he was bearing up bravely against them.

"Cease that battle!" cried Tristram, loudly, as he came up. "Ten to one are cowards' odds." And as he came nearer he saw by his shield that the one knight was Sir Palamides.

"You would be wise not to meddle," said the leader of the ten, who was the villanous knight called Breuse San Pitié. "Go your way while your skin is whole. As for this knight, he is our prey."

"Say you so!" cried Tristram. "There may be two words to that."

As he spoke he sprang from his horse, lest they should kill it, and attacked them on foot with such fury that with every stroke a knight fell before him.

This was more than they had bargained for, and Breuse fled hastily to the tower, followed by all that were able, while Tristram hotly pursued. But they quickly closed and barred the door, shutting him out. When he saw this he returned to Palamides, whom he found sitting under a tree, sorely wounded.

"Thanks for your timely aid," said the Saracen. "You have saved my life."

"What is your name?" asked Tristram.

"It is Sir Palamides."

"Then have I saved my greatest enemy; and I here challenge you to battle."

"What is your name?" asked Palamides.

"I am Tristram of Lyonesse."

"My enemy indeed! yet I owe you thanks for your rescue, nor am I in condition for jousting. But I desire nothing better than to meet you in battle. If you are as eager for it, fix day and place, and I will be there."

"Well said," answered Tristram. "Let it be in the meadow by the river at Camelot, there where Merlin set the tombstone."

"Agreed. I shall not fail you."

"How came you in battle with these ten dastards?"

"The chance of journeying brought me into this forest, where I saw a dead knight with a lady weeping beside him. I asked her who slew her lord, and she told me it was the most villanous knight in the world, named Breuse Sans Pitié. I then took her on my horse and promised to see that her lord was properly interred. But as I passed by this tower its rascally owner suddenly rode from the gate and struck me unawares so hard that I fell from my horse. Before I could recover he killed the lady. It was thus the battle began, at which you arrived in good time."

"It is not safe for you to stay here," said Tristram. "That fellow is out of our reach for the present, but you are not in condition to meet him again."

So they mounted and rode into the forest, where they soon came to a sparkling fountain, whose clear water bubbled freshly from the ground. Here they alighted and refreshed themselves.

As they did so Tristram's horse neighed loudly and was answered by another horse nearby. They mounted and rode towards the sound, and quickly came in sight of a great war-horse tied to a tree. Under an adjoining tree lay a knight asleep, in full armor, save that his helmet was placed under his head for a pillow.

"A stout-looking fellow that," said Tristram. "What shall we do?"

"Awake him," said Palamides.

Tristram did so, stirring him with the butt of his spear.

But they had better have let him sleep, for he sprang angrily to his feet, put on his helmet in haste, and mounting his war-horse seized his spear. Without a word he spurred upon Tristram and struck him such a blow as to fling him from his saddle to the earth. Then he galloped back and came hurling upon Palamides, whom he served in the same rude fashion. Leaving them laying there, he turned his horse and rode leisurely away.

When the two overthrown knights gained their feet again, they looked at one another with faces of shame and anger.

"Well, what now?" asked Tristram. "That is the worst waking I ever did in my life. By my troth, I did not fancy there was a knight in Arthur's realm that could have served you and me such a trick. Whatever you do, I am going after this woodland champion to have a fairer trial."

"So would I were I well," said Palamides. "But I am so hurt that I must seek rest with a friend of mine nearby."

"I can trust you to meet me at the place appointed?"

"I have cause to have more doubt of you than you of me; for if you follow this strong knight you may not escape with whole bones from the adventure. I wish you success."

"And I wish you health."

With these words they parted, each riding his own way.

But news came to Tristram as he rode on that would have turned many a knight from that adventure. For the first day he found a dead knight and a lady weeping over him, who said that her lord had jousted with a strong champion, who had run him through. On the third day he met the good knights Gawaine and Bleoberis, both wounded, who said they had been so served by a knight with a covered shield.

"He treated me and Palamides the same way," said Tristram, "and I am on his track to repay him."

"By my faith, you had best turn back," said Gawaine.

"By my head, I will not," said Tristram, and he rode on in pursuit.

The next day he met Kay the seneschal and Dinadan in a meadow.

"What tidings have you?" he asked.

"Not good," they answered.

"Tell me what they are. I ride in search of a knight."

"What cognizance does he bear?"

"He carries a shield covered by a cloth."

"Then you are not far from him," said Kay. "We lodged last night in a widow's house, and that knight sought the same lodging. And when he knew we were of Arthur's court he spoke villanous things of the king, and worse of Queen Guenever. The next day we waged battle with him for this insult. But at the first encounter he flung me from my horse with a sore hurt. And when Dinadan here saw me down he showed more prudence than valor, for he fled to save his skin."

After some further words Tristram rode on; but days passed and he found not the knight with the covered shield, though he heard more tales of his irresistible prowess. Then, finding that his armor was bruised and broken with long use, he sent Gouvernail, his squire, to a city nearby to bring him fresh apparel, and rested at a priory till he came.

On Gouvernail's return he donned his new armor, and turned his horse's head towards Camelot, seeking the point where he had engaged to do battle with Palamides. This was at the tomb of Lanceor, son of the king of Ireland, who had been slain by Balin, and whose lady Columbe had slain herself, as we have already told. His tomb had been set up near the river by Merlin, and it had become a place of pilgrimage for true lovers and faithful wedded pairs.

Tristram did not get there without more battling, for the roads around Camelot then swarmed with errant knights, eager to show their strength. Yet he was none the worse for these encounters when he rode up to the tomb where he hoped to find Palamides in waiting. But instead of the Saracen he saw a knight approaching in white armor, who bore a shield covered with a dark cloth.

"Sir knight, you are welcome; none more so," cried Tristram. "I have sought you far and near, and have an ugly fall to repay you for; and also owe you a lesson for your revilement of King Arthur and his fair queen."

"Shorter words and longer deeds would serve better," said the stranger knight. "Make ready, my good fellow, if one fall is not enough to satisfy you."

Then they rode apart to a fair distance, and putting spurs to their horses hurtled together with headlong speed. So fiercely met they, indeed, that horses and knights together went toppling to the earth, both those brave warriors kissing the dust.

With all haste they regained their feet, put their shields before them, and struck at each other with bright swords like men of might. The battle that followed was such a one as that ground had never seen, for those two knights seemed rather giants than men. For four hours they kept up the combat, neither speaking a word, till at the end their armor was hewn off in many places, and blood had flowed from their wounds till the grass was turned from green to crimson.

The squires looked on in wonder, and boasted of the might of their lords, though their hearts grew heavy when they saw the bright swords so reddened with blood.

At last the unknown knight rested on his weapon, and said:

"Sir stranger, you are the best fighter I ever saw in armor. I would know you better, and beg to learn your name."

"I care not to tell it," said Tristram.

"Why not? I never make my name a secret."

"Then pray tell it, for I would give much to know the name of the stoutest knight I ever drew sword upon."

"Fair sir, my name is Lancelot du Lac."

"Alas, can this be so? Have I fought thus against the man I love best in the world?"

"Then who are you?"

"My name is Tristram de Lyonesse."

"Oh, what strange chance is this! Take my sword, Sir Tristram, for you have earned it well."

And he knelt and yielded Tristram his sword.

Tristram in turn knelt and yielded up his. And thus with exchange of words they gave each other the degree of brotherhood. Then they sat together on the stone, and took off their helms to cool their heated faces, and kissed each other with brotherly ardor.

When they had rested and conversed long in the most loving amity, and their squires had salved and bandaged their wounds, they mounted and rode towards Camelot.

Near the gates of the city they met Gawaine and Gaheris, who were setting out in search of Tristram, having promised King Arthur never to return till they could bring the valiant knight of Cornwall with them.

"Return, then, for your quest is done," said Lancelot. "I have found Sir Tristram, and here he is in person."

"Then, by my life, you are heartily welcome!" cried Gawaine. "You have eased me from great labor, and there are ten others seeking you. Why came you hither of yourself?"

"I had a challenge with Sir Palamides to do battle with him at Lanceor's tomb this day, and I know not why he has failed me. By lucky chance my lord Lancelot and I met there, and well have we tried each other's strength."

Thus conversing they came to the court, where King Arthur, when he learned the name of Lancelot's companion, was filled with joy. Taking Tristram warmly by both hands, he welcomed him to Camelot.

"There is no other man in the world whom I would so gladly have here," he said. "Much have you been sought for since you left the tournament, but in vain. I would fain learn your adventures."

These Tristram told, and the king was amazed when he learned that it was he who had overthrown him at the Castle of Hard Rock. Then he told of his pursuit of the knight with the covered shield, and of the deeds he had done.

"By our faith," cried Gawaine, Bleoberis and Kay, "we can testify to that, for he left us all on the ground."

"Aha! who could this strong fellow have been?" asked Arthur. "Did any of you know him?"

They all declared that he was a stranger to them, though Tristram kept silent.

"If you know not, I do; it was Lancelot or none," cried the king.

"In faith, I fancy so," said Tristram, "for I found him today, and we had a four hours' fight together, before each found out the other."

"So," they all cried, "it is he who has beguiled us with his covered shield!"

"You say truly," answered Lancelot, with a smile. "And I called myself an enemy of King Arthur so that none should suspect me. I was in search of sport."

"That is an old trick of yours," said Arthur.

"One must go in disguise in these days, or go untried," laughed Lancelot.

Then Queen Guenever, and many ladies of the court, learning that Tristram was there, came and bade him welcome, ladies and knights together crying, "Welcome, Sir Tristram! welcome to Camelot!"

"Welcome, indeed," said Arthur, "to one of the best and gentlest knights of the world, and the man of highest esteem. For of all modes of hunting, you bear the prize, and of all bugle hunting calls you are the origin, and all the terms of hunting and hawking began with you; on all instruments of music no man surpasses you: therefore, you are trebly welcome to this court. And here I pray you to grant me a boon."

"I am at your command," said Tristram.

"It is that you abide in my court, and be one of my knights."

"That I am loath to do, for I have work laid out elsewhere."

"Yet you have passed your word. You shall not say me nay."

"Then be it as you will," said Tristram.

These words spoken, Arthur took Tristram by the hand and led him to the Round Table, going with him round its circle, and looking into every seat that lacked a knight. When at length he came to that in which Sir Marhaus had formerly sat, he saw there engraved in letters of gold, "This is the seat of the noble knight Sir Tristram."

Then Arthur made Tristram a Knight of the Round Table with noble ceremony and great pomp, and with feasts that lasted many days. Glad were all there to have a knight of such prowess and high esteem in their company, and many friends Tristram made among his new brothers-in-arms.

But chief of all these was Lancelot, and for days together Lancelot and Tristram kept genial company, while their brotherhood gave joy to all, and most of all to King Arthur, who felt that the glory of his reign was now at its height, and that two such knights as these would spread the renown of the Round Table throughout the world.

Book VIII
Tristram and Isolde at Joyous Gard

Chapter I
The Treachery of King Mark

T HE STORY OF TRISTRAM'S valorous deeds, and of the
high honor in which he was held at Camelot, in good time
came to Cornwall, where it filled King Mark's soul with
revengeful fury, and stirred the heart of La Belle Isolde to the
warmest love. The coward king, indeed, in his jealous hatred
of his nephew, set out in disguise for England, with murderous
designs against Tristram should an opportunity occur.

Many things happened to him there, and he was brought into deep
disgrace, but the story of his adventures may be passed over in brief
review, lest the reader should find it wearisome.

Not far had he ridden on English soil before he met with Dinadan,
who, in his jesting humor, soon played him a merry trick. For he
arrayed Dagonet, the king's fool, in a suit of armor, which he made Mark
believe was Lancelot's. Thus prepared, Dagonet rode to meet him and
challenged him to a joust. But King Mark, on seeing what he fancied was
Lancelot's shield, turned and fled at headlong speed, followed by the fool
and his comrades with hunting cries and laughter till the forest rang with
the noise.

Escaping at length from this merry chase, the trembling dastard
made his way to Camelot, where he hoped some chance would arise to
aid him in his murderous designs on Tristram. But a knight of his own

train, named Sir Amant, had arrived there before him, and accused him of treason to the king, without telling who he was.

"This is a charge that must be settled by wager of battle," said King Arthur. "The quarrel is between you; you must decide it with sword and spear."

In the battle that followed, Sir Amant, by unlucky fortune, was run through, and fell from his horse with a mortal wound.

"Heaven has decided in my favor," cried King Mark. "But here I shall no longer stay, for it does not seem a safe harbor for honest knights."

He thereupon rode away, fearing that Dinadan would reveal his name. Yet not far had he gone before Lancelot came in furious haste after him.

"Turn again, thou recreant king and knight," he loudly called. "To Arthur's court you must return, whether it is your will or not. We know you, villain. Sir Amant has told your name and purpose; and, by my faith, I am strongly moved to kill you on the spot."

"Fair sir," asked King Mark, "what is your name?"

"My name is Lancelot du Lac. Defend yourself, dog and dastard."

On hearing this dreaded name, and seeing Lancelot riding upon him with spear in rest, King Mark tumbled like a sack of grain from his saddle to the earth, crying in terror, "I yield me, Sir Lancelot! I yield me!" and begging piteously for mercy.

"Thou villain!" thundered Lancelot, "I would give much to deal thee one buffet for the love of Tristram and Isolde. Mount, dog, and follow me."

Mark hastened to obey, and was thus brought like a slave back to Arthur's court, where he made such prayers and promises that in the end the king forgave him, but only on condition that he would enter into accord with Tristram, and remove from him the sentence of banishment. All this King Mark volubly promised and swore to abide by, though a false heart underlay his fair words. But Tristram gladly accepted the proffered truce with his old enemy, for his heart burned with desire to see his lady love again.

Soon afterwards Dinadan, with Dagonet and his companions, came to court, and great was the laughter and jesting at King Mark when they told the story of his flight from Arthur's fool.

"This is all very well for you stay-at-homes," cried Mark; "but even a fool in Lancelot's armor is not to be played with. As it was, Dagonet paid for his masquerade, for he met a knight who brought him like a log to the ground, and all these laughing fellows with him."

"Who was that?" asked King Arthur.

"I can tell you," said Dinadan. "It was Sir Palamides. I followed him through the forest, and a lively time we had in company."

"Aha! then you have had adventures."

"Rare ones. We met a knight before Morgan le Fay's castle. You know the custom there, to let no knight pass without a hard fight for it. This stranger made havoc with the custom, for he overthrew ten of your sister's knights, and killed some of them. He afterwards tilted with Palamides for offering to help him, and gave that doughty fellow a sore wound."

"Who was this mighty champion? Not Lancelot or Tristram?" asked the king, looking around.

"On our faith we had no hand in it," they both answered.

"It was the knight next to them in renown," answered Dinadan.

"Lamorak of Wales?"

"No less. And, my faith, a sturdy fellow he is. I left him and Palamides the best of friends."

"I hope, then, to see the pair of them at next week's tournament," said the king.

Alas for Lamorak! Better for him far had he kept away from that tournament. His gallant career was near its end, for treachery and hatred were soon to seal his fate. This sorrowful story it is now our sad duty to tell.

Lamorak had long loved Margause, the queen of Orkney, Arthur's sister and the mother of Gawaine and his brethren. For this they hated him, and with treacherous intent invited their mother to a castle near Camelot, as a lure to her lover. Soon after the tournament, at which Lamorak won the prize of valor, and redoubled the hatred of Gawaine and his brothers by overcoming them in the fray, word was brought to the victorious knight that Margause was near at hand and wished to see him.

With a lover's ardor, he hastened to the castle where she was, but, as they sat in the queen's apartment in conversation, the door was suddenly flung open, and Gaheris, one of the murderous brethren, burst in, full armed and with a naked sword in his hand. Rushing in fury on the unsuspecting lovers, with one dreadful blow he struck off his mother's head, crimsoning Lamorak with her blood. He next assailed Lamorak, who, being unarmed, was forced to fly for his life, and barely escaped.

The tidings of this dread affair filled the land with dismay, and many of the good knights of Arthur's court threatened reprisal. Arthur himself was full of wrath at the death of his sister. Yet those were days when law ruled not, but force was master, and retribution only came from the strong hand and the ready sword. This was Lamorak's quarrel, and the king, though he vowed to protect him from his foes, declared that the good knight of Wales must seek retribution with his own hand.

He gained death, alas! instead of revenge, for his foes proved too vigilant for him, and overcame him by vile treachery. Watching his movements, they lay in ambush for him at a difficult place, and as he was passing, unsuspicious of danger, they set suddenly upon him, slew his horse, and assailed him on foot.

Gawaine, Mordred and Gaheris formed this ambush, for the noble-minded Gareth had refused to take part in their murderous plot; and with desperate fury they assaulted the noble Welsh knight, who, for three hours, defended himself against their utmost strength. But at the last Mordred dealt him a death-blow from behind, and when he fell in death the three murders hewed him with their swords till scarce a trace of the human form was left.

Thus perished one of the noblest of Arthur's knights, and thus was done one of the most villanous deeds of blood ever known in those days of chivalrous war.

Before the death of Lamorak another event happened at Arthur's court which must here be told, for it was marvellous in itself, and had in it the promise of wondrous future deeds.

One day there came to the court at Camelot a knight attended by a young squire. When he had disarmed he went to the king and asked him to give the honor of knighthood to his squire.

"What claim has he to it?" asked the king. "Of what lineage is he?"

"He is the youngest son of King Pellinore, and brother to Sir Lamorak. He is my brother also; for my name is Aglavale, and I am of the same descent."

"What is his name?"

"Percivale."

"Then for my love of Lamorak, and the love I bore your father, he shall be made a knight tomorrow."

So when the morrow dawned, the king ordered that the youth should be brought into the great hall, and there he knighted him, dealing him the accolade with his good sword Excalibur.

And so the day passed on till the dinner-hour, when the king seated himself at the head of the table, while down its sides were many knights of prowess and renown. Percivale, the new-made knight, was given a seat among the squires and the untried knights, who sat at the lower end of the great dining-table.

But in the midst of their dinner an event of great strangeness occurred. For there came into the hall one of the queen's maidens, who was of high birth, but who had been born dumb, and in all her life had spoken no word. Straight across the hall she walked, while all gazed at her in mute surprise, till she came to where Percivale sat. Then she took him by the hand, and spoke in a voice that rang through the hall with the clearness of a trumpet:

"Arise, Sir Percivale, thou noble knight and warrior of God's own choosing. Arise and come with me."

He rose in deep surprise, while all the others sat in dumb wonder at this miracle. To the Round Table she led him, and to the right side of the seat perilous, in which no knight had hitherto dared to sit.

"Fair knight, take here your seat;" she said. "This seat belongs to you, and to none other, and shall be yours until a greater than you shall come."

This said, she departed and asked for a priest. Then was she confessed and given the sacrament, and forthwith died. But the king and all his court gazed with wonder on Sir Percivale, and asked themselves what all this meant, and for what great career God had picked out this youthful knight, for such a miracle no man there had ever seen before.

Meanwhile, King Mark had gone back to Cornwall, and with him went Sir Tristram, at King Arthur's request, though not till Arthur had made the Cornish king swear on Holy Scripture to do his guest no harm, but hold him in honor and esteem.

Lancelot, however, was full of dread and anger when he heard what had occurred, and he told King Mark plainly that if he did mischief to Sir Tristram he would slay him with his own hands.

"Bear this well in mind, sir king," he said, "for I have a way of keeping my word."

"I have sworn before King Arthur to treat him honorably," answered Mark. "I, too, have a way of keeping my word."

"A way, I doubt not," said Lancelot, scornfully; "but not my way. Your reputation for truth needs mending. And all men know for what you came into this country. Therefore, take heed what you do."

Then Mark and Tristram departed, and soon after they reached Cornwall a damsel was sent to Camelot with news of their safe arrival, and bearing letters from Tristram to Arthur and Lancelot. These they answered and sent the damsel back, the burden of Lancelot's letter being, "Beware of King Fox, for his ways are ways of wiles."

They also sent letters to King Mark, threatening him if he should do aught to Tristram's injury. These letters worked harm only, for they roused the evil spirit in the Cornish king's soul, stirring him up to anger and thirst for revenge. He thereupon wrote to Arthur, bidding him to meddle with his own concerns, and to take heed to his wife and his knights, which would give him work enough to do. As for Sir Tristram, he said that he held him to be his mortal enemy.

He wrote also to Queen Guenever, his letter being full of shameful charges of illicit relations with Sir Lancelot, and dishonor to her lord, the king. Full of wrath at these vile charges, Guenever took the letter to Lancelot, who was half beside himself with anger on reading it.

"You cannot get at him to make him eat his words," said Dinadan, whom Lancelot took into his confidence. "And if you seek to bring him to terms with pen and ink, you will find that his villany will get the better of your honesty. Yet there are other ways of dealing with cowardly curs. Leave him to me; I will make him wince. I will write a mocking lay of King Mark and his doings, and will send a harper to sing it before him at his court. When this noble king has heard my song I fancy he will admit that there are other ways of gaining revenge besides writing scurrilous letters."

A stinging lay, indeed, was that which Dinadan composed. When done he taught it to a harper named Eliot, who in his turn taught it to other harpers, and these, by the orders of Arthur and Lancelot, went into Wales and Cornwall to sing it everywhere.

Meanwhile King Mark's crown had been in great danger. For his country had been invaded by an army from Session, led by a noted warrior named Elias, who drove the forces of Cornwall from the field and besieged the king in his castle of Tintagil. And now Tristram came nobly to the rescue. At the head of the Cornish forces he drove back the besiegers with heavy loss, and challenged Elias to a single combat to end the war. The challenge was accepted, and a long and furious combat followed, but in the end Elias was slain, and the remnant of his army forced to surrender.

This great service added to the seeming accord between Tristram and the king, but in his heart Mark nursed all his old bitterness, and hated him the more that he had helped him. His secret fury soon found occasion to flame to the surface. For at the feast which was given in honor of the victory, Eliot, the harper, appeared, and sang before the king and his lords the lay that Dinadan had made.

This was so full of ridicule and scorn of King Mark that he leaped from his seat in a fury of wrath before the harper had half finished.

"Thou villanous twanger of strings!" he cried. "What hound sent you into this land to insult me with your scurrilous songs?"

"I am a minstrel," said Eliot, "and must obey the orders of my lord. Sir Dinadan made this song, if you would know, and bade me sing it here."

"That jesting fool!" cried Mark, in wrath. "As for you, fellow, you shall go free through minstrels' licence. But if you lose any time in getting out of this country you may find that Cornish air is not good for you."

The harper took this advice and hastened away, bearing letters from Tristram to Lancelot and Dinadan. But King Mark turned the weight of his anger against Tristram, whom he believed had instigated this insult, with the design to set all the nobles of his own court laughing at him. And well he knew that the villanous lay would be sung throughout the land, and that he would be made the jest of all the kingdom.

"They have their sport now," he said. "Mine will come. Tristram of Lyonesse shall pay dearly for this insult. And all that hold with him shall learn that King Mark of Cornwall is no child's bauble to be played with."

The evil-minded king was not long in putting his project in execution. At a tournament which was held soon afterwards Tristram was badly wounded, and King Mark, with great show of sorrow, had him borne to a castle nearby, where he took him under his own care as nurse and leech.

Here he gave him a sleeping draught, and had him borne while slumbering to another castle, where he was placed in a strong prison cell, under the charge of stern keepers.

The disappearance of Tristram made a great stir in the kingdom. La Belle Isolde, fearing treachery, went to a faithful knight named Sir Sadok, and begged him to try and discover what had become of the missing knight. Sadok set himself diligently to work; and soon learned that Tristram was held captive in the castle of Lyonesse. Then he went to Dinas, the seneschal, and others, and told them what had been done, at which they broke into open rebellion against King Mark, and took possession of all the towns and castles in the country of Lyonesse, filling them with their followers.

But while the rebellious army was preparing to march on Tintagil, and force King Mark to set free his prisoner, Tristram was delivered by the young knight Sir Percivale, who had come thither in search of adventures, and had heard of King Mark's base deed. Great was the joy between these noble knights, and Tristram said:

"Will you abide in these marches, Sir Percivale? If so, I will keep you company."

"Nay, dear friend, I cannot tarry here. Duty calls me into Wales."

But before leaving Cornwall he went to King Mark, told him what he had done, and threatened him with the revenge of all honorable knights if he sought again to injure his noble nephew.

"What would you have me do?" asked the king. "Shall I harbor a man who openly makes love to my wife and queen?"

"Is there any shame in a nephew showing an open affection for his uncle's wife?" asked Percivale. "No man will dare say that so noble a warrior as Sir Tristram would go beyond the borders of sinless love, or will dare accuse the virtuous lady La Belle Isolde of lack of chastity. You have let jealousy run away with your wisdom, King Mark."

So saying, he departed; but his words had little effect on King Mark's mind. No sooner had Percivale gone than he began new devices to gratify his hatred of his nephew. He sent word to Dinas, the seneschal, under oath, that he intended to go to the Pope and join the war against the infidel Saracens, which he looked upon as a nobler service than that of raising the people against their lawful king.

So earnest were his professions that Dinas believed him and dismissed his forces, but no sooner was this done than King Mark set aside his oath and had Tristram again privately seized and imprisoned.

This new outrage filled the whole realm with tumult and rebellious feeling. La Belle Isolde was at first thrown into the deepest grief, and then her heart swelled high with resolution to live no longer with the dastard who called her wife. Tristram at the same time privately sent her a letter, advising her to leave the court of her villanous lord, and offering to go with her to Arthur's realm, if she would have a vessel privately made ready.

The queen thereupon had an interview with Dinas and Sadok, and begged them to seize and imprison the king, since she was resolved to escape from his power.

Furious at the fox-like treachery of the king, these knights did as requested, for they formed a plot by which Mark was privately seized, and they imprisoned him secretly in a strong dungeon. At the same time Tristram was delivered, and soon sailed openly away from Cornwall with La Belle Isolde, gladly shaking the dust of that realm of treachery from his feet.

In due time the vessel touched shore in King Arthur's dominions, and gladly throbbed the heart of the long-unhappy queen as her feet touched that free and friendly soil. As for Tristram, never was lover fuller of joy, and life seemed to him to have just begun.

Not long had they landed when a knightly chance brought Lancelot into their company. Warm indeed was the greeting of those two noble companions, and glad the welcome which Lancelot gave Isolde to English soil.

"You have done well," he said, "to fly from that wolf's den. There is no noble knight in the world but hates King Mark and will honor you for leaving his palace of vile devices. Come with me, you shall be housed at my expense."

Then he rode with them to his own castle of Joyous Gard, a noble stronghold which he had won with his own hands. A royal castle it was, garnished and provided with a richness which no king or queen could surpass. Here Lancelot bade them use everything as their own, and charged all his people to love and honor them as they would himself.

"Joyous Gard is yours as long as you will honor it by making it your home," he said. "As for me, I can have no greater joy than to know that my castle is so nobly tenanted, and that Tristram of Lyonesse and Queen Isolde are my honored guests."

Leaving them, Lancelot rode to Camelot, where he told Arthur and Guenever of what had happened, much to their joy and delight.

"By my crown," cried Arthur, joyfully, "the coming of Tristram and Isolde to my realm is no everyday event, and is worthy of the highest honor. We must signalize it with a noble tournament."

Then he gave orders that a stately passage-at-arms should be held on May Day at the castle of Lonazep, which was near Joyous Gard. And word was sent far and near that the knights of his own realm of Logris, with those of Cornwall and North Wales, would be pitted against those of the rest of England, of Ireland and Scotland, and of lands beyond the seas.

Chapter II
How Tristram Befooled Dinadan

NEVER WERE TWO happier lovers than Tristram and Isolde at Joyous Gard. Their days were spent in feasting and merriment, Isolde's heart overflowing with joy to be free from the jealousy of her ill-tempered spouse, and Tristram's to

have his lady love to himself, far from treacherous plots and murderous devices.

Every day Tristram went hunting, for at that time men say he was the best courser at the chase in the world, and the rarest blower of the horn among all lovers of sport. From him, it is said, came all the terms of hunting and hawking, the distinction between beasts of the chase and vermin, all methods of dealing with hounds and with game, and all the blasts of the chase and the recall, so that they who delight in huntsmen's sport will have cause to the world's end to love Sir Tristram and pray for his soul's repose.

Yet Isolde at length grew anxious for his welfare, and said:

"I marvel that you ride so much to the chase unarmed. This is a country not well known to you, and one that contains many false knights, while King Mark may lay some plot for your destruction. I pray you, my dear love, to take more heed to your safety."

This advice seemed timely, and thereafter Tristram rode in armor to the chase, and followed by men who bore his shield and spear. One day, a little before the month of May, he followed a hart eagerly, but as the animal led him by a cool woodland spring, he alighted to quench his thirst in the gurgling waters.

Here, by chance, he met with Dinadan, who had come into that country in search of him. Some words of greeting passed between them, after which Dinadan asked him his name, telling his own. This confidence Tristram declined to return, whereupon Dinadan burst out in anger.

"You value your name highly, sir knight," he said. "Do you design to ride everywhere under a mask? Such a foolish knight as you I saw but lately lying by a well. He seemed like one asleep, and no word could be got from him, yet all the time he grinned like a fool. The fellow was either an idiot or a lover, I know not which."

"And are not you a lover?" asked Tristram.

"Marry, my wit has saved me from that craft."

"That is not well said," answered Tristram. "A knight who disdains love is but half a man, and not half a warrior."

"I am ready to stand by my creed," retorted Dinadan. "As for you, sirrah, you shall tell me your name, or do battle with me."

"You will not get my name by a threat, I promise you that," said Tristram. "I shall not fight till I am in the mood; and when I do, you may get more than you bargain for."

"I fear you not, coward," said Dinadan.

"If you are so full of valor, here is your man," said Tristram, pointing to a knight who rode along the forest aisle towards them. "He looks ready for a joust."

"On my life, it is the same dull-plate knave I saw lying by the well, neither sleeping nor waking," said Dinadan.

"This is not the first time I have seen that covered shield of azure," said Tristram. "This knight is Sir Epinegris, the son of the king of Northumberland, than whom the land holds no more ardent lover, for his heart is gone utterly out to the fair daughter of the king of Wales. Now, if you care to find whether a lover or a non-lover is the better knight, here is your opportunity."

"I shall teach him to grin to more purpose," said Dinadan. "Stand by and you shall see."

Then, as the lover approached, he cried:

"Halt, sir knight, and make ready to joust, as is the custom with errant knights."

"Let it be so, if you will," answered Epinegris. "Since it is the custom of you knight-errant to make a man joust whether he will or no, I am your man."

"Make ready, then, for here is for you."

Then they spurred their horses and rode together at full speed, Dinadan breaking his spear, while Epinegris struck him so shrewd a blow that he rolled upon the earth.

"How now?" cried Tristram. "It seems to me that the lover has best sped."

"Will you play the coward?" queried Dinadan. "Or will you, like a good knight, revenge me?"

"I am not in the mood," answered Tristram. "Take your horse, Sir Dinadan, and let us get away from here, where hard blows are more plentiful than soft beds."

"Defend me from such fellowship as yours!" roared Dinadan. "Take your way and I will take mine. We fit not well together."

"I might give you news of Sir Tristram."

"Sir Tristram, if he be wise, will seek better company. I can do without your news, as I have had to do without your help," and he rode on in high dudgeon.

"Farewell, then," cried Tristram, laughing. "It may happen we shall soon meet again."

Tristram rode back in much amusement to Joyous Gard, but on coming near he heard in the neighboring town a great outcry.

"What means this noise?" he asked.

"Sir," he was told, "a knight of the castle has just been slain by two strangers, and for no other cause than saying that Sir Lancelot was a better knight than Sir Gawaine."

"Who would dispute that?" said Tristram. "It is a small cause for the death of a good man, that he stands for his lord's fame."

"But what remedy have we?" said the townsmen. "If Lancelot had been here, these fellows would soon have been called to a reckoning. But, alas, he is away."

"I may do something in his service," answered Tristram. "If I take his place, I must defend his followers."

Thereupon he sent for his shield and spear, and rode in pursuit of the two knights, whom he overtook before they had gone far.

"Turn, sir dastards," he cried, "and amend your misdeeds."

"What amends wish you?" asked one of the knights. "We are ready with spear and sword to make good whatever we have done."

He rode against Tristram, but was met so sturdily in mid-career that he was thrust over his horse's tail. Then the other rode against him, and was served in the same rough manner.

They rose as quickly as they could, drew their swords, and challenged him to battle on foot.

"You shall tell me your names," he said, sternly. "I warn you that if it comes to sword-play you will find more than your match. Yet you may have that in your lineage which will keep you from my hands, however much you deserve punishment for your evil deeds."

"As for our names, we dread not to tell them. We are Agravaine and Gaheris, brothers to the good knight Gawaine, and nephews of King Arthur."

"For Arthur's sake, then, I must let you pass unscathed. Yet it is a crying shame that men of such good blood as you should play the part of murderers. You slew among you a better knight than the best of your kin, Lamorak de Galis, and I would to God I had been by at that time."

"You would have gone the same road," said Gaheris.

"Not without more knights to do it than you had in your murderous crew."

With these words he turned from them and rode back towards Joyous Gard. When he had gone they regained their horses, and feeling themselves safe in the saddle their courage returned.

"Let us pursue this boaster," they said, "and see if he fares so much better than Lamorak."

They did so, and when they came near Tristram, who was jogging slowly along, Agravaine cried:

"Turn, traitor knight!"

"Traitor in your teeth!" cried Tristram, in a rage. "I let you off too cheaply, it seems." And drawing his sword, he turned upon Agravaine and smote him so fiercely on the helm that he fell swooning from his horse, with a dangerous wound.

Then he turned to Gaheris and dealt him a blow that in like manner tumbled him from his saddle to the earth. This done, Tristram turned and rode into the castle, leaving them like dead men in the road.

Here he told La Belle Isolde of his several adventures. When he spoke of Dinadan, she asked:

"Was it not he that made the song about King Mark?"

"The same," answered Tristram. "He is the greatest jester at Arthur's court, but a good knight withal, and I know no man whom I like better as a comrade."

"Why did you not bring him with you?"

"No need of that. He is seeking me through this country, and there is no fear that he will give up the search lightly."

As they spoke, a servant came and told Tristram that a knight-errant had entered the town, and described the device on his shield.

"That is our man now," said Tristram. "That is Dinadan. Send for him, Isolde, and you shall hear the merriest knight and the maddest talker that you ever spoke with. I pray you to make him heartily welcome, for he is a cherished friend of mine."

Then Isolde sent into the town with a message to Dinadan, begging that he would come to the castle and rest a while there, at a lady's wish.

"That will I, with a good will," answered Dinadan. "I were but a churl else."

He hastened to mount and ride to the castle, and here he was shown to a chamber where he laid aside his armor. Then he was brought into the presence of La Belle Isolde, who courteously bade him welcome.

"Whence, come you, and what name do you bear?" she asked.

"Madam," he answered, "I am from King Arthur's court, and am one of the small fry of Round Table Knights. My name is Dinadan."

"And why came you hither?"

"I am seeking my old friend and comrade, Sir Tristram, who I am told has made his way to this country."

"That I cannot answer for," said Isolde. "He may and he may not be here. Sir Tristram will be found where love leads him."

"I warrant me that. Your true lover has no will of his own, but is led like an ox, with a ring in his nose. I marvel what juice of folly gets into the pates of these lovers to make them so mad about the women."

"Why, sir," said Isolde, "can it be that you are a knight and no lover? I fancy that there can be no true man-of-arms who seeks not by his deeds to win the smiles of the fair."

"They who care to be fed on smiles are welcome to them, but I am not made of that fashion," answered Dinadan. "The joy of love is too short, and the sorrow thereof too long, to please my fancy."

"Say you so? Yet near here but today was the good knight Sir Bleoberis, he who fought with three knights at once for a maiden's sake, and won her before the king of Northumberland."

"I know him for a worthy fellow," said Dinadan, "as are all of Lancelot's kindred. Yet he has crotchets in his head, like all that crew."

"Now, I pray you," said Isolde, "will you not do me the grace to fight for my love with three knights that have done me great wrong? As you are a knight of King Arthur's, you can never say me nay in such a duty."

"Can I not?" cried Dinadan. "This much I will say, madam, that you are as fair a sample of womankind as ever I saw, and much more beautiful than is my lady Queen Guenever. And yet, heaven defend me, I will not fight for you against three knights; and would not, were you Helen of Troy herself."

At these words, and the odd grimace which he made, La Belle Isolde burst into a merry peal of laughter, and broke out with:

"I know you better than you fancy, Sir Dinadan. And well you keep up your credit of being a merry fellow. You are very welcome to my castle, good sir."

They had much more of gameful conversation together, and Dinadan was treated with all honor, and slept serenely at the castle that night. But Tristram took good care to keep out of his sight.

Early the next day Tristram armed himself and prepared to ride away, saying to the Lady Isolde that he would contrive to meet with Dinadan, and would ride with him to Lonazep, where the tournament was to be held. He promised also to make arrangements to provide her with a good place from which to see the passage-at-arms. Then he departed, accompanied by two squires, who bore his shield and a brace of great and long spears.

Shortly afterwards Dinadan left the castle, bidding a merry adieu to the lady, and rode so briskly forward that he soon overtook Tristram. He knew him at sight for his yesterday's comrade, and made a sour grimace at beholding him.

"So," he said, "here again is my easy-going friend, who wears his armor for a holiday parade. You shall not get off so lightly today, fellow. You shall joust with me, despite your head."

"Faith, I am not eager," said Tristram, "but a wilful man will have his way; so let us have it over, if fight we must."

Then they rode at each other, and Dinadan broke a spear on Tristram's shield, but Tristram purposely missed him.

Dinadan now bade him draw his sword.

"Not I," he answered. "What makes you so warlike? I am not in the humor to fight."

"You shame all knights by your cowardice."

"So far as that goes, it troubles me little," said Tristram. "Suppose, my good sir, you take me under your protection. Though I bear arms I shall gladly accept the patronage of so worthy a knight as you."

"The devil deliver me of you!" cried Dinadan. "You are a fellow of goodly build, and sit your horse like a warrior; but heaven knows if you have blood or water in your veins. What do you propose to do with those great spears that your squire carries?"

"I shall give them to some good knight at the tournament. If you prove the best there, you are welcome to them."

As they thus conversed they saw a knight-errant in the road before them, who sat with spear in rest as if eager to joust.

"Come," said Tristram, "since you are so anxious for a fight, yonder is your man."

"Shame betide you for a dastard," cried Dinadan. "Fight him yourself. You can't get more than a fall."

"Not so. That knight seems a shrewish fellow. It will need a stronger hand than mine to manage him."

"Good faith, then, here's to teach you a lesson," said Dinadan, and he rode fiercely against the other knight, with the unlucky result that he was thrust from his horse, and fell headlong to the earth.

"What did I tell you?" said Tristram. "You had better have taken a lesson from my prudence, and let that good fellow alone."

"The fiends take you, coward!" cried Dinadan, as he started to his feet and drew his sword. "Come, sir knight, you are my better on horseback, let us have it out on foot."

"Shall it be in love or in anger?" said the other.

"Let it be in love. I am saving all my anger for this do-nothing who came with me."

"Then I pray you to tell me your name."

"Folks call me Dinadan."

"Ah, and I am your comrade Gareth. I will not fight with an old friend like Dinadan."

"Nor I with you, by my faith!" cried Dinadan, seizing Gareth's hand and giving it a warm pressure. "Beaumains is safe from my spear. Here is a chap now, if you want to try your skill; but if you can get him to fight you must first learn the art of converting a coward into a man of valor."

Tristram laughed quietly at this, and bided his time. Nor was there long to wait, for just then a well-armed knight rode up, on a sturdy horse, and put his spear in rest as he approached.

"Now, my good sirs," said Tristram, "choose between yourselves which will joust with yonder knight; for I warn you that I will keep clear of him."

"Faith, you had better," said Gareth. "Leave him to me."

And he rode against the knight but with such ill-fortune that he was thrust over his horse's croup.

"It is your turn now," said Tristram to Dinadan. "Honor requires that you should avenge your comrade Gareth."

"Honor does, eh? Then reason does not, and I always weigh reason against honor. He has overturned a much bigger fellow than I, and with your kind permission I will not stir up that hornet."

"Aha, friend Dinadan, your heart fails you after all your boasting. Very well, you shall see what the coward can do. Make ready, sir knight."

Then Tristram rode against the victorious knight, and dealt him so shrewd a buffet that he was thrust from his horse.

Dinadan looked at this in amazement. Was this the fellow that professed cowardice and begged protection? "The cunning rogue," he said to himself, "has been making game of me. The rascal! where has he learned the art of turning my weapons on myself?"

The dismounted knight rose to his feet in anger, and drawing his sword, challenged Tristram to a fight on foot.

"First, tell me your name?" asked Tristram.

"My name is Palamides."

"And what knight hate you most?"

"I hate Sir Tristram to the death. If we meet, one of us must die."

"You need not go far to seek him. I am Tristram de Lyonesse. Now do your worst."

At this Dinadan started, and struck his hand sturdily on his knee, like one who has had a shock of surprise. Nor was Palamides less astonished, and he stood before Tristram like one in a sudden revulsion of feeling.

"I pray you, Sir Tristram," he said, "to forgive my ill-will and my unkind words. You are a noble knight and worthy of the love of all honorable warriors. I repent my truculent temper towards you, and, if I live, will rather do you service than assail you."

"I know your valor well," answered Tristram, "and that it is anything but fear makes you speak so. Therefore I thank you much for your kind words. But if you have any shreds of ill-will towards me I am ready to give you satisfaction."

"My wits have been astray," answered Palamides. "There is no just reason why we should be at odds, and I am ready to do you knightly service in all things you may command."

"I take you at your word," cried Tristram, as he grasped Palamides by the hand. "I have never been your enemy, and know none whom I would rather have as a friend."

"Would you?" cried Dinadan. "And would have me as your fool, mayhap? By my knightly faith, you have made a sweet butt of me! I came into this country for your sake, and by the advice of Sir Lancelot, though he would not tell me where to find you. By Jove's ears, I never thought to find you masquerading as a milk-brained coward."

"He could have told you," said Tristram, "for I abode within his own castle. As for my little sport, friend Dinadan, I cry you mercy."

"Faith, it is but one of my own jests, turned against me," said Dinadan, with a merry laugh. "I am pinked with my own dart. I forgive you, old comrade; but I vow I did not know you had such a jolly humor."

"It comes to one in your company," said Tristram, laughing. "The disease is catching."

And so the four knights rode gayly onward, conversing much as they went, and laying their plans for the tournament.

Chapter III
On the Road to Lonazep

THE FOUR KNIGHTS rode onward in company until they came in sight of the castle of Lonazep, where they saw striking preparations for the tournament. For not less than four hundred tents and pavilions covered the plain outside the

great circle of the lists, and war-horses and knights in armor were there in hundreds.

"Truly," said Tristram, "this is the royalest show that I ever saw."

"You forget," answered Palamides. "It had its equal at the Castle of Maidens, where you won the prize."

"And in that tournament which Galahalt of the Long Isles held in Surluse there was as great a gathering," said Dinadan.

"I was not there; who won the prize?" asked Tristram.

"Lancelot du Lac, and the next after him was the noble knight Lamorak de Galis."

"A noble fellow, indeed, I never met his better, save Sir Lancelot. His murder was shameful, and were they not the nephews of my lord Arthur that slew him, by my faith they should die the death. And this without prejudice to you, Sir Gareth."

"Say what you will on that point; I am with you," answered Gareth. "Though my own brothers did that bloody work, I hold not with them. None of them love me, as you well know, and I have left their company as murderers. Had I been by when Lamorak was killed there might have been another tale to tell."

"Truly that is well said of you," rejoined Tristram. "I would rather have been there than to have all the gold between here and Rome."

"And I also," said Palamides. "It is a burning disgrace to the Round Table fellowship that such a knight should have been ambushed and slain on his way from a passage-at-arms where he had won the prize of valor."

"Out on such treason!" cried Tristram. "The tale of it makes my blood run cold."

"And mine as well," said Gareth. "I can never love or respect my brothers again for that ruthless deed."

"Yet to speak of it is useless," said Palamides. "His life is gone; we cannot bring it back again."

"There lies the pity," said Dinadan. "No matter how good and noble a man may be, when he stops breathing all else stops with him. By good luck, though, the same rule holds with villains and cowards. As for Gawaine and his brothers, except you, Sir Gareth, they hate the best knights of the Round Table, and Lancelot and his kindred above all. Only that Lancelot is well aware of this, they might draw him into as deadly a trap as they drew poor Lamorak."

"Come, come, remember that Gareth is their brother," said Palamides. "Let us change the subject. Here is this tournament,—what part shall we play here? My advice is that we four hold together against all that may assail us."

"That is not my counsel," said Tristram. "By their pavilions we may count on some four hundred knights, and doubtless many of them worthy ones. If we play the game of four against all comers we are likely to find ourselves borne down by numbers. Many good knights have lost the game by taking too great odds. Manhood is of little avail if it be not tempered by wisdom. If you think it best we may try it, and see what we can do in company, but, as a rule, I prefer to fight for my own hand."

As they thus talked they rode away from Lonazep, and in due time came to the banks of the Humber, where they were surprised by a loud and grievous cry that seemed full of doleful meaning. Looking over the waters they saw approaching before the wind a vessel richly draped with red silk. Not long had they waited when it came to the shore, at a point close by where they stood.

Seeing this strange thing and hearing the doleful cries which came from the vessel, the knights gave their horses in care of their squires, and approached on foot, Tristram boarding the vessel. When he reached the deck he saw there a bed with rich silken coverings, on which lay a dead knight, armed save the head, which was crimsoned with blood. And through great gaps in his armor deadly wounds could be seen.

"What means this?" said Tristram. "How came this knight by his death?"

As he spoke he saw that a letter lay in the dead knight's hand.

"Master mariners," he asked of those on board the vessel, "what does this strange thing signify?"

"Sir knight," they answered, "by the letter which the dead knight bears you may learn how and for what cause he was slain, and what name he bore. Yet first heed well this warning: No man must take and read that letter unless he be a knight of proved valor, and faithfully promises to revenge the murder of this good warrior."

"There be those among us able to revenge him," answered Tristram. "And if he shall prove to have been foully treated his death shall not go unredressed."

Therewith he took the letter from the knight's hand and opened it. Thus it read:

"I, Hermance, king and lord of the Red City, request of all knights-errant and all noble knights of Arthur's court, that they find one knight who will fight for my sake with two false brethren, whom I brought up from nothingness and who have feloniously and treacherously slain me. And it is my will and desire that the valiant knight who avenges my death shall become lord of my Red City and all my castles."

"Sir," said the mariners, "the king and knight that lies here dead was a man of great virtue and noble prowess, and one who loved all knights-errant, and, above all, those of King Arthur's court."

"It is a piteous case, truly," said Tristram. "I would fain take the enterprise in hand myself, but that I have made a solemn promise to take part in this great tournament. It was for my sake in especial that my lord Arthur made it, and I cannot in honor and courtesy fail to attend it. Therefore I am not free to undertake any adventure which may keep me from the lists."

"I pray you, dear sir," said Palamides, who had followed Tristram into the vessel, "to put this enterprise into my hands. I promise to achieve it worthily or to die in the effort."

"Be it so," said Tristram. "You may go if you will. But first I wish your promise to return so as to be with me at the tournament this day week, if possible."

"That promise I freely give. If I be alive and unhurt, and my task be not too arduous and long, I shall be with you by that day."

This said, Tristram left the vessel, leaving Palamides in it, and he, with Gareth and Dinadan, stood watching it as the mariners hoisted its sails and it glided swiftly away over long Humber. Not till it was out of sight did they return to their horses, and look about them.

As they did so they beheld near them a knight, who came up unarmed save a sword, and saluted them with all courtesy.

"Fair sirs," he said, "I pray you, as knights-errant, to come and see my castle, and take such fare as you may find there. This I heartily request."

"That shall we willingly do, and thank you for your courtesy," they answered, and rode with him to his castle, which was nearby.

Here they entered a richly-furnished hall, and, having laid off their armor, took their seats at a well-laden table. But when the host saw Tristram's face, he knew him, and first grew pale and then angry of countenance.

"Sir, mine host," said Tristram, on seeing this threatening aspect, "what is wrong with you, I pray?"

"I know you, Tristram de Lyonesse," answered the knight, hotly. "You slew my brother. Honor demands that I shall not seek revenge here, but I give you warning that I will kill you when I meet you outside my castle."

"I have no knowledge of you or your brother," answered Tristram. "But no man can say that I ever killed any one except in fair and open fight. If I have done as you say I stand ready to make what amends are in my power."

"I desire no amends," rejoined the knight. "But I warn you to keep from me."

Tristram at this rose from the table and asked for his arms, his companions following him. Seeking their horses they rode away, but they had not gone far from the castle when Dinadan saw a knight following them, who was well armed, but bore no shield.

"Take care of yourself, Sir Tristram," he said. "Yonder comes our host to call you to account."

"Then I must abide him as I may," answered Tristram.

Soon the knight came up, and, loudly bidding Tristram to be on his guard, he rode furiously upon him with couched spear. But his valor went beyond his strength, for he was hurled over his horse's croup.

Not content with this, he rose, mounted again, and driving his horse at full speed upon Tristram, struck him two hard blows on the helm.

"Sir knight," said Tristram, "I pray you leave off this sport. I do not care to harm you after having just eaten at your table, but beg you not to try my patience too far."

The furious assailant would not cease, however, and continued his assaults until Tristram was provoked to anger. In the end he returned the knight a blow with the full strength of his mighty arm, so fierce a buffet, indeed, that the blood burst out from the breathing holes of his helm, and he fell to the earth and lay there like one dead.

"I hope I have not killed him," said Tristram. "I did not think to strike the man so hard a blow, but I am not a log to stand at rest and let him whet his sword on."

Leaving the fallen knight to the care of his squire, they rode on; but not far had they gone when they saw coming towards them two well-armed and well-horsed knights, each with a good following of servants. One of these was Berrant le Apres, he who was called the king with the hundred knights, and the other Sir Segwarides, both men of might and renown.

When they came up the king looked at Dinadan, who, through sport, had put on Tristram's helmet. This he recognized as one he had seen before with the queen of Northgalis, whom he loved. She had given it to La Belle Isolde, and she to Tristram.

"Sir knight," asked Berrant, "whence had you that helm?"

"Not from you, I fancy. What have you to say to it?"

"That I will have a tilt with you, for the love of her who once owned it. Therefore, defend yourself."

So they drew asunder, and rode at each other with all the speed of their horses. But Dinadan, good knight as he was, was no match for the tough and hardy warrior before him, and was sent, horse and all, to the ground.

"I fancy I have something to say about the helmet now," said Berrant, grimly. "Go take it off him, and keep it," he ordered his servant.

"What will you do?" cried Tristram. "Hands off, fellow. Touch not that helm."

"To what intent do you meddle, sir knight?" demanded Berrant.

"To this intent, that the helm is mine. Nor will you get it from me till you buy it at a dearer price."

"Do you mean that as a challenge?" asked Berrant. "Be it so, then; make ready."

Together they rode with all speed, but with a change of fortune, for Berrant found himself thrust over the tail of his horse. In a moment he was on his feet, sprang briskly to his saddle, and, riding in anger upon Tristram, struck at him fiercely with his sword.

Tristram was not taken unawares, but in an instant had his sword in hand. A fierce combat followed, for the king with the hundred knights was a warrior of tough sinews and tried valor, but at the last he received such a buffet on the helm that he fell forward on his horse's neck, stunned and helpless.

"By my faith, that helmet has proved unlucky for two of us," said Dinadan. "It brought me a tumble, and now, sir king, you owe it a buzzing head-piece."

"Who will joust with me?" asked Segwarides.

"It is your right," said Gareth to Dinadan, "but I pray you let me have it."

"You are heartily welcome to it. One tumble a day is enough for my weak appetite," answered Dinadan. "I make you a free present of the opportunity."

"That is no fair exchange," said Tristram. "The joust is yours by right."

"But not by choice," rejoined Dinadan. "Good faith, sir bruiser, I have lived long enough to know when I have had my share, and that is a lesson it would pay many of you battle-hungry knights to learn."

Then Gareth and Segwarides rode together, the result being that Gareth and his horse went in a heap to the earth.

"Now," said Tristram, "the joust is yours."

"But the appetite is lacking," said Dinadan. "I have even less stomach for it than before."

"Then will I try him."

With these words Tristram challenged Segwarides, who received a sore fall in the joust that followed. Then the three knights rode on, leaving their late antagonists the worse in heart and limb for the encounter.

They continued their ride till they reached Joyous Gard. Here Gareth courteously declined to enter the castle, but Tristram would not hear of his departure, and made him alight and enter as his guest. So they disarmed and had good cheer, with La Belle Isolde as their hostess.

But Dinadan, when he came into the presence of Isolde, roundly cursed the hour that he had been persuaded to wear Tristram's helm, and told her of how he had been mocked by his comrade knight.

Much laughing and jesting at Dinadan followed, but this was a game in which he was quite able to hold his own, however he might lack with sword and spear. For Arthur's court held no other so witty of tongue and merry of heart. And thus in jest and feast they passed the hours happily away.

Chapter IV
How Palamides Fared at the Red City

LEAVING TRISTRAM and his companions to their merry talk in Joyous Gard, we must now return to Palamides. The ship into which he had entered sailed far along the Humber, until in time it reached the open sea. It continued its course through the sea-waves till it came to a part of the coast where stood a stately castle.

All day and night they had sailed, and it was now early in the morning, before day-dawn. Palamides was sound asleep in the vessel's cabin when the mariners came to call him.

"Sir knight," they said, "you must arise. We have reached a castle, which you must enter."

"I am at your command," he replied.

Rising, he armed himself quickly, and then blew a loud call upon a horn which the mariners gave him.

At the ringing music of that bugle-blast the sleeping castle seemed to stir into life. Soon many eyes could be seen looking from the windows, and ere long the walls were crowded with knights, who called to Palamides as with one voice, "Welcome, fair sir, to this castle."

The day had now fully dawned, and Palamides entered the castle, where a crowd of knights came to greet him, and led him to a stately dining-hall, where an abundant breakfast awaited him. But as he ate he heard much lamentation, and saw many whose eyes were wet with tears.

"What means this?" he asked. "I love not such sorrow, and would fain know what gives rise to it."

"We mourn here daily," answered a knight named Sir Ebel, "and for this cause. We had a king named Hermance, who was lord of the Red City, and in every way a noble and generous monarch. And he loved nothing in the world so much as the knights-errant of King Arthur's court, together with the sports of jousting, hunting, and all knightly diversions. A king so kind of heart as he was never before known in this country, and we shall ever be filled with sorrow for his loss. Yet he acted unwisely, and is himself at fault for his death."

"Tell me how he was slain and by whom," asked Palamides.

"In this wise it came to pass," answered Ebel. "He brought up, in pure charity, two children, who are now strong knights. And to them he gave all his trust and confidence, in default of those of his own blood. These two men governed him completely, and, through him, his lands and people, for they took the best of care that none of his kindred should come into power. He was so free and trustful, and they so politic and deceitful, that they ruled him as though they were the kings and he the subject. When the lords of our king's blood saw that he had fallen into this dotage they left the court in disgust, and sought their livelihood elsewhere. This it proved not wise to do, for when these villains found that all the king's kindred had left the realm they schemed to have more power still; for, as the old saw says, 'Give a churl rule in part, and he will not be content till he has it all.' It is the instinct of the base-born to destroy gentlemen-born, if the power be put in their hands, and all rulers should take warning by the fate of King Hermance. In the end our king, by the advice of these traitors, rode into the forest here by, to chase the red deer. When he had become warm from the hunt he alighted to drink at a woodland spring, and, while he was bent over the water, one of these villains thrust him through the body with a spear. They then fled from the spot, thinking he was dead. Shortly after they had gone, fortune brought me to the spot, where I found my lord still alive, but mortally hurt, and learned from him his story. Knowing that we had no knights able to revenge him on his murderers, I had him brought to the water, and put into the ship alive, and the letter which he bore in his hand I wrote from his own words. Then he died, and, as he had ordered, the ship set sail up the Humber, bound for the realm of Logris, where it was hoped that some valiant Knight of the Round Table would take this adventure on himself."

"Truly your doleful tale grieves me sorely," said Palamides. "I saw the letter you speak of. It was read to me by one of the best knights upon the earth, and it is by his command I am here. I came to revenge your king, and I shall never be at ease till I meet with and punish his murderers."

"You have my hearty thanks and best wishes," said Ebel. "Since you accept this adventure, you must enter the ship again, and sail forward till you reach the Delectable Isle, which is nearby the Red City. We shall await here your return. If you speed well this castle is yours. King Hermance built it for the two traitors, but we hold it against them, and they threaten us sorely unless we yield it."

"Look that you keep it, whatsoever may come to me," said Palamides. "For if fortune decides that I am to be slain in this quest, I trust that one of the best knights in the world will come to revenge me; either Tristram de Lyonesse or Lancelot du Lac."

Then Palamides entered the ship and sailed away towards the Red City. But as he came near it, and landed on the coast, another ship touched shore nearby, from which came a goodly knight, with his shield on his shoulder and his hand on his sword.

"Sir knight, what seek you here?" he asked Palamides. "If you have come to revenge King Hermance you must yield this quest to me, for it was mine before it was yours, and I shall yield it to no man."

"You speak like a true knight," said Palamides. "But when the letter was taken from the dead king's hand there was nothing known of any champion for him, and so I promised to revenge him. And this I must and shall do, lest I win shame instead of honor."

"You have right on your side," said the knight. "What I propose is this. I will fight with you; and he who proves the better knight shall have the quest."

"That fits with my fancy," said Palamides; "for from what I hear no second-rate champion can watch this pair of villains."

With this they advanced their shields and drew their swords, and began a stern and well-contested combat. For more than an hour the fight between them continued, but at the end of this time Palamides seemed stronger and better-winded than at the beginning, and he finally dealt his opponent a blow that brought him to his knees. Then the discomfited combatant cried out:

"Knight, hold your hand."

Palamides let fall his sword at this request.

"You are the better of us two, and more worthy of this battle," said the knight. "But fain would I know your name."

"My name is Palamides. I am a Knight of the Round Table, and one well known in Arthur's realm."

"In good faith it is, and much beyond that realm," answered the knight. "I know only three living men besides yourself who are fitted for this task, and they are Lancelot, Tristram, and my cousin Lamorak. As for me, my name is Hermind, and I am brother to the murdered King Hermance."

"I shall do my best to revenge your brother," said Palamides. "If I am slain, I commend you to Lancelot or Tristram. As for Lamorak, he will never strike blow again."

"Alas, what mean you?"

"That he has been murdered – waylaid and slain treacherously by Gawaine and his brothers, except Sir Gareth, the best of them all." And he told the story of the death of Lamorak, much to the grief and indignation of his hearer.

Then Palamides took ship again, and sailed on till he came to the Delectable Isle. Meanwhile Hermind made all haste to the Red City, where he told of the arrival of the famous knight Palamides and of his combat with him. The people were filled with joy at these tidings, and quickly sent a messenger to the two brethren, bidding them to make ready, as a knight had come who would fight them both. The messenger found them at a castle nearby, and delivered his message.

"Who is this champion?" they asked. "Is it Lancelot or any of his blood?"

"No."

"If it were, we would not fight. But we care for no one else."

"It is a good knight though, Sir Palamides, a Saracen by birth, and still unchristened."

"He had best have been christened before he came here, for it will be too late when we have done with him. Let him know that we will be at the Red City in two days, and will give him all the fighting he is likely to want for the rest of his life."

When Palamides came to the city he was received with the greatest joy, and the more so when the people saw what a handsome and well-built man he was, neither too young nor too old, with clean and powerful limbs, and no defect of body.

At the time appointed there came to the city the two brethren, Helius and Helake by name, both of them strong and valiant men, of great prowess in war, false as they were at heart. And with them they brought forty knights, to guard them against any treachery from the Red City, for they knew well that it was filled with their enemies.

The lists had already been prepared, and at the appointed hour Palamides entered full armed, and confronted his antagonists boldly.

"Are you the two brethren Helius and Helake, who slew your king by treason?" he asked.

"We are the men who slew King Hermance," they replied. "And bear in mind, Sir Saracen, we are able to stand by our deeds, and will handle you so before you depart that you will wish you had been christened before you came so far."

"I trust to God I shall die a better Christian than either of you," Palamides replied. "And you had best kill me if you get the chance, for I vow not to spare you."

As he spoke the trumpet sounded, and, reining back their horses, they rode against each other with terrific speed. Palamides directed his spear against Helake, and struck him so mighty a blow that the spear pierced through his shield and hauberk, and for a fathom's length through his breast, hurling him dead to the earth. As for Helius, he held up his spear in pride and presumption, and rode by Palamides without touching him.

But when he saw his brother stretched in death on the earth his assurance changed to doubt, and rage drove the pride from his heart. "Help thyself, villain!" he cried, and rushed upon Palamides before he could prepare to encounter him, striking him a blow with his spear that bore him from his saddle to the earth. Then he forced his horse over him backward and forward before the dismounted champion could regain his feet.

As he came again, the fallen knight reached up and caught the horse by the bridle, dragging himself by its aid to his feet. Then, as the animal reared, he pressed so strongly upon it that it toppled backward to the ground, the rider barely saving himself from being crushed beneath his fallen horse. But he was on his feet in an instant, and, sword in hand, struck Palamides a blow on the helm that brought him down to one knee.

Before he could repeat the blow the gallant Saracen was on his feet and had drawn his trenchant blade, with which he attacked his antagonist in turn. A fierce and deadly combat succeeded, the two knights hurtling together like two wild boars, now both hurled grovelling to the earth, now on foot again and hewing at each other with the strength of giants.

Thus for two hours they fought, without time for rest or a moment's space to recover breath. At the end of that time Palamides grew faint and weary from the violence of his efforts, but Helius seemed as strong as ever, and redoubling his strokes he drove back the Saracen knight step by step, over all the field. At this the people of the city were filled with fear, while the party of Helius shouted with triumph.

"Alas!" cried the citizens, "that this noble knight should be slain for our king's sake."

While they thus bewailed his threatened fate and the seeming victory of their tyrant, Helius showered so many vigorous blows on his weakened foe that it was a wonder he kept his feet. But when he saw how the common people wept for him his heart was filled with a sense of shame, while a glow of fury burned like fire in his veins.

"Fie on you for a dastard, Palamides!" he said to himself. "Why hang you your head so like a whipped hound?"

Then, with a new spirit burning hotly within him, and fresh strength animating his limbs, he lifted his drooping shield and turned on Helius with lion-like fury, smiting him a vigorous blow on the helm, which he followed quickly by others. This violent onset was too much for the strained strength of the false knight, and he retreated in dismay, while the sword of Palamides fell with ever more and more might. At length came so mighty a blow that he was hurled like a log to the earth. The victorious Saracen gave him no time to recover, but sprang upon him like a fury, tore the helm from his head, and with a final stroke smote the head from his body.

Then he rose and stood leaning upon his sword, hardly able to bear himself on his feet, while from all the people of the city went up loud shouts of joy and congratulation.

"Palamides, the conqueror! Palamides, our deliverer! Palamides, our king!" they shouted, while one adorned his brows with a wreath of laurel, and others tore off his armor and applied ointments to his bleeding limbs.

"Fair friends, your crown is not for me," he said. "I have delivered you from your tyrants, but you must choose some other king, as I am under promise to return with all speed to my lord King Arthur at the castle of Lonazep."

This decision filled them with grief, but they brought him to the city and treated him with all the honor which they could bestow upon him. And as he persisted in his refusal of the crown, they proffered him a third part of their goods if he would remain with them. All this he declined, and in a short time departed, bearing with him a thousand good wishes and prayers for success and fortune.

He was received with like joy and congratulation at the castle, Sir Ebel warmly pressing him to change his decision and remain as their king. To this Palamides would by no means consent, and after a day's stay he took ship again, and sailed up the Humber to the castle of Lonazep.

Chapter V
The Tournament at Lonazep

WHEN PALAMIDES LEARNED that Tristram was not at Lonazep, he tarried not there, but crossed the Humber, and sought him at Joyous Gard. Here he found lodgings in the town, and word was quickly brought to Tristram that a knight-errant had come.

"What manner of man is he? and what sign does he bear?" he asked.

The messenger described his armor and appearance.

"That is Palamides," said Dinadan. "The brave fellow is already back, and victorious, I doubt not."

"It looks that way, indeed. Go and bid him welcome to Joyous Gard," said Tristram.

So Dinadan went to Palamides, and joyfully greeted him, listening eagerly to the story of his exploits, and congratulating him on his signal success. He remained with him that night, and in the morning they were visited by Tristram and Gareth before they had arisen.

Many were the warm congratulations which Tristram gave Palamides on his noble achievement, and after they had breakfasted he invited him to ride into the fields and woods, that they might repose under the cool shelter of the forest. Here they alighted by a refreshing spring, and as they sat conversing an armed knight came riding towards them.

"Who are those knights that are lodged in Joyous Gard?" he asked.

"That I cannot say," answered Tristram.

"At any rate you can tell me who you are. You are not knights-errant, I fancy, since you ride unarmed."

"Whether we be or no, we prefer not to tell our names."

"You are not courteous, sir knight, and this is the way I pay discourtesy," said the stranger. "Guard yourself, or you shall die by my hands."

Then, spear in hand, he rode on Sir Tristram, with brutal intent to run him through. But Palamides sprang up hastily, and smote the knight's horse so fierce a blow with his clinched fist that horse and man fell together to the earth. He then drew his sword to slay him.

"Let the dog go," said Tristram. "He is but a fool, and it were a shame to slay him for his folly. Take the fellow's spear from him, though. It is a weapon he has not learned the use of."

The knight rose groaning, and when he had regained his saddle he again requested their names.

"My name is Tristram de Lyonesse, and this knight's name is Palamides. Would you know more?"

"No, by my faith!" cried the other, and, hastily putting spurs to his horse, he rode away as fast as the animal would carry him.

Hardly had he gone when a knight, who bore a bended shield of azure, came riding up at a furious gallop.

"My fair sirs," he asked, "has a knight passed here bearing a shield with a case of red over it?"

"Yes. We but now had some trouble with such a fellow. Who is he?"

"And you let him escape? That was ill-advised, fair sirs. He is the falsest rogue and the greatest foe to knights-errant living. His name is Breuse Sans Pitié."

"And I had him under my sword!" cried Palamides. "Fool I was to let him go."

"If I overtake him there will be another story to tell," answered the knight, as he spurred onward on the track of the fugitive.

Then the four friends mounted and rode leisurely back towards Joyous Gard, much conversing as they went. When they reached the castle Palamides wished not to enter, but Tristram insisted on it, and, taking him by the hand, led him in.

When Palamides saw La Belle Isolde, whom he had not met for years, but for whom his love burned as warmly as ever, he was so ravished with joy that he could scarcely speak. And when they were at dinner he could not eat a morsel, but sat like a dumb man, scarcely venturing to raise his eyes to Isolde's lovely countenance.

Poorly he slept that night, and with many dreams of her he loved. When morning broke they all prepared to ride to Lonazep. Tristram took with him three squires, and Queen Isolde had three gentlewomen, all attired with great richness. These, with the other knights and their squires, and valets to bear their shields and spears, formed their train.

Not far had they gone before they saw on the road before them a group of knights. Chief of these was the knight Galihodin, who was attended by twenty companions.

"Fair fellows," said Galihodin, "yonder come four knights escorting a richly-attired lady. What say you? shall we take her from them?"

"That is not the best counsel," said one.

"At any rate, it is my counsel," answered Galihodin. "We shall show them that we have the right of the road." And he sent a squire to them, asking them if they would joust, or else lose their lady.

"We are but four," said Tristram. "Tell your lord to come with three of his comrades, and win her if he can."

"Let me have this joust," said Palamides. "I will undertake them all four."

"As you will," said Tristram. "Go tell your lord that this one knight will encounter him and any three of his fellows."

The squire departed with his challenge, and in a trice Galihodin came riding forward spear in rest. Palamides encountered him in mid-career, and smote him so hard a blow that he had a terrible fall to the earth, and his horse with him. His three comrades were served in the same summary manner, while Palamides still bore an unbroken spear. At this unlooked-for result six knights rode out from the opposite party with purpose of revenge on the victor.

"Hold your hands," cried Galihodin. "Let not one of you touch this noble knight, who has proved himself a man of worth. And I doubt if the whole of you could handle him."

When Palamides saw that the field was yielded to him he rode back to Sir Tristram.

"Well and worshipfully have you done," said Tristram. "No man could have surpassed you."

Onward they rode again, and in a little while after met four knights in the highway, with spears in rest. These were Gawaine and three companions. This joust also Tristram gave to Palamides, and he served these four as he had served the others, leaving them all unhorsed in the road. For the presence of La Belle Isolde gave the strength of ten men to the arm of her lover, the Saracen.

They now continued their route without molestation, and in good time reached the spot where Tristram had ordered his pavilions to be set up. Here were now many more pavilions than they had seen on their previous visit, and a great array of knights, who had been gathering for many days, for far and wide had spread the news of the great tournament.

Leaving Palamides and Gareth at the pavilions with Queen Isolde, Tristram and Dinadan rode to Lonazep to learn what was afoot, Tristram riding on the Saracen knight's white horse. As they came into the castle the sound of a great bugle-blast met their ears, and many knights crowded forward.

"What means the blast?" asked Tristram.

"Sir," answered a knight, "it comes from the party who hold against King Arthur at this tournament. These are the kings of Ireland, of Surluse, of Listinoise, of Northumberland, of North Wales, and of other countries. They are calling a council to decide how they shall be governed in the lists."

Tristram thereupon followed them to their council, and listened to the debate. He then sought his horse again, and rode by where King Arthur stood surrounded by a press of knights. Among those were Galihodin and Gawaine, who said to the king: "That knight in the green harness, with the white horse, is a man of might, whoever he be. Today he overthrew us both, with six of our fellows."

"Who can he be?" said the king, and he called Tristram to him, and requested to know his name.

"I beg pardon, my liege lord," answered Tristram, "and pray that you will hold me excused from revealing my name at this time," and he turned his horse and rode away.

"Go after him, Sir Griflet," said the king. "Tell him that I wish to speak with him apart."

Griflet rode to Tristram and told him the king's wish, and the two returned in company.

"Fair sir," said the king, "what is the cause that you withhold your name?"

"I have an excellent reason, but beg that you will not press me for it."

"With which party do you hold?"

"Truly, my lord, that I cannot say. Where my heart draws or my fancy bids I will go. Tomorrow you shall see which side I take. Today I know not myself."

Leaving the king, he rode back to where his pavilions were set. When the morning dawned he and his three companions armed themselves all in green and rode to the lists. Here young knights had begun to joust, and, seeing this, Gareth asked leave of Tristram to break a spear.

"Go in and do your best if you care to play with beginners," said Tristram, laughing.

But Gareth found himself encountered by a nephew of the king with the hundred knights, who had some of his uncle's tough fibre, and both got ugly falls, and lay on the ground till they were helped up by their friends. Then Tristram and Palamides rode with Gareth back to the pavilions, where they removed their helmets. When Isolde saw Gareth all bruised in the face, she asked him what ailed him.

"Madam, I had a hard buffet, and gave another, but none of my fellows would rescue me."

"Only unproved knights are yet in the field," said Palamides. "The man that met you, though, was a strong and well-trained knight, Sir Selises by name, so you have no dishonor. Rest here and get yourself in condition for tomorrow's work."

"I shall not fail you if I can bestride my horse," said Gareth.

"What party is it best for us to join tomorrow?" asked Tristram.

"Against King Arthur, is my advice," said Palamides. "Lancelot and many other good men will be on his side, and the more men of prowess we meet the more honor we will win."

"Well and knightly spoken," said Tristram. "Hard blows is what we court. Your counsel is well given."

"So think we all," said the others.

On the morrow, when day had broken, they arrayed themselves in green trappings, with shields and spears of green, while Isolde and her three damsels wore dresses of the same color. For the ladies Tristram found seats in a bay window of a priory which overlooked the field, and from which they could see all that took place. This done, they rode straight to the party of the king of Scots.

When Arthur saw this he asked Lancelot who were these knights and the queenly lady who came with them.

"That I cannot say for certain. Yet if Tristram and Palamides be in this country then it is they and La Belle Isolde."

Then Arthur turned to Kay and said:

"Go to the hall and see how many Knights of the Round Table are missing, and bring me word."

Kay did so, and found by the roll of knights that ten were wanting Tristram, Dinadan and eight others.

"Then I dare say," remarked Arthur, "that some of these are here today against us."

The tournament began with a combat in which two knights, cousins to Gawaine, named Sir Edward and Sir Sadok, rode against the king of Scots and the king of North Wales and overthrew them both. This Palamides saw, and in return he spurred upon these victorious knights and hurled both of them from their saddles.

"What knight is that in green?" asked Arthur. "He is a mighty jouster."

"You will see him do better yet," said Gawaine. "It was he that unhorsed me and seven others two days ago."

As they stood talking Tristram rode into the lists on a black horse, and within a few minutes he smote down four knights of Orkney, while Gareth and Dinadan each unhorsed a good knight.

"Yonder is another fellow of marvellous arm," said Arthur; "that green knight on the black horse."

"He has not begun his work yet," said Gawaine. "It is plain that he is no common man."

And so it proved, for Sir Tristram pushed fiercely into the press, rescued the two kings who had been unhorsed, and did such mighty work among the opposing party that all who saw him marvelled to behold one man do so many valiant deeds. Nor was the career of Palamides less marvellous to the spectators.

King Arthur, who watched them both with admiring eyes, likened Tristram to a furious lion, and Palamides to a maddened leopard, and Gareth and Dinadan, who seconded them strongly, to eager wolves. So fiercely did Tristram rage, indeed, among the knights of Orkney that at length they withdrew from the field, as no longer able to face him.

Then loud went up the cry of the heralds and the common people:

"The green knight has beaten all Orkney!" And the heralds took account that not less than fifty knights had been smitten down by the four champions in green.

"This will not do," said Arthur. "Our party will be overmatched if these fellows rage on at such a rate. Come, Lancelot, you and Hector and Bleoberis must try your hands, and I will make a fourth."

"Let it be so," answered Lancelot. "Let me take him on the black horse, and Bleoberis him on the white. Hector shall match him on the gray horse" (Sir Gareth).

"And I," said Arthur, "will face the knight on the grizzled steed" (Sir Dinadan).

With this conversation they armed and rode to the lists. Here Lancelot rode against Tristram and smote him so hard a blow that horse and man went to the earth, while his three companions met with the same ill fortune from their new antagonists.

This disaster raised a cry throughout the lists: "The green knights are down! Rescue the green knights! Let them not be held prisoners!" For the understanding was that any unhorsed knight not rescued by his own strength or by his fellows should be held as prisoner.

Then the king of North Wales rode straight to Tristram, and sprang from his horse, crying:

"Noble knight, I know not of what country you are, but beg you to take my horse, for you have proved yourself worthier to bestride it than I am."

"Many thanks," said Tristram. "I shall try and do you as welcome a turn. Keep near us, and I may soon win you another horse."

Then he sprang to the saddle, and meeting with King Arthur struck him so fierce a sword-blow on the helm that he had no power to keep his saddle.

"Here is the horse promised you," cried Tristram to the king of North Wales, who was quickly remounted on King Arthur's horse.

Then came a hot contest around the king, one party seeking to mount him again and the other to hold him prisoner. Palamides thrust himself, on foot, into the press, striking such mighty blows to the right and left that the whole throng were borne back before him. At the same time Tristram rode into the thickest of the throng of knights and cut a way through them, hurling many of them to the earth.

This done, he left the lists and rode to his pavilion, where he changed his horse and armor; he who had gone forth as a green knight coming back to the fray as a red one.

When Queen Isolde saw that Tristram was unhorsed, and lost sight of him in the press, she wept greatly, fearing that some harm had come to him. But when he rode back she knew him in an instant, despite his red disguise, and her heart swelled anew with joy as she saw him with one spear smite down five knights. Lancelot, too, now knew him, and withdrew from the lists lest he should encounter him again.

All this time Tristram's three friends had not been able to regain their saddles, but now he drove back the press and helped them again to horse, and, though they knew him not in his new array, they aided him with all their knightly prowess.

When Isolde, at her window, saw what havoc her chosen knight was making, she leaned eagerly forth and laughed and smiled in delight. This Palamides saw, and the vision of her lovely and smiling countenance filled his soul so deeply with love's rejoicing that there seemed to flow into him the strength and spirit of ten men, and, with a shout of knightly challenge, he pressed forward, smiting down with spear and sword every man he encountered. For his heart was so enamoured by the vision of that charming face that Tristram or Lancelot would then have had much ado to stand before him.

"Truly Palamides is a noble warrior," said Tristram, when he beheld this. "I never saw him do such deeds as he has done this day, nor heard of his showing such prowess."

"It is his day," said Dinadan, simply. But to himself he said, "If you knew for whose love he does these valorous deeds, you would soon be in the field against him."

"It is a crying pity that so brave a knight should be a pagan," said Tristram.

"It is my fancy," said Dinadan to himself, "that you may thank Queen Isolde for what you have seen; if she had not been here today that shouting throng would not be giving Palamides the palm of the tourney."

At this juncture Lancelot came again into the field, and hearing the outcry in favor of Palamides he set his spear in rest and spurred upon him. Palamides, seeing this, and having no spear, coolly awaited Lancelot, and as he came up smote his spear in two with a sword-stroke. Then he rushed upon him and struck his horse so hard a blow in the neck that the animal fell, bearing his rider to the ground.

Loud and fierce was the outcry then: "Palamides the Saracen has smitten Sir Lancelot's horse! It is an unknightly deed!"

And Hector de Maris, seeing his brother Lancelot thus unfairly dismounted, rushed upon Palamides in a rage, and bore him from his horse with a mighty spear-thrust.

"Take heed to yourself, sirrah," cried Lancelot, springing towards him sword in hand. "You have done me a sorry deed, and by my knightly honor I will repay you for it."

"I humbly beg your pardon, noble sir," answered Palamides. "I have done so much this day that I have no power or strength left to withstand you. Forgive me my hasty and uncourteous deed, and I promise to be your knight while I live."

"You have done marvellously well indeed," said Lancelot. "I understand well what power moves you. Love is a mighty mistress, and if she I love were here today you should not bear away the honor of the field, though you have nobly won it. Beware that Tristram discovers not your love, or you may repent it. But I have no quarrel with you, and will not seek to take from you the honor of the day."

So Lancelot suffered Palamides to depart, and mounted his own horse again, despite twenty knights who sought to hinder him. Lancelot, Tristram, and Palamides did many more noble deeds before that day's end, and so great became the medley at length that the field seemed a dense mass of rearing and plunging horses and struggling knights.

At length Arthur bade the heralds to blow to lodging and the fray ended. And since Palamides had been in the field from first to last, without once withdrawing, and had done so many, noble and valiant deeds, the honor and the prize for the day were unanimously voted him, a judgment which Arthur and the kings of his counsel unanimously confirmed.

But when Palamides came to understand that the red knight who had rescued him was Sir Tristram his heart was glad, for all but Dinadan fancied he had been taken prisoner. Much was the talk upon the events of the day, and great the wonder of king and knights at the remarkable valor of the Saracen knight.

"And yet I well know," said Lancelot, "that there was a better knight there than he. And take my word for it, this will be proved before the tournament ends."

This also thought Dinadan, and he rallied his friend Tristram with satirical tongue.

"What the fiend has ailed you today?" he asked. "Palamides grew in strength from first to last, but you have been like a man asleep, or a coward knight."

"I was never called coward before," said Tristram, hotly. "The only fall I got was from Lancelot, and him I hold as my better, and for that matter the better of any man alive."

But Dinadan kept up his railing accusations till the growing anger of Tristram warned him to desist. Yet this was all from friendship, not from spite, for he wished to stir up his friend to do his best in the lists the coming day, and not permit the Saracen again to carry off the prize.

Chapter VI
The Second Day of the Tournament

WHEN THE NEXT morning dawned, Tristram, Palamides, and Gareth, with La Belle Isolde and her ladies, all arrayed as before in green, took horse at an early hour,

**and rode into the fresh forest. But Dinadan was left still asleep
in bed. As they passed the castle at a little distance, it chanced
that King Arthur and Lancelot saw them from an upper window.**

"Yonder rideth the fairest lady of the world," said Lancelot, "always
excepting your queen, Guenever."

"Who is it?" asked Arthur.

"It is La Belle Isolde, Cornwall's queen and Tristram's lady-love."

"By my troth, I should like to see her closer," said the king. "Let us
arm and mount, and ride after them."

This they did, and in a short time were on the track of the gay
cavalcade they had seen.

"Let us not be too hasty," warned Lancelot. "There are some knights who
resent being intruded on abruptly; particularly if in the company of ladies."

"As for that, we must take our chances," said Arthur. "If they feel
aggrieved I cannot help it, for I am bent on seeing Queen Isolde."

Seeing Tristram and his companions just in advance, Arthur rode
briskly up and saluted Isolde courteously, saying, "God save you, fair lady."

"Thanks for your courtesy, sir knight," she replied.

Then Arthur looked upon her charming countenance, freshened by
the morning air, and thought in his mind that Lancelot had spoken but
the truth, and that no more beautiful lady lived. But at this moment
Palamides rode up.

"Sir knight, what seek you here?" he asked. "It is uncourteous to
come on a lady so suddenly. Your intrusion is not to our liking, and I
bid you to withdraw."

Arthur paid no heed to these words, but continued to gaze upon
Isolde, as one stricken with admiration. Seeing this, Palamides flamed
into anger, and spurred fiercely upon the king, with spear in rest,
smiting him from his horse.

"Here is an awkward business," said Lancelot to himself. "If I ride
down Palamides I shall have Tristram on me; and the pair of them
would be too much for me. This comes from too headstrong a will. But
whether I live or die I must stand by my lord and king." Then riding
forward, he called to Palamides, "Keep thee from me!"

Fierce was the onset with which they met, but it ended in Lancelot's favor, for Palamides was flung from his saddle and had a hard fall.

When Tristram saw this he called to Lancelot, "Be on your guard, sir knight. You have unhorsed my comrade, and must joust with me."

"I have no dread of that," said Lancelot; "and yet I did but avenge my lord, who was unhorsed unwarily and unknightly. You have no cause for displeasure; for no honorable knight could stand by and see his friend ill-treated."

Tristram now felt sure that it was Lancelot who spoke, and that it was King Arthur whom Palamides had unhorsed. He therefore laid aside his spear and helped Palamides again to his saddle, while Lancelot did the same for the king.

"That deed of thine was not knightly nor courteous," said Tristram, sternly to Palamides, after the others had departed. "I cannot see any harm in a knight accosting a lady gently and courteously; nor am I pleased to have you play such masteries before my lady. If I deem her insulted, I am quite able myself to protect her. And if I am not mistaken, it was King Arthur you assailed so rudely, and the other was Lancelot du Lac. You may yet have to pay for your violence."

"I cannot think," said Palamides, "that the great Arthur would ride thus secretly arrayed as a poor knight-errant."

"Then you know him not," said Tristram. "No knight living is fonder of adventure. King Arthur is always ready to take his part as an errant knight, nor does he bear malice against those who may overthrow him when in disguise. I tell you, Palamides, that our king is the true model of knightly honor, and that the best of us might learn from him."

"If it were he I am sorry," said Palamides. "I may have been over-hasty. But a thing that is done cannot be undone, and I must abide the consequences."

Then Tristram sent Isolde to her lodging in the priory, from which she might behold the tournament, and made ready to enter the lists.

Fierce was the shock of the first encounter of the knights, and the three champions in green began the day with many deeds of might.

"How feel you?" asked Tristram of Palamides. "Are you able to repeat yesterday's work?"

"Hardly," was the reply. "I am weary and sore yet from my hard labors."

"I am sorry for that, as I shall miss your aid."

"Trust not to me," answered Palamides. "I have not much work left in me."

"Then I must depend on you," said Tristram to Gareth. "We two should be able to make our mark. Keep near me and rescue me if I get in trouble, and I will do the same for you."

"I shall not fail you," was the reply.

Leaving them, Palamides rode off by himself, and, pushing into the thickest press of the men of Orkney, did such deeds of arms that Tristram looked on in amazement.

"Is that his soreness and weariness?" he asked. "I fancy he is weary of my company, and wishes to win all the honor to his own hand."

"That is what Dinadan meant yesterday when he called you coward," said Gareth. "He but wished to stir you to anger so that Palamides should not rob you of credit."

"By my faith, if Palamides bears me ill will and envy I shall show him what a knight of Cornwall can do. He has gained the acclamations of the crowd already. He has left our company and we owe him no courtesy. You shall see me rob him of his honors."

Then Tristram rode into the thickest of the press, and laid about him with such might that all eyes were turned upon him, and men began to say, "There is a greater than Palamides come into the field."

"Is it not as I told you?" said Lancelot to Arthur. "I said you would this day see the Saracen distanced."

"It is true enough," answered Arthur. "Palamides has not such strength of arm."

"It is Tristram himself you look upon."

"That I can well believe," said Arthur. "Such knights as he do not grow like mushrooms in every field."

The noise from the other part of the lists now drew the attention of Palamides, and when he saw what puissant deeds his late comrade was doing he wept for spite, for he saw that the honor of that day was not for him.

Seeing to what straits their party was put, Arthur and Lancelot and many other knights now armed and rode into the field, and by their aid so changed the tide of victory that the other side was driven quite back, until Tristram and Gareth stood alone, bravely abiding all who came upon them. But Lancelot and his kinsmen kept purposely away from them.

"See," said Lancelot to Arthur, "how Palamides hovers yonder like one in a dream, sick, I fancy, from envy of Tristram."

"Then he is but a fool," said the king. "He is not and never was the match of Tristram. I am glad to see the fellow repaid for the way he served me this morning."

As they stood thus conversing, Tristram withdrew quietly from the lists, his going noted only by Isolde and Palamides, who kept their eyes upon him. He rode back to his pavilions, where he found Dinadan still asleep, his slumbers not broken by all the uproar of the tournament.

"As I am a living man, here is a lusty sleeper," cried Tristram. "Wake, Dinadan. The day is half spent and the field half won, and here you are still a-bed."

At this Dinadan sprang hastily up and rubbed his eyes.

"I dreamt of wars and jousts," he said. "And, i' faith, I like that way the best, for one gets all the good of the fight and is safe from sore limbs and aching bones. But what's to do?"

"Get on your harness and ride with me to the field. You will find something there to waken you up."

Dinadan, as he armed, noted Tristram's battered shield, and remarked:

"I slept both well and wisely, it seems. If I had been there I must have followed you, from shame if not from courage. And by the looks of your shield I would have been worse battered than I was yesterday. Why did you not let me sleep out the balance of it, friend Tristram?"

"A truce with your jests. Come, we must to the field again."

"How now, is there a new deal in the game? Yesterday you did but dream; today you seem awake."

Meanwhile Tristram had changed his armor, and now was attired all in black.

"You have more fight in you than you had yesterday, that is sure," said Dinadan. "Did I stir up your sleeping spirit?"

"It may be so," said Tristram, smiling. "Keep well up to me, and I shall make you a highway through the press. If you see me overmatched, do what you can to aid me."

When ready they took their horses and rode back to the lists, where Isolde and Palamides noted their entrance. When the Saracen saw that Tristram was disguised, a new fancy came into his scheming brain. Leaving the lists, he rode to where a knight sat sorely wounded under a tree outside. Him he prayed for an exchange of armor, saying that his own was too well known in the field, and that he wished for a disguise.

"That is very true," said the knight, as he recognized the green armor. "You have made your array somewhat too well known. You are welcome to my arms, if they will be of use to you. They will gain more credit in your hands than they have won in mine."

Palamides thereupon exchanged armor with him, and, taking his shield, which shone like silver, rode into the field. He now joined the party of King Arthur, and rode spitefully against Tristram, who had just struck down three knights. They met with such force that both spears splintered to their hands, though neither lost his seat. Then they dashed eagerly together with drawn swords and fought with the courage and fury of two lions. But Tristram wondered much what knight this was that faced him so valiantly, and grew angry as he felt that he was wasting in this single combat the strength he wished to treasure up for the day's work.

La Belle Isolde, who had watched Palamides from her window, had seen him change his armor with the wounded knight. And when his treacherous purpose came to her mind she wept so heartily and was so deeply disturbed that she swooned away.

At this juncture in the fray Lancelot rode again into the field, and when the knights of Arthur's party saw him the cry went up. "Return, return, here comes Sir Lancelot du Lac!"

And some said to him, "Sir Lancelot, yonder knight in the black harness is your man. He is the best of our opponents, and has nearly overcome the good knight with the silver shield."

At this Lancelot rode between the combatants, and cried to Palamides:

"Let me have this battle; you need repose."

Palamides knew Lancelot, and readily gave way, hoping through his mighty aid to gain revenge upon his rival. Then Lancelot fell upon Tristram, and, unknowing who he was, dealt him blows that would have stunned a less hardy fighter. Tristram returned them but feebly, for he knew well with whom he fought. And Isolde, who saw it all, was half out of her mind with grief.

Dinadan now told Gareth who the knight in black armor was, and said, "Lancelot will get the better of him, for one is weary and the other fresh, and Tristram is not fighting with his old vim. Let us to his aid."

"I am with you," said Gareth. "Yonder fellow with the silver shield is waiting to fall on Tristram, if he can to advantage. It is our business to give our friend what help we can."

Then they rode in, and Gareth struck Lancelot a sword-blow that made his head swim, while Dinadan followed with a spear-thrust that bore horse and man together to the earth.

"Why do you this?" cried Tristram, angrily. "It is not a knightly act, and does not that good knight any dishonor. I was quite his match without you."

Then Palamides came to Lancelot's aid, and a close medley of fighting began, in which Dinadan was unhorsed and Tristram pulled Palamides from his saddle, and fell with him. Dinadan now sprang up and caught Tristram's horse by the bridle, calling out, with purpose to end the fight:

"My lord Sir Tristram, take your horse."

"What is this?" cried Lancelot. "What have I done? Sir Tristram, why came you here disguised? Surely I would not have drawn sword on you, had I known you."

"Sir," said Tristram, "this is not the first honor you have done me."

Then they mounted their horses again, while the people on one side gave Lancelot the honor of the fray, and those on the other side gave it to Tristram.

"The honor is not mine," said Lancelot. "He has been longer in the field, and has smitten down many more knights; so I give my voice for Sir Tristram, and pray to all my lords and fellows to do the same."

This was the verdict of the judges, and the prize of that day's tourney was by all voted to the noble Sir Tristram.

Then the trumpets blew to lodging, and the knights left the field, while Queen Isolde was conducted to her pavilion. But her heart burned hot with wrath against Palamides, all whose treachery she had seen. As Tristram rode forward with Gareth and Dinadan, Palamides joined them, still disguised.

"Sir knight," said Tristram, "you are not of our party, and your company is not welcome. So begone."

"Not I," he answered. "One of the best knights in the world bade me keep fellowship with you, and till he relieve me from that service I must obey him."

"Ha, Palamides, I know you now!" said Tristram. "But, by my faith, I did not know you before, for I deemed you a worthy knight and not a traitor. I could have handled you well enough, but you brought Lancelot to your aid against me."

"Are you my lord, Sir Tristram?" said Palamides, in a tone of surprise.

"That you know, well enough."

"How should I know it any more than you knew me? I deemed you the king of Ireland, for you bear his arms."

"I won them in battle, from his champion Sir Marhaus," said Tristram.

"Sir," answered Palamides, "I fancied you had joined Lancelot's party, and that caused me to turn to the same side."

"If that be so, I forgive you," said Tristram.

But when they reached the pavilion and had disarmed and washed, and were come to table, Isolde grew red with wrath on seeing Palamides.

"You traitor and felon!" she cried, "how dare you thrust yourself into this goodly company? You know not how falsely he has treated you, my lord Tristram. I saw it all. He watched you when you rode to your tent and donned the black armor. Then he changed armor with a wounded knight and rode back and wilfully changed sides, and drew sword upon you. I saw it all, my lord, and I impeach him of treason."

"Madam," said Palamides, calmly, "you may say what you will. I cannot in courtesy deny you. Yet by my knighthood I declare I knew not Sir Tristram."

"I will take your excuse," said Tristram, "though it seems a lame one. You spared me little in the field, but all that I have pardoned."

At this, Isolde held down her head in despite and said no more.

While they were still at table two knights rode to the pavilions, and entered in full armor.

"Fair sirs," said Tristram, "is this courtesy, to come upon us thus armed at our meal?"

"We come with no ill intent," said one, "but as your friends, Sir Tristram."

"I am come," said the other, "to greet you as a friend and comrade, and my companion is eager to see and welcome La Belle Isolde."

"Then remove your helms, that I may see what guests I have."

"That we do, willingly."

No sooner were their helmets off than Tristram sprang hastily to his feet.

"Madam, arise," he cried; "this is none less than my lord King Arthur; and this my very dear friend Sir Lancelot."

Then the king and queen kissed, and Lancelot and Tristram warmly embraced, while deep joy filled all hearts there. At the request of Isolde the visitors removed their armor and joined them at their meal.

"Many is the day that I have longed to see you," said Arthur to Isolde, "for much praise have I heard of you, and not without warrant. For a nobler match for beauty and valor than you and Sir Tristram the world does not hold."

"We thank you heartily," replied Tristram and Isolde. "Such praise from King Arthur is the highest honor that men's lips could give."

Then they talked of other things, but mainly of the tournament.

"Why were you against us?" asked Arthur. "You are a Knight of the Round Table, and have fought today against your own."

"Here is Dinadan, and your own nephew Gareth. You must blame them for that," said Tristram, smiling.

"You may lay all the blame on my shoulders, if Tristram wishes it," said Gareth.

"Not on mine, then," said Dinadan. "Mine are only broad enough to carry my own sins. It was this unhappy Tristram brought us to the tournament, and I owe to him a whole body full of aches and pains as it is, without taking any of his sins in my sack, to boot."

At this the king and Lancelot laughed heartily, and the more so at the sour grimace with which Dinadan ended.

"What knight was he with the shield of silver that held you so short?" asked Arthur.

"Here he sits," said Tristram.

"What! was it Palamides?"

"None less than he," said Isolde.

"That was not a courteous action."

"Sir," said Palamides, "Tristram was so disguised that I knew him not."

"That may well be," said Lancelot, "for I knew him no better."

"However it be, we are friends again," said Tristram, "and I hope will continue so."

And so the evening passed, till the time came for Arthur and Lancelot to take their leave.

That night Palamides slept not for the pain and envy that burned in his heart. But when his friends entered his chamber in the morning they found him fast asleep, with his cheeks stained with tears.

"Say nothing," said Tristram. "The poor fellow has been deeply wounded by the rebuke that I and Isolde gave him. Lay no heavier load upon his heart."

Chapter VII
The Woes of Two Lovers

EARLY ON THE THIRD morning of the tournament the knights of Tristram's party were up and armed, they now being all arrayed in red, as was also Isolde and her maidens. And rare was the show they made as they rode gayly to the priory, where they left Isolde and her maidens to occupy their proper seats. As the knights turned thence towards the field they heard three

loud bugle-blasts, and saw the throng of armed knights press eagerly forward, while already from the listed space came the thunder of hoofs and the cries of combatants.

Into the field they rode, Palamides in advance, and such havoc did he make in the opposing ranks that shouts of approval went up from all the seats. But Tristram now rode forward at the full speed of his great war-horse, hurled Kay the seneschal from his saddle, smote down three other knights with the same spear, and then, drawing his sword, laid about him like a roused giant.

Quickly changed the cry from Palamides. "O Tristram! O Tristram!" shouted the throng of spectators, and the deeds of this new champion threw those of the former victor into the shade.

Gareth and Dinadan also nobly aided the two champions, rousing the admiration of Arthur and Lancelot by their gallantry, and the four knightly comrades soon cleared a wide space in the ranks before them.

"Come," said Arthur, "we must to the rescue, or our side will be driven from the field before the day is an hour old. See how the others crowd in on Tristram's steps, like wolves to the prey."

Then he and Lancelot hastily armed and sought the field, where they quickly fought their way into the thickest press of the tumult. Tristram, not knowing them, rode upon them and thrust King Arthur from his horse, and when Lancelot rushed to his rescue he was surrounded with such an eager host that he was pulled from his saddle to the ground.

Seeing this, the kings of Ireland and Scotland, with their knights, rushed forward to take Lancelot and Arthur prisoners. But they counted without their host, for the dismounted knights laid about them like angry lions, driving back all who came near them. Of all that passed in that hot turmoil it were too much to say. Many a knight there did deeds of great prowess, and Arthur and Lancelot being mounted again, strewed the earth with fallen knights, Lancelot that day unhorsing thirty warriors. Yet the other side held so firmly together that, with all their ardent labor, Arthur and his party were overmatched.

At this juncture, Tristram turned to his companions and said:

"My good comrades, I begin to fancy that we are today on the wrong side. King Arthur's party is overborne more by numbers than valor, for I must say I never saw so few men do so well. It would be a shame for us, who are Knights of the Round Table, to see our lord Arthur and our good comrade Lancelot dishonored. I am in the humor to change sides, and help our king and liege lord."

"We are with you in that," cried Gareth and Dinadan. "We have been fighting against the grain these three days."

"Do as you will," said Palamides. "I shall not change my hand in the midst of the fray."

"As you will," said Tristram. "You are your own master. Speed well in your way, and we will do our best in ours."

Then he, Gareth and Dinadan drew out of the press and rode round to Arthur's side, where they lent such noble aid that the fortune of the field quickly changed, and the opposing party began to give ground. As for Palamides, King Arthur struck him so fierce a blow that he was hurled from his horse, while Tristram and Lancelot unhorsed all before them. Such havoc did they make, indeed, that the party of the opposing kings was soon in full flight from the field, bearing Palamides, who wept for rage and grief, with them.

Then rarely sounded the trumpets, and loudly shouted the spectators, while the names of Tristram and Lancelot were in every mouth, some voting one the prize, some the other. But neither of these good comrades would have it alone, so that in the end it was divided between them.

When evening drew near, and the knights had all withdrawn to their pavilions, Palamides rode up to that of Sir Tristram, in company with the kings of Wales and Scotland. Here he drew up his horse, praying his companions to wait a while while he spoke to the knight within. Then he cried loudly at the entrance:

"Where are you, Tristram of Lyonesse?"

"Is that you, Palamides?" answered the knight. "Will you not dismount and join us?"

"I seek better company, sir traitor," cried Palamides, in tones that trembled with fury. "I hate you now as much as I once esteemed you, and bear this in mind, if it were daylight as it is night, I would slay you with my own hands. You shall die yet for this day's deeds."

"You blame me wrongly, Palamides," said Tristram, mildly. "If you had done as I advised you would have won honor instead of disgrace. Why come you here seeking to lay your own fault on me? Since you give me such broad warning, I shall be well on my guard against you."

"Well you may, sir dastard, for I love you not," and, fiercely spurring his horse, the hot-blooded Saracen joined his kingly companions.

When the next day dawned the festive array which had long spread bustle and splendor round Lonazep broke up, and knights and ladies rode off in all directions through the land, to carry far and wide the story of the wondrous deeds of valor that had been performed at the great tournament. Tristram and his two comrades, with Hector de Maris and Bleoberis, escorted La Belle Isolde to Joyous Gard, where for seven days the guests were nobly entertained, with all the sports and mirthfulness that could be devised. King Arthur and his knights drew back to Camelot, and Palamides rode onward with the two kings, his heart torn with mingled sorrow and despair. Not alone was he in grief for his disgrace in the field, under the eyes of her he loved, but was full as sorrowful for the hot words he had spoken in his wrath to Tristram, who had been so kind and gentle to him that his heart was torn to think how falsely and treacherously he had requited him.

His kingly companions would have had him stay with them, but he could not be persuaded, so the king of Ireland presented him with a noble courser, and the king of Scotland with valuable gifts, and he rode his way, still plunged in a grief that was almost despair. Noon brought him to a forest fountain, beside which lay a wounded knight, who sighed so mournfully that the very leaves on the trees seemed to sigh in echo.

"Why mourn you so, fair knight?" asked Palamides, mildly. "Or if you care not to tell, at least let me lie beside you and join my moans to yours, for I dare say I have a hundredfold deeper cause for grief, and we may ease our hearts by mutual complaints."

"What is your name, gentle sir?"

"Such as I am, for better or worse, men call me Palamides, son to King Astlabor."

"Noble sir, it solaces me much to meet you. I am Epinegris, son to the king of Northumberland. Now repose you on this mossy bank and let us tell our woes, and so ease somewhat our sad hearts."

Then Palamides dismounted and laid himself beside the wounded knight.

"This is my source of woe," he said. "I love the fairest queen that ever drew breath, La Belle Isolde, Cornwall's queen."

"That is sheer folly," said Epinegris, "for she loves none but Tristram de Lyonesse."

"Know I it not? I have been in their company this month, daily reaping sorrow. And now I have lost the fellowship of Tristram and the love of Isolde for ever, through my envy and jealousy, and never more shall a glad thought enter my sorrowful heart."

"Did she ever show you signs of love?"

"Never. She hated me, I fear. And the last day we met she gave me such a rebuke that I will never recover from it – yet well I deserved it by my unknightly acts. Many great deeds have I done for her love, yet never shall I win a smile from her eyes."

"Deep is your grief, indeed," said Epinegris, with a heartbreaking sigh, "yet it is but a jest to my sorrow. For my lady loved me, and I won her with my hands. But, alas! this day I have lost her and am left here to moan. I took her from an earl and two knights that were with her; but as we sat here this day, telling each other of our loves, there came an errant knight, named Helior de Preuse, and challenged me to fight for my lady. You see what followed. He wounded me so that he left me for dead and took my lady with him. So my sorrow is deepest, for I have rejoiced in my love, and you never have. To have and lose is far worse than never to own."

"That is true," said Palamides. "But yet I have the deepest cause for grief, for your love is not hopeless, like mine. And I shall prove this, for if I can find this Helior he shall be made to yield you your lady, unless he prove able to deal with me as he has with you."

Then he helped Epinegris on his horse and led him to a hermitage nearby, where he left him under the care of the holy hermit. Here Palamides stayed not long, but walked out under the shadow of the green leaves, to be a while alone with his woes. But not far had he gone before he saw near him a knight, who bore a shield that he had seen Hector de Maris wear. With him were ten other knights, who sheltered themselves from the noontide heat under the green leaves.

As they stood there another knight came by whose shield was green, with a white lion in its midst, and who led a lady on a palfrey. As he came up, the knight who bore Sir Hector's shield rode fiercely after him, and bade him turn and defend his lady.

"That I must, in knightly duty," cried the other.

Then the two knights rode together with such might that horses and men together were hurled to the earth. Drawing their swords, they now fought sturdily for the space of an hour. In the end the knight of the white lion was stricken to the earth and forced to beg for his life.

Palamides stood under the leaves, watching this combat till it came to its end. Then he went to the lady, whom he believed to be her whom he had promised to rescue. Taking her gently by the hand, he asked her if she knew a knight named Epinegris.

"Alas! that ever I did," she sadly replied. "For his sake I have lost my liberty, and for mine he has lost his life."

"Not so badly as that," said Palamides. "He is at yonder hermitage. I will take you to him."

"Then he lives!" she cried in joy. "You fill my heart with gladness."

But not many steps had Palamides led her before the victorious knight cried out in tones of fierce anger:

"Loose the lady, sirrah! Whither take you her?"

"Whither I will?" answered Palamides.

"You speak largely, sir knave," cried the knight. "Do you fancy you can rob me of my prize so lightly? Think it not, sirrah; were you as good a knight as Lancelot or Tristram or Palamides, you should not have that lady without winning her at a dearer rate than I did."

"If fight it is, I am ready for you," answered Palamides. "I promised to bring this lady to her lover from whom yonder knight stole her, and it will need more swords than one to make me break my word."

"We shall see if that be so," said the other, attacking him so fiercely that Palamides had much ado to protect himself. They fought for so long a time that Palamides marvelled much who this knight could be that withstood him so sturdily after his late hard battle.

"Knight," he said, at length, "you fight like a hero. I would know your name."

"You shall have it for yours in return."

"I agree to that."

"Then, sir, my name is Safere. I am son of King Astlobar, and brother to Palamides and Segwarides."

"Then heaven defend me for having fought you, for I am your brother Palamides."

At these words Safere fell upon his knees and begged his brother's pardon; and then they unlaced their helms and kissed each other with tears of joy.

As they stood thus, Epinegris advanced towards them, for he had heard the sounds of fighting, and, wounded as he was, he came to help Palamides if he should stand in need.

Palamides, seeing him approach, took the lady by the hand and led her to him, and they embraced so tenderly that all hearts there were touched.

"Fair knight and lady," said Safere, "it would be a cruel pity to part you, and I pray heaven to send you joy of each other."

"You have my sincere thanks," said Epinegris. "And deeper thanks has Sir Palamides for what he has done for me this day. My castle is nearby; will you not ride there with me as a safeguard?"

"That we gladly will," they said, and when Epinegris had got his horse they rode with him and the lady to the castle, where they were nobly received and treated with the highest honor. They had such good cheer and such enjoyment as they had rarely before known. And never burned the flame of love more warmly than that between Epinegris and his rescued lady.

Chapter VIII
The Rivalry of Tristram and Palamides

WHEN MORNING again dawned over the forest and the smiling fields that surrounded the castle of Epinegris, the two brothers rode out, taking with them the blessings and prayers for good fortune of those they left behind. But had

they known into what deadly peril they ventured they would not for days have left those hospitable gates.

For they rode on hour by hour, until afternoon came, and then found themselves in front of a noble manor house from which came to their ears doleful sounds of woe and lamentation.

"What means this woful noise? Shall we enter and see?" said Safere.

"Willingly," answered Palamides.

Leaving their horses at the gates, they entered the courtyard, where they saw an old man tremblingly fumbling his beads. But when they came within the hall they beheld many men weeping and lamenting.

"Fair sirs, why make you such a moaning?" asked Palamides.

"We weep for our lord, who is slain," they dolefully replied.

But one of the knights observed the newcomers closely, and said secretly to his fellows:

"Know you not this man? Fortune has thrown into our hands the knight who slew our lord at Lonazep. That tall fellow is Palamides. Let him not go as easily as he came."

Hearing this, most of them quietly withdrew and armed themselves, and then came suddenly upon their visitors to the number of threescore, crying:

"Defend yourself, if you can, Sir Palamides. We know you for the murderer of our lord, and it is our duty to revenge him. Die you shall, though you had the might of a giant."

Palamides and his brother, finding themselves in this desperate strait, set themselves back to back in the midst of their assailants, and fought like very giants, keeping their ground for two hours, though they were attacked by twenty knights and forty gentlemen and yeomen. But strength cannot hold out for ever against odds, and at the end they were forced to yield, and were locked up in a strong prison.

Within three days thereafter a court of twelve knights sat upon the charge against them, and found Sir Palamides guilty of their lord's death.

Sir Safere, who was adjudged not guilty, was given his liberty, and bidden to depart from the castle. He parted with his brother in the deepest woe.

"Dear brother, grieve not so greatly," said Palamides. "If die I must, I shall meet death bravely. But had I dreamed of such a doom as this, they should never have taken me alive."

Then Safere departed in untold sorrow, though not without hope of rescue if he could raise a force to storm the castle. This he had no chance to do, for on the next morning Palamides was sent under an escort of twelve knights to the father of the dead knight, who dwelt in a strong castle by the seaside, named Pelownes, where it had been decided that the sentence should be put into execution.

Palamides was placed on a sorry old steed with his feet bound beneath it, and, surrounded by the guard of twelve armed knights, was taken towards the place of death.

But through the favor of fortune their route lay by the castle of Joyous Gard, and here they were seen by one who knew Palamides, and who asked him whither he was borne.

"To my death," he answered, "for the slaying of a knight at the tournament. Had I not left Sir Tristram this would not have happened to me. I pray you, recommended me to your lord and to my lady Isolde, and beg them to forgive me my trespasses against them. And also to my lord King Arthur, and to all my fellows of the Round Table."

When the yeoman heard this he rode in all haste to Joyous Gard, where he told Tristram of what he had seen and heard.

"To his death, you say?" cried Tristram. "And for an accident of the tournament? Why, I and twenty others might be served in the same manner. I have reason to be angry with Palamides, but he shall not die the death of a dog if I can rescue him."

This said, he armed in all haste, and taking two squires with him, he rode at a fast gallop towards the castle of Pelownes, hoping to overtake the party before they could pass its gates.

But fortune had decreed that the prisoner should be otherwise rescued. For as the guard of knights rode on their way they passed by a well where Lancelot had alighted to drink of the refreshing waters.

When he saw the cavalcade approach he put on his helmet and stood watching them as they passed. But his heart swelled with anger when he saw Palamides disarmed and bound in their midst, and seemingly led to his death.

"What means this?" he cried. "What has this knight done that deserves a shameful death? Whatever it be, I cannot suffer him to be foully dealt with."

Then he mounted and rode after the twelve knights, soon overtaking them.

"Sir knights," he said, "whither take you that gentleman? To ride thus bound is not befitting for a man of his metal."

At this the guard of knights turned their horses and faced Lancelot.

"We counsel you not to meddle with us," they said, sternly. "This man has deserved death, and to death he is adjudged."

"I tell you, sirs, it shall not be. He is too good a knight to die a shameful death. Defend yourselves, then, for I will try my one hand against your twelve, and rescue him or die in the effort."

The knights of the guard now put their spears in rest, and Lancelot rode upon them with such fury that the foremost and three of those behind him were hurled to the ground before his spear broke. Then he drew his sword and laid about him so shrewdly that in a little time the whole twelve of them were stretched upon the earth, most of them being sorely wounded. Lancelot now cut the bonds of Palamides, mounted him upon the best of their horses, and rode back with him towards Joyous Gard.

As they went forward they saw Sir Tristram approaching. Lancelot knew him at sight, but was himself unknown, because he bore a golden shield which neither Tristram nor Palamides recognized. He therefore mystified them for a time, and declined to enter Joyous Gard on the plea that he had other pressing business on hand. But when strongly entreated, he at length consented, and entered the castle with them.

Great was their surprise and joy when he had unhelmed, to find that they had their host for guest. Tristram took him in his arms, and so did Isolde, while Palamides kneeled before him and thanked him for his life. When Lancelot saw this he took him by the hand and made him rise.

"Good sirs," he said, "could I, or any knight of worship in this land, hesitate to rescue from an ignoble death such a knight as Palamides? Had there been fifty instead of twelve, I fear I should have braved them all."

Much joy was there in Joyous Gard at the visit of the lord of the castle, but Lancelot stayed there but four days. Palamides, however, remained for two months and more, his love and grief growing deeper, till he faded away to a shadow of himself.

One day, at the end of this time, he wandered far into the neighboring forest, and here by chance saw the reflection of his face in a clear pool. The wasted visage disturbed and affrighted him.

"What does this mean?" he asked himself. "Am I, who was called one of the handsomest knights in the world, wasted to such a frightful figure? I must leave this life, for it is idle to grieve myself to death for that which I can never possess."

Then he threw himself beside the well, and from the fulness of his heart began to make a song about La Belle Isolde and himself, a rhyme made up of music, love and grief.

As chance would have it, Tristram had ridden into the forest that day in chase of the hart. And as he rode up and down under the green leaves the summer air brought to his ears the sound of a voice singing loud and clear. He rode softly towards the sound, for he deemed that some knight-errant lay there solacing himself with song.

When he came nigh he tied his horse to a tree and advanced on foot. Then he became aware that the singer was his guest Palamides, and that his song was about La Belle Isolde, a doleful and piteous, yet marvellously well-made song, which the singer sang loudly and in a clear voice. Tristram stood listening till he had heard it from beginning to end. But at the last his anger grew so high that he needed to restrain himself from slaying the singer where he lay.

Remembering that Palamides was unarmed, he resisted this impulse, and advanced slowly towards him.

"Sir Palamides," he said, in a gentle voice, "I have heard your song, and learned your treason to your host. If it were not for the shame of an unknightly act I would deal you here the meed you have earned. How will you acquit yourself of treachery?"

"Thus will I," said Palamides, springing to his feet in his surprise. "As for Queen Isolde, you may know well that I love her above all other ladies in the world. I loved her before you ever saw her, as you know, and have never ceased nor shall ever cease to love her. What honor I have won is due for the most part to my love of her. Yet never for a moment has she returned my love, and I have been her knight without guerdon. Therefore I dread not death, for I had as lief die as live."

"Well have you uttered your treason," said Tristram.

"No treason is it," said Palamides. "Love is free to all men, and I have a right to love any lady I will. If she return it not, no man is harmed. Such wrong as is done I have suffered, not you, for your love is returned and mine has brought me but pain. Yet I shall continue to love La Belle Isolde to the end of my days as deeply as you can."

That there was reason in these words Tristram could not but have seen, had not anger blinded his wisdom.

"None shall love my lady but myself," he cried, in passion. "And for what you have said I challenge you to battle to the uttermost."

"I can never fight in a better quarrel," said Palamides. "And if you slay me I can never die by a nobler hand. Since I cannot hope for favor from La Belle Isolde, I have as good will to die as to live."

"Then set a day in which we shall do battle in this cause."

"Let it be fifteen days hence. And let the place be in the meadow under Joyous Gard."

"Why so long a time?" demanded Tristram. "Tomorrow will suit me better."

"It is because I am meager and weak, and have fallen away to a shadow through hopeless love. I must rest until I get my strength again before I can face so doughty a knight."

"So let it be, then," said Tristram. "Yet once before you broke a promise to meet me in battle at the grave near Camelot."

"What could I do?" rejoined Palamides. "I was in prison, and could not keep my word."

"If you had done so, there would have been no need of a fight now," said Tristram, as he strode haughtily away.

Then Palamides took his horse and rode to Arthur's court, where he did his utmost to rest and regain strength. When the appointed time approached he returned, attended by four knights and four sergeants-at-arms.

Meanwhile Tristram spent his time at the chase. And by evil fortune, about three days before the time of battle, a wild arrow shot by an archer at a hart struck him in the thigh and wounded him so deeply that he could scarcely return to Joyous Gard.

Great was his heaviness of heart, and neither man nor woman could bring him cheer, for it was now impossible to keep his word with his rival; and his heart grew full of the fancy that Palamides himself had shot that arrow, so as to prevent him doing battle on the appointed day. But this no knight about Tristram would believe.

When the fifteenth day came Palamides appeared at the place fixed, with the knights and sergeants whom he had brought with him to bear record of the battle. One sergeant bore his helm, a second his spear, and a third his shield. And for two hours he rested in the field, awaiting the approach of his antagonist.

Then, seeing that Tristram failed to come, he sent a squire to Joyous Gard to remind him of his challenge. When Tristram heard of this message he had the squire brought to his chamber, and showed him his wound.

"Tell Sir Palamides," he said, "that were I able to come he would not need to send for me, and that I had rather be whole today than have all King Arthur's gold. Tell him, moreover, that as soon as I am able I shall seek him throughout the land, as I am a true knight; and when I find him he shall have his fill of battle."

This message the squire brought to his master, who heard it with much secret satisfaction.

"I would have had hard handling of him, and very likely have been vanquished," he said, "for he has not his equal in battle, unless it be Sir Lancelot. So I am well content to give up the fight."

A month passed before Tristram was well. Then he took his horse and rode from country to country in search of Palamides, having many strange adventures by the way, but nowhere could he meet or hear of his rival in love. But during his search Tristram did so many valiant deeds that his fame for the time quite overtopped that of Lancelot, so much so that Lancelot's kinsmen in their anger would have waylaid and slain the valiant warrior.

For this jealousy Lancelot sternly rebuked them, saying,—

"Bear it well in mind, that if any of you does any harm to Sir Tristram, that man shall I slay with my own hands. To murder a man like this for his noble deeds! Out upon such base designs! Far rather should you worship him for his valor and royal prowess."

And so time went on for the space of two years, during which Tristram sought in vain for his rival.

At the end of that time he came home to Joyous Gard from one of his journeys of adventure, and there was told by La Belle Isolde of a great feast to be held at the court on the coming day of Pentecost, which she counselled him strongly to attend.

Much debate passed between him and his lady-love on this subject, for he was loath to go without her, and she cared not to go. In the end he declared that he would obey her wishes, but would ride thither unarmed, save for his sword and spear.

This he did, and though she in her loving anxiety sent after him four knights, he sent them back within half a mile. Yet he soon had reason to repent his rashness. For hardly had he gone a mile farther when he came upon a wounded knight, who told him he owed his hurt to Sir Palamides. What to do now, Tristram knew not. Nearby was the foe he had so long sought in vain, and he was unarmed. Should he ride back for his armor, or go on as he was?

While he stood thinking, Palamides appeared, and knew him at sight.

"Well met, Sir Tristram!" he cried. "I have heard much of your search for me. You have found me now, and we shall not part till we have settled our old scores."

"As for that," answered Tristram, "no Christian can boast that I ever fled from him, nor shall a Saracen make this boast, even if I be unarmed."

Then he put his horse to the gallop and rode on Palamides with such fury that his spear broke into a hundred pieces. Throwing it away, he drew his sword and struck Palamides six great strokes upon the helm, while the Saracen stood unresisting, and wondering at the folly and madness of his foe. Then Tristram cried out in fury,—

"Coward knight, why stand you thus idly? You dare not do battle with me, for doubt not but I can endure all your strength and malice."

"You know well, Sir Tristram," answered Palamides, "that I cannot in honor strike at your unarmed head. If I should slay you thus, shame would be my lot. As for your valor and hardiness, those I shall never question."

"You speak well," answered Tristram.

"Tell me this," continued Palamides. "Were I here naked of armor, and you full armed as I am, what would you do?"

"I shall not answer from fear, but from truthfulness. I would bid you depart, as I could not have ado with you."

"No more can I with you," said Palamides, "therefore ride on your way."

"I shall ride or abide as I may choose," said Tristram. "But tell me this, Palamides: how is it that so good a knight as you refuses to be christened, as your brothers have long been?"

"I cannot become a Christian till a vow I made years ago is fulfilled. I believe fully in Jesus Christ and His mild mother Mary; but there is one battle yet I must fight, and when that is done I will be baptized with a good will."

"If that is the battle with me," said Tristram, "you shall not long wait for it. For God defend that through my fault you should continue a Saracen. Yonder is a knight whom you have hurt. Help me to put on his armor and I will aid you to fulfil your vow."

So they rode together to the wounded knight, who was seated on a bank. Tristram saluted him, and he weakly returned the salute.

"Will you tell me your name, sir knight?" asked Tristram.

"I am Sir Galleron of Galway, and a Knight of the Round Table."

"I am sorry for your hurts, and beg you to lend me your armor, for I am unarmed, and would do battle with this knight who wounded you."

"You shall have it with a good will. But you must beware, for this is no common knight."

"I know him well," answered Tristram, "and have an old quarrel with him."

"Will you kindly tell me your name?"

"My name is Tristram de Lyonesse."

"Then it was idle to warn you. Well I know your renown and worship; and Sir Palamides is likely to have no light task."

Tristram now took off the armor of the wounded knight, who, as well as he could, helped him to put it on himself. This accomplished, Tristram mounted his horse and took in his hand Sir Galleron's spear.

Riding to where Palamides stood waiting, he bade him make ready. In a minute more the two strong knights came hurtling together like two lions. Each smote the other in the centre of the shield, but Palamides's spear broke, while that of Tristram overturned the horse of Palamides. In a moment the unhorsed knight had sprung to his feet and drawn his sword, while Tristram alighted, tied his horse to a tree, and advanced to the fray.

The combat that succeeded was a hard and well-fought one, as only it could be between two such knights. For more than two hours it continued, Tristram often bringing Palamides to his knees by his mighty strokes, while Palamides cut through Tristram's shield and wounded him. Then, in a fury of anger, Tristram rushed upon his rival and hurled him to the earth. But in an instant the agile Saracen was on his feet again, fighting with all his old strength and skill. And so the combat went on, hour by hour, and, hard as Tristram fought, Palamides stood as nobly to his work, and gave him stroke for stroke.

But, as fortune willed, in the end a fierce blow struck the sword from Palamides's hand, nor dare he stoop for it, for fear of being slain. So he stood moveless, regarding it with a sorrowful heart.

"Now," said Tristram, "I have you at advantage, as you had me this day. But it shall never be said that Tristram de Lyonesse killed a weaponless knight. Therefore take your sword, and let us make an end of this battle."

"As for that, I am willing to end it now," said Palamides. "I have no wish to fight longer. Nor can I think that my offence is such that we may not be friends. All I have done is to love La Belle Isolde. You will not say that I have done her aught of dishonor by holding that she is peerless among ladies, or by the valor which love for her has given me. As for such offence as I have given you, I have atoned for it this day, and no one can say that I have not held my own like a man. But this I will affirm, that I never before fought with a man of your might. Therefore I beg you to forgive me for all wrongs which I have done you, and as my vow is now fulfilled, I stand ready to go with you to the nearest church, there to be confessed, and to receive baptism as a true and earnest Christian knight."

"I gladly forgive you all you have done against me," said Tristram; "the more so that you have done it rather from love than from hatred. It fills my heart with joy to be the means of bringing the valiant Palamides into the Church of Christ, and hereafter I shall hold you among my best friends. Within a mile from here is the suffragan of Carlisle, who will gladly give you the sacrament of baptism; and all Christendom must rejoice to gain so noble a convert."

Then they took their horses and helped Galleron to his, and rode to the church, where Tristram told the suffragan the purpose of their coming. Proud to bring into the fold of the church so notable a convert, the suffragan filled a great vessel with water, and hallowed it. This done, he confessed and baptized Sir Palamides, while Tristram and Galleron stood as his godfathers.

Afterwards the three knights rode to Camelot, much to the joy of the king and queen, who gladly welcomed Tristram to their court, and were no less glad to learn that the valiant Palamides had become a Christian, and that the long rivalry between him and Tristram was at an end. The great feast of Pentecost that followed was the merriest that had ever been held at Arthur's court, and the merriest that ever would be, for the breath of coming woe and trouble was in the air, and the time was near at hand in which that worthy fellowship of noble knights was destined to break up in dire disaster.

But first of all the tide of disaster came upon Tristram the brave and Isolde the fair, as we must now relate. The chronicles tell the story at length, but the record of treachery and crime had always best be short, and so we shall make that of King Mark, the murderer.

Many years before the time to which we have now come, King Mark's treachery had filled Cornwall with mischief and all the land with horror, through a deed of frightful crime. And in thus wise it came about. Cornwall had been invaded by a host of Saracens, but before they could do any mischief, Prince Baldwin, King Mark's brother, attacked them, burned their ships, and utterly destroyed them. Furious at heart that his brother should win such honor, while he lay cowering with fear in his castle, Mark invited him to Tintagil, with his wife and child. There suddenly charging him with treason for attacking the Saracens without orders, he stabbed him to the heart, and would have slain his wife and child as well had not the lady Anglides fled for life with her child.

Mark sent after them an old knight named Sir Sadok, with orders to bring them back to Tintagil. But he suffered them to escape, and brought back to the king a false tale that he had drowned the boy.

Many years now passed by, during which Baldwin's son, Alexander the orphan, grew up to be a youth large of limb and strong of arm. In due time he was made a knight, whereupon Anglides produced the bloody doublet and shirt of her murdered husband, which she had carefully preserved, and laid upon the young knight the duty of revenging his father's death. The story of the crime had been diligently kept from him, but he now accepted this heavy charge with alacrity, and vowed solemnly to devote his life to the duty of revenging his murdered father.

News of all this was quickly brought to King Mark, by a false knight who hoped to win favor by turning informer.

"By my halidom," cried Mark, "whom can I trust? I fancied the young viper was dead years ago. That false hound, Sadok, let him escape. As I am a living man, he shall pay the penalty of his treason."

Seizing a sword, he burst furiously from the chamber, and rushed madly through the castle in search of the knight who had deceived him. When Sadok saw him coming, with fury in his face, he guessed what had happened, and drew his own sword in haste.

"King Mark," he cried, "beware how you come nigh me. I saved the life of Alexander, and glory in it, for you slew his father cowardly and treacherously. And it is my hope and prayer that the youth may have the strength and spirit to revenge the good Prince Baldwin on his murderer."

"What, traitor! What, dog! Do you dare rail thus at me?" cried the king, and in a voice of fury he bade four knights of his following to slay the traitor.

These knights drew their swords and advanced in a body on Sadok; but he got the wall of them, and fought so shrewdly that he killed the whole four in King Mark's presence.

Then, shaking his clinched fist at the king, he said:

"I would add your false body to the heap, but that I leave you for Alexander's revenge."

This said, he took horse and rode briskly away, and in all his court Mark could not find a knight willing to pursue him, for all that held with the king feared the old knight's sturdy arm.

King Mark now finding his wrath of no avail, set himself to devising some scheme of treachery by which the danger that threatened him might be removed. In the end he made a compact with Morgan le Fay and the queen of Northgalis, both false sorceresses, in which they agreed to fill the land with ladies that were enchantresses, and with false knights like Malgrim and Breuse Sans Pitié, so that the young knight Alexander le Orphelin should be surrounded with magic and treachery, and without doubt be taken prisoner or slain.

Soon after his knighting, Alexander set out for King Arthur's court, and on the way there had many adventures, in which he proved himself a knight of great valor and skill. Among these was a mighty battle with the false knight Malgrim, whom in the end he killed.

But now Morgan le Fay sought to entrap him by her false devices. She gave him a sleeping draught, and had him taken in a horse-litter to a castle of hers named La Belle Regard.

Here she cured him of his wounds by healing salves, but not until he had promised that he would not set foot beyond the boundaries of that castle for a twelvemonth and a day. When he had recovered, Alexander chafed bitterly at his confinement, for he felt sure that the pledge had been exacted from him to save King Mark from his vow of revenge. Yet his word held him close prisoner.

As one day he wandered through the halls of the castle, like a young lion in a cage – now heavy and sad, now burning with desire for action – there came to him a damsel who was cousin to Morgan le Fay, and to whom the castle of La Belle Regard by right belonged.

"Sir knight," she said to him, "I find you doleful of aspect; yet I bear tidings that should make you merry!"

"I pray you tell them to me," he answered. "I am here now a prisoner by promise, but must say that time hangs very heavy on my hands."

"You are more of a prisoner than you deem," she replied. "My cousin, Morgan le Fay, keeps you here for purposes of her own which you will scarcely find to your liking."

"I fancy she keeps me here through an understanding with King Mark," he rejoined. "I have no faith in her, but I cannot break my word of honor."

"Truly, fair sir," she said, "I pity your unhappy lot, and have a plan in mind through which you may escape from this durance without loss of honor."

"Do that and I shall owe you my life's service," he answered, warmly. "Tell me, dear lady, by what means I can be freed."

"This I may justly say, that this castle of right belongs to me. I have been unjustly deprived of it, and in right and honor you are my prisoner, not Morgan's. I have an uncle who is a powerful nobleman, the Earl of Pase, and who hates Morgan le Fay above all persons. I shall send to him, and pray him for my sake to destroy this castle, which harbors only evil customs. He will come at my wish and set fire to the building throughout. As for you, I shall get you out at a private postern, and there have your horse and armor ready."

"Truly, fair maiden, you are as wise as you are beautiful," he answered, in eager accents. "Release me from imprisonment to Morgan and I will hold myself your prisoner for life."

Then she sent to her uncle the earl, and bade him come and burn that haunt of mischief – a design which he already had in mind.

When the appointed day came the Earl of Pase sought the castle with four hundred knights, and set fire to it in all parts, ceasing not his efforts till there was not a stone left standing of the once proud stronghold.

But Alexander was not willing to take this as a release from his vow, but stationed himself within the limits of the space where had stood the castle of La Belle Regard, and made it known far and wide that he would hold that ground against all comers for a twelvemonth and a day.

Word of this knightly challenge soon came to Arthur's court, where was then a lady of famous beauty and great estate, known as Alice la Belle Pilgrim, daughter of Duke Ansirus, called the pilgrim, since he went on a pilgrimage to Jerusalem every third year.

When this fair maiden heard of Alexander's challenge, she went into the great hall of Camelot and proclaimed in the hearing of all the knights that whoever should overcome the champion of La Belle Regard should wed her and be lord of all her lands.

This done, she went to La Belle Regard, where she set up her pavilion beside the piece of earth held by the young knight. And as the weeks passed by there came from all directions knights who had heard of Alexander's challenge and Alice's offer, and many a hard battle was fought. Yet from them all Alexander came as victor.

But the more he triumphed over his knightly foes the deeper he fell captive to his fair neighbor, for whom he grew to feel so deep a love that it almost robbed him of his wits. Nor was his love unrequited, for his valor and youthful beauty had filled her heart with as ardent a passion for him in return, and she prayed as warmly for his victory in every combat as though he had been her chosen champion.

And so time passed on, varied by fighting and love-making, till one day, after Alexander had unhorsed two knights, there came to him the lady to whom he owed the burning of the castle, who told Alice the whole story of what had then occurred.

"You worked wisely and well," answered Alice. "Sir Alexander, indeed, has not gained much more freedom, except it be freedom to fight. But that is more his fault than yours."

"Have I not?" exclaimed the young knight. "I have gained freedom to love also; for which I am ever beholden to this fair damsel."

At this Alice turned away with a rosy blush, while the maiden stood regarding them with merry smiles.

"I have, by right, the first claim on you, Sir Alexander," she said. "But if this fair lady wants you, I should be sorry to stand in love's light. I yield my claim in her favor."

As they thus conversed in merry mood, three knights rode up, who challenged Alexander to joust for the proffered prize of the hand and estate of Alice la Belle Pilgrim. But the three of them got such falls that they lost all desire to wed the lady, and, like all knights whom Alexander overcame, they were made to swear to wear no arms for a twelvemonth and a day.

Yet love may bring weakness as well as strength, as the young lover was to find to his cost. For there came a day in which, as he stood looking from his pavilion, he saw the lady Alice on horseback outside, and so charming did she appear in his eyes that his love for her became almost a frenzy. So enamoured was he that all thought of life and its doings fled from his brain, and he grew like one demented.

While he was in this state of love-lorn blindness the false-hearted knight Sir Mordred rode up with purpose to joust. But when he saw that the youthful champion was besotted with admiration of his lady, and had no eyes or mind for aught beside, he thought to make a jest of him, and, taking his horse by the bridle, led him here and there, designing to bring the lover to shame by withdrawing him from the place he had sworn to defend.

When the damsel of the castle saw this, and found that no words of hers would rouse Alexander from his blind folly, she burned with indignation, and bethought her of a sharper means of bringing him back to his lost senses.

So she put on her armor and took a sword in her hand, and, mounting a horse, rode upon him with the fury of a knight, giving him such a buffet on the helm that he thought that fire flew from his eyes.

When the besotted lover felt this stroke he came of a sudden to his wits, and felt for his sword. But the damsel fled to the pavilion and Mordred to the forest, so that Alexander was left raging there, with no foe to repay for that stinging blow.

When he came to understand how the false knight would have shamed him, his heart burned with wrath that Sir Mordred had escaped his hands. But the two ladies had many a jest upon him for the knightly stroke which the damsel had given him on the helm.

"Good faith," she said, "I knew not how else to bring back his strayed wits. I fancy I would have given him some shrewd work to do if I had chosen to stand against him. These men think that none but they can wear armor and wield swords. I took pity on your champion, Alice, or it might have gone hard with him," and she laughed so merrily that they could not but join her in her mirth.

After that nearly every day Alexander jousted with knights of honor and renown, but of them all not one was able to put him to the worse, and he held his ground to the twelvemonth's end, proving himself a knight of the noblest prowess.

When the year had reached its end and his pledge was fully kept, he departed from that place with Alice la Belle Pilgrim, who afterwards became his loving wife, and they lived together with great joy and happiness in her country of Benoye.

But though he let love set aside for the time his vow of revenge on King Mark, he did not forget the duty that lay before him, nor did that evil-minded king rest at ease under the knowledge that an avenger was in the land. Many a false scheme he devised to keep Alexander from his court, and in the end his treacherous plots proved successful, for the young knight was murdered by some of King Mark's emissaries, with his father's death still unrevenged.

But vengeance sleeps not, and destiny had decided that the false-hearted king should yet die in retribution for the murder of Prince Baldwin. Alexander left a son, who was named Bellengerus le Beuse, and who grew up to become a valiant and renowned knight. He it was who avenged the slaughter of Prince Baldwin, and also of Sir Tristram, for this noble knight was also slain by the felonious king, as we must now tell.

Through the good services of King Arthur and Queen Guenever, after Tristram and Isolde had long dwelt at Joyous Gard, peace was made between them and King Mark, and they returned to Tintagil, where for a long time all went on in seeming friendship and harmony.

But the false king nursed the demon of jealousy deep within his breast, and bided his time for revenge. At length, on a day when Tristram, dreaming not of danger, sat harping before La Belle Isolde, the treacherous king rushed suddenly upon him with a naked sword in his hand and struck him dead at her feet.

Retribution for this vile deed came quickly, for Bellengerus was at Tintagil Castle at the time, brought there by thirst of vengeance, and with a heart filled with double fury by the news of this dastardly deed, he rushed upon King Mark as he stood in the midst of his knights and courtiers, and struck him to the heart with his father's avenging blade.

Then, aided by Dinas, Fergus and others of Tristram's friends, he turned upon Andred and the remainder of King Mark's satellites, and when the work of blood was done not one of these false-hearted knights remained alive, and the court of Cornwall was purged of the villany which had long reigned there supreme.

But La Belle Isolde loved Tristram with too deep a love to survive his death, and she fell swooning upon the cross above his tomb and there sobbed out her life; and she was buried by his side, that those who had been so united in life should not be parted in death.

Great was the grief and pity aroused throughout England, and through all lands where knighthood was held in honor, by this distressful event, for never before had two such faithful lovers breathed mortal air. And long thereafter lovers made pilgrimages to their tomb, where many prayed fervently for a draught from that magic goblet from which Tristram and Isolde drank, and whose wine of love for ever after ran so warmly in their veins.

Tristan and Isolde: A Poem

LADY JANE Franchesca Agnes Wilde (née Elgee) was a nineteenth-century Irish writer who wrote under the pen name Speranza. Born in Dublin, Lady Wilde was a poet, folklorist, nationalist and feminist who used her voice in favour of Irish independence and equality for women. Famous for such poems as 'The Famine Year' (first published in 1847 as 'The Stricken Land'), Lady Wilde also had a keen interest in Celtic folklore and Arthurian legend, publishing her own version of the Tristan and Isolde legend in her 1871 poetry collection, *Poems by Speranza*.

The poetry collection begins with a 'Dedication – to Ireland' and ends with 'An Appeal to Ireland', with the tale of the Irish queen, Isolde, and her lover, Tristan, situated towards the end of the collection. In 'Tristan and Isolde' Lady Wilde emphasizes Tristan and Isolde's love as natural, and prioritizes the faithfulness of their relationship, undermining King Mark's presence by never naming him, and asking if

> *Nature joined them hand in hand,*
> *Is not that truer band*
>   *Than the formal name of wife?*

The poem also has a tragic tone, however, that highlights the inevitability of the lovers' tragic end and the destruction of their 'youth's sunny, golden time' with 'ghastly, cold despair'. The appearance of these two lovers in the collection once again shows the enduring presence of the legend in popular imagination.

Tristan and Isolde:
The Love Sin

NONE, *unless the saints above,*
Knew the secret of their love;
For with calm and stately grace
Isolde held her queenly place,
Tho' the courtiers' hundred eyes
Sought the lovers to surprise.
Or to read the mysteries
Of a love—so rumour said—
By a magic philtre fed,
Which for ever in their veins
Burn'd with love's consuming pains.

Yet their hands would twine unseen,
In a clasp 'twere hard to sever;
And whoso watched their glances meet,
Gazing as they'd gaze for ever,
Might have marked the sudden heat
Crims'ning on each flushing cheek,
As the tell-tale blood would speak
Of love that never should have been—
The love of Tristan and his Queen.

But, what hinders that the two,
In the spring of their young life,
Love each other as they do?
Thus the tempting thoughts begin—
Little recked they of the sin;
Nature joined them hand in hand,
Is not that a truer band
Than the formal name of wife?

253

Ah! what happy hours were theirs!
  One might note them at the feast
Laughing low to loving airs,
  Loving airs that pleased them best;
Or interchanging the swift glance
In the mazes of the dance.
So the sunny moments rolled,
And they wove bright threads of gold
  Through the common web of life;
Never dreaming of annoy,
  Or the wild world's wicked strife;
Painting earth and heaven above
  In the light of their own joy,
In the purple light of love.

Happy moments, which again
Brought sweet torments in their train:
All love's petulance and fears,
Wayward doubts and tender tears;
Little jealousies and pride,
That can loving hearts divide:
Murmured vow and clinging kiss,
Working often bane as bliss;
All the wild, capricious changes
Through which lovers' passion ranges.

Yet would love, in every mood,
Find Heaven's manna for its food;
For love will grow wan and cold,
And die ere ever it is old,
That is never assailed by fears,
Or steeped in repentant tears,
Or passed through the fire like gold.

So loved Tristan and Isolde,
In youth's sunny, golden time,
In the brightness of their prime;
Little dreaming hours would come,
Like pale shadows from the tomb,
When an open death of doom
Had been still less hard to bear,
Than the ghastly, cold despair
Of those hidden vows, whose smart
Pale the cheek, and break the heart.

FLAME TREE PUBLISHING